MAX SPANKY

The Weatherman

For Chris, who has great ideas.

For Nell, the best proof-reader anyone could ever hope for.

For my parents, who always believed I could write a book (thanks for the forty years of patience).

And for Ollie and Zoe.

A change in the weather is sufficient
to recreate the world and ourselves.

– Marcel Proust

Chapter One

Sam is about thirty seconds away from picking up the pencil on his desk and shoving it right into his own eyeball, just to make the stress stop. The clock on his desk taunts him, ticking too quickly through the hours and rushing him headlong towards evening. It's past three already and he's achieved nothing.

The "To Do" reminders popping up on his computer every fifteen minutes are slowly driving him to despair. He seriously considers for a moment whether it might be worth cancelling tonight's flights and just working all weekend instead, but then he sees Claudia's steely gaze watching him from the family photo perched on his desk.

No. There will be serious consequences if he clocks off tonight without finishing his overdue report, but that's nothing compared to the wrath of his wife scorned. The holiday is non-negotiable.

The reminders pop up again: Finish report; Submit budget proposal for new Financial Year; Approve planograms. He hits snooze again and stands with a heavy sigh, returning mug-in-hand to the break room for yet another coffee. Abby is there, because of course she is.

Abby: jet-black hair scraped back into the perkiest of pony-tails, long legs disappearing into the type of footwear his boss insists on calling *fuck-me boots*, the faintest suggestion of breasts showcased in a deep v-neckline. It hasn't escaped Sam's attention that Abby bears more than a passing resemblance to Claudia of ten years ago, but that does nothing to calm the stirring in his groin.

She must have heard the door swing closed behind him, but Abby doesn't look up until Sam moves next to her, rinsing his coffee cup in the sink she's leaning against.

"Sam!" she says, affecting surprise. "Where did you come from?"

"In the door," he says. "As per usual."

She giggles.

"But aren't you meant to be on holiday?" she asks, pushing the button to drop a new capsule into the coffee machine.

"Leaving tonight," he says. "I was meant to have today off, but there were reports that needing doing..."

"Ahh," she says. "Board reports will wait for no man, right?"

He smiles weakly, not entirely sure what she's talking about but pleasantly distracted by the movement of her breasts as her arms move, pressing buttons on the coffee machine.

"Scuse," she mutters, reaching in front of him to open the fridge and take out the milk. The side of her body presses against the front of his for just a moment and he's stunned into silence by the warmth of that brief contact.

"Need this?" she asks, waving the milk bottle at him.

"Um," he says. "Uh. I think..."

She smiles.

"I'll just leave it here for you then," she says. Then, as she turns for the door, coffee cup in hand, "Good luck with the reports, Sam."

His name sounds like music in her mouth.

When he returns to his desk, the phone is ringing. The teeth-gritted expression on next-desk-Jane's face implies that it's been ringing for some time. He sets his coffee down, yelping as the hot liquid splashes over his fingers, and grabs for the phone with his unburnt hand.

It's Claudia.

Of course it is.

"When are you home?" she demands, barrelling straight to the point in her usual manner, with no time for greetings or pleasantries.

"I told you," he says, clicking through the To-Do reminders that have popped up on screen for the thousandth time. "I have a million things to do. I will be home when I'm finished."

"Which is when?" she asks, all business. In the background her can hear the muffled sounds of six-year-old Noah shouting and eight-year-old Avril shrieking with laughter.

"I. Don't. Know." he says, opening his emails to find twelve new messages waiting for him, three flagged as *Urgent*. He fights the overwhelming urge to slam his face into the desk.

"So, all day, then," she says. It's not a question.

"Yes, Claudia. All day," he says

"Are we going to miss this flight?" she asks. After many years of these conversations, Sam understands that this is not a rhetorical question. They will not be missing the flight.

"Of course not," he says. "I'll be home by six. Seven at the latest."

"Great," she says, voice icy. "Let me just clean the house

from top to bottom, pack suitcases for all of us and take the dog to the kennels. Oh, and I'd best organise the passports, hadn't I?"

"You're amazing, Claude," he says, trying to force some gratitude into his voice.

She slams the phone down without response.

As soon as he replaces the phone in its cradle, it starts to ring again. Sam turns the volume to zero, to be ignored for the rest of the day.

Chapter Two

The clock on Sam's computer reads 6:28pm when he closes the board report file.

It's not finished. It's not even close to finished. But it does have numbers in all the places that numbers are required, as well as an assortment of vague terms like *evolution* and *step change* and *company culture*. This should provide sufficient misdirection to buy Sam another couple of weeks. If he takes the laptop to Florida with him and stays up a few nights tweaking the numbers...

"Sam!" the cheery sing-song tone of his boss takes Sam completely by surprise. He'd thought he was alone in the office.

"You're not still here, are ya?" Mike "Buddy" Rogers seems alarmed at the sight of anyone still working four hours after he clocked off for the day.

Sam unplugs his laptop from its docking station and turns to smile at Buddy.

"Just about done, boss," he says in a tone of voice that really says *Go fuck yourself.*

Oblivious to all subtleties, Buddy smiles broadly. Dressed

in the most disconcerting of workout gear, hairy white shins glowing in the office lights, he's clearly just popped back into the office post-gym session to change.

"Board report all done, then?" Buddy asks, pulling one foot up behind himself in some kind of cooling-down stretch.

"Should be in your inbox, Buddy," Sam says, remembering too late that he's forgotten to set up an out-of-office message.

"Great!" Buddy grins, apparently not noticing that Sam has called him by his office nickname.

"Now, Sam," Buddy says, face straightening itself into an attempt at an earnest expression. "Everything OK with you, my man?"

Sam grimaces, then tries to cover it with a Buddy-style grin.

"Sure," he says. "Everything's just peachy."

"Great!" Buddy grins again, then pulls over Jane-next-door's chair and sits down uncomfortably close to Sam.

Sam makes a show of checking his watch, hoping to send clear please-stop-talking signals.

"So, Sam," Buddy has clearly been trained at some point to use people's names as often as possible. The result is often a surreal conversation where one's own name begins to sound like a nonsensical noise.

"Yes," Sam says, still standing with laptop under one arm and car keys in hand.

"Have a seat, Sam," Buddy waves invitingly at Sam's own chair.

"Well, I've done quite a bit of sitting already today…"

"Come on, Sam!" Buddy chuckles to himself, for some mysterious reason. "Just give me two minutes, mmkay?"

Sam sits with a heavy sigh.

"I've just wanted to say, Sam," Buddy is looking scarily

earnest again. "You're my best worker, Sam. Honestly. You just...work. You know?"

"That's what they pay me for," Sam says.

Buddy waves this away, shaking his head.

"No," he says. "It's about you, Sam. You've got a lot of integrity, Sam. And that work ethic; it's just..." Buddy shakes his head and gives a low whistle. "Just, wow. You know?"

Sam suspects that Buddy would think less of his work ethic if he better understood the work they were meant to be doing. Sam skates through his working life quite happily on the back of Buddy's utter incompetence.

"It's just," Sam says, taking a few tentative steps toward the door. "I really need to get going..."

"Of course you do, Sam," Buddy's condescending smile sets off a nasty shiver down Sam's spine.

Buddy pats Sam on the shoulder with enough force to bruise.

"I just need you to consider, Sam," Buddy says. "I need you to consider that there are more important things than work, you know?"

This is the strangest motivational speech Sam has ever received in the workplace.

"Right..."

Buddy waves one hand vaguely in the direction of the family photo on Sam's desk.

"Lovely family, Sam." Buddy smiles, nodding wisely to himself. "Lovely family."

"Well, I suppose they're all right," Sam demurs.

"Just, don't take it for granted." Sam is horrified to see Buddy's big dumb cow eyes misting over. "Don't ever take them for granted, Sam."

"Right. I mean, yes." Sam can't look away from the tears brimming over Buddy's bottom lashes.

"Work's not that important, Sam," Buddy says quietly. "Work will always still be there."

"Sure," Sam says in a soothing tone, hoping to talk his boss down from this uncomfortable level of emotional openness.

"Give me the laptop, Sam," Buddy demands.

"I... hold on, what?" Sam backs away from Buddy's grasping hands as he reached out to seize the laptop from under Sam's arm.

"I don't want you working, Sam," Buddy says, a tear still threatening to escape from his right eye. "If you take this with you, I know you will work all through your holiday."

It's true.

"That's not true," Sam protests.

Buddy has caught the corner of the laptop between the index fingers of both hands and is scrabbling at it. Sam makes a wordless squawk of protest.

"Sam," Buddy says. "Give me the laptop."

Sam tries to shuffle the laptop further away from Buddy's grasping pincer-movements but loses his grip and watches in helpless horror as it falls heavily to the floor.

Buddy retrieves the laptop, making some exploratory poking gestures at the important-looking internal parts that are now protruding from a large crack down one side of the machine.

"No biggie," he smiles. "We'll have IT take a look at it and it'll be up and running for you again when you get back from holiday."

Sam is lost for words.

"Right then," Buddy says, "No rest for the wicked, eh, Sam?"

In a none-too-subtle attempt to get Sam out of the office, Buddy turns out the lights and sets the alarm.

Sam only just remembers to take his wallet from his desk drawer before jogging out of the building, the alarm counting down behind him. As the door swings shut behind Sam, the alarm makes its final high-pitched trilling sound to indicate full alert.

Sam sits in his car for a good five minutes, staring into space and wondering what the fuck has gotten into his boss.

His spell of peaceful contemplation is interrupted by the vibration of the phone in his pocket, which is then automatically answered (goddammit) by his car's Bluetooth sound system.

"Fuck," he says.

"Hello to you too, Fuckface," Claudia says in her best fake-cheery tone.

"Just on my way…" he starts.

"Can't hear the car engine," she interrupts.

He turns the key with more force than necessary, disappointed when the car just makes its usual starting-up noise.

"Happy now?" he says.

"Oh, of course!" she says. "I'm just *so happy* that my useless excuse for a husband hasn't even left the office yet and we needed to leave for the airport ten minutes ago."

"We didn't need to…"

"Yes, Sam. Yes, we did."

"You're being ridiculous. There's still at least an hour until…"

"Do you want to explain to the kids that we're not going to Florida? Or should I do it?"

There's the distant echo down the line of Avril shrieking

"What?"

"We'll make the flight, Claude," he says, easing the car slowly down the office ramp to avoid scraping the bottom on a too-high speed bump half-way down. He flinches as the bottom scrapes across the concrete anyway.

"Fuck you," she says, ending the call.

* * *

Considering Claudia's urgency over the phone, Sam is surprised to find her only half-dressed when he arrives home. In jeans and bra, wearing only one sock, she's halfway through straightening her hair. Her suitcase is open on the bed, clothes half-in and half-out of it. The kids recline casually on the sofas, watching a startlingly inappropriate episode of South Park. Noah appears to be wearing pyjamas.

"We're not in Florida yet, Claude," Sam says, raising his eyebrows at her toplessness.

"Get fucked," she says.

He shrugs off the implied criticism of what he'd thought a half-decent Dad Joke.

"Did you say the kids could watch…"

"Don't care what they're watching," she says, eyes shooting daggers at him in the bathroom mirror.

"Right," he says. "So…"

"Get their bags in the car," she says. "I'll be done in two minutes."

"OK. So they've already eaten..?"

"No they haven't already eaten, Sam," she rolls her eyes

at him in the mirror. "We've been a wee bit fucking busy, actually."

"Right. So you want me to…"

"Just sort the bags. We'll eat at the airport."

"But the prices at the airport…"

Claudia has a habit of escalating her tone until dangerously angry, at which point she switches to a deceptively cool-and-collected tone. Sam has been caught out by this before. When she turns to him and smiles calmly, steaming-hot potential weapon in hand and repeats,

"We'll eat at the airport," he does not argue.

When he turns off the TV, Noah bursts into tears.

"Dad!" Avril says. "It was almost finished!"

"Don't care," Sam says, grabbing one of their suitcases under each arm and taking them out to the car.

"Mum's not even ready yet!" Avril calls after him.

"Get in the car, Avril," he calls back.

Noah stomps past as Sam is closing the car boot. He sits in the backseat, arms folded and a scowl on his face.

"You need to get dressed first," Sam says, opening the car door to remove Noah from the backseat.

Noah bursts into tears again.

Grateful that he's still so small for his age, Sam hoists Noah out of the car seat and carries him back inside.

Avril is right where he left her, having turned the TV back on.

"Avril!" he says, turning the TV off again. "Get in the car!"

"I hate you!" she screeches, disappearing off in the direction of her bedroom.

Sam carries a still-sobbing Noah to his room, where he

patiently dresses him in a mish-mash of items. Even Sam can see that the t-shirt doesn't match the trousers, but it's slim pickings in Noah's drawers as all of his clothes seem to have been packed away for the Florida trip.

No longer crying, but taking those odd, hitching breaths of the recently-stopped-crying, Noah follows Sam back out to the lounge, where Claudia is now sitting on the couch, pulling on her other sock and watching South Park. Sam switches off the TV once again. Claudia stares at him.

"What the fuck is this?" she says.

"I thought you were in a hurry!" Sam says. "We don't need the bloody TV..."

"No," she interrupts, pointing at Noah's too-small t-shirt. "What the fuck is this?"

"Well, everything's already packed and he was wearing pyjamas," Sam says.

"He was meant to be wearing pyjamas," she says, speaking very slowly as if in doubt of Sam's understanding of English. "So that he can sleep on the plane."

Noah starts to cry again.

There's a knock at the door.

Sam answers.

Julia, the goth neighbour kid, pushes past him and sits down beside Claudia on the sofa.

"I love this one!" she says. Somehow, South Park is back on the TV.

"Sorry," Sam says, "Why are you..."

"Julia's housesitting for us," Claudia says in her best why-does-nobody-listen-to-me voice. "I told you."

"You didn't," Sam says. "The dog's at the bloody kennels.

Why would we need a…"

"Home security is important, Mister Frost," Julia says, staring darkly at Sam from behind a greasy black fringe.

"Just put your suitcase in the car, Sam," Claudia says.

"OK," Sam says. "Did you already pack…" he trails off into silence as Claudia's icy expression makes it very clear that no, she has not packed a suitcase for him.

Grabbing armfuls of shirts from the wardrobe, underwear from his drawers and three randomly chosen pairs of shoes from under the bed, Sam manages to pack his suitcase in less than two minutes. This does nothing to save him from Claudia's disdain as she waits in the passenger seat, leaning on the car horn.

With the expert Space Management skills carefully honed over a lifetime of playing Tetris, Sam manages to reshuffle four large suitcases into the ridiculously small boot space of his company car.

They are two houses away from home when Avril remembers that she's left her tablet charging in the lounge. Sam reverses the car back down the street and into their driveway. Back in the lounge, he finds Goth-Kid Julia sprawled across his sofa with her dirty shoes on his coffee table and her grubby little mitts deep in the bag of crisps he'd been saving for weeks. She grunts some kind of acknowledgement but doesn't bother moving. Sam nods vaguely at her, still irritated by the presence of an unnecessary teenager in his house.

Upon his return to the car, he is quick to let Claudia know that he has saved the house from burning down by unplugging the hair straighteners she's so irresponsibly left steaming away on the bathroom counter.

He is less open about the wallet and cellphone he'd left sitting on the kitchen bench, which are only now in his pocket because the greasy teenager on his sofa had helpfully pointed them out.

As per usual, it's a long and painful drive to the airport. Avril is upset beyond all reason that *"Noah keeps annoying me"*. Noah, still fragile over the pyjamas incident, is a tearful mess of confusion. Claudia stares silently out the window, jaw clenched, clearly on a break from parenting duties.

"So," Sam ventures, "Who's excited about going on a plane?"

This is greeted by silence. Noah looks even more confused. Sam is suddenly unsure whether they've actually told the kids about the holiday at all.

"To America," he clarifies. "We're going on a plane to America."

Noah looks frankly startled.

"They know we're going to America," Claudia says with one of her best eye-rolls.

"Well, that's pretty exciting, isn't it?" Sam tries.

"No," Avril says, arms folded fiercely across her skinny chest.

"Yes?" Noah tries.

"I think it's pretty exciting!" Sam says. Claudia snorts.

"I think it's lame," Avril says.

"Yeah, it's pretty lame,"Noah echoes.

"You think it's lame?" Sam says, in the same deceptively-calm voice Claudia uses to show great rage. "You think it's lame that we would spend thousands of pounds to take you ungrateful little buggers halfway across the world so you can see Mickey bloody Mouse?"

"Mickey Mouse?" Noah asks. He doesn't seem to know who this is.

"Yes," Avril says, doubling-down on her belligerence. "Mickey Mouse is lame."

"Well, good then," Sam says. "Holiday cancelled. I'm going to turn this car around…"

There is a pointed silence as they all wait for him to turn the car around.

"It's a dual carriageway," Sam says through gritted teeth. "I can't just turn around here. But I will…"

It's an empty threat and they all know it.

After a few minutes' silence, Sam tries again.

"So, nobody wants to go to Disneyworld, then?"

Silence.

"Alligators? Nobody wants to go on those big fan boat things to see alligators?"

More silence.

"Nobody likes beaches?"

"I like beaches!" Noah cannot stay silent in the face of this temptation. "I love beaches!"

"OK, good," Sam says. "The boys can go to the beach and the girls can stay at the hotel being grumpy."

"Sounds great," Claudia says.

"What's Disneyworld?" Noah asks.

Chapter Three

They've been seated separately. Sam is sandwiched between Noah and Avril in the three middle seats directly in front of the toilet. Claudia is luxuriating three rows ahead in a window seat. The two seats beside her are unoccupied so she has stretched her legs out across the row and appears to be very comfortable.

Sam is not comfortable.

It's an hour into the flight and already he feels desperately close to murdering someone. Noah is asleep against Sam's left shoulder, snoring snottily into his ear. Avril is asleep against his other side, warm dribble tickling the side of his neck. Sitting bolt upright in an attempt to balance both children, Sam's left leg has already fallen asleep and both buttocks feel strangely numb.

There's a very large man sitting across the aisle from Noah. He's intently focused on the three-year-old romcom playing on his entertainment screen, while digging deep into his right nostril with one finger. Sam finds himself staring in horror, unable to look away, as the man removes his finger - large chunk of snot balanced on the end - and puts it into his mouth.

Sam makes an involuntary gargling sound as he fights the

urge to throw up. As a father-of-two, snot-eating is not foreign territory to Sam. Somehow though, it's exponentially more revolting when an adult does it.

He watches in abject fascination as the man digs into his nose twice more and eats it twice more.

Then, apparently bored with his romcom, the man uses that very same snot-and-spit finger to prod at the entertainment screen and choose a new movie. Sam looks at his own entertainment screen with a dawning understanding of its potential disgustingness.

He presses the call button and requests some hand sanitiser, which he then diligently wipes across everything that any previous passenger might have touched.

After another hour of wide-eyed boredom, Sam orders a double vodka-orange. Then two more. It doesn't help him sleep, but it does make the movie he's watching seem significantly more entertaining. He orders a third and then a fourth but is fairly sure that the flight attendant is now skipping the vodka and serving him unadulterated orange juice.

Still, he considers. "Mustn't grumble."

"What?" Avril mumbles.

He stays silent in the hope that she'll go back to sleep. It seems to work.

With his bladder eventually full to the point of intense discomfort, Sam attempts to wriggle his way out of the seat without waking either child. Noah topples forward, his head bouncing off the seat in front of him with an audible crunching sound. Eyes still closed, he mutters something under his breath, settles himself awkwardly against the armrest and resumes his phlegmy snoring.

Avril jerks awake and stares at Sam with wild-eyed rage as he shuffles his way down the cabin. Avoiding the distinctly sick-smelling bathroom behind their seats, he sways his way down the aisle towards the other bathroom, where a bright green vacant light beckons. Of course, Claudia is still wide awake. As he passes her seat, an arm shoots out to seize him by the sleeve and he lets out an involuntary shriek of surprise. This results in several nearby passengers waking and looking around in alarm for the source of their sudden return to consciousness.

Sam slides into the empty aisle seat beside his wife. She looks displeased.

"Are you drunk?" she hisses.

"Nope," he says. His voice comes out a little louder than expected and the woman in front of him turns to look, clearly startled.

"Really," Claudia deadpans. "So, why are your eyes all red and out-of-focus?"

"Well, my love," he says, "I've been sandwiched between two snotty, snoring children for the past few hours, watching some bullshit movie and quite unable to sleep."

She frowns.

"I would imagine," he continues, "that I'm currently demonstrating some of the ill effects of exhaustion, backache and a very strong urge to pee."

With that, he stands with something of a flourish for dramatic effect. Unfortunately, the vodka-dispensing attendant is standing in the aisle and Sam collides with him heavily, knocking his tray of plastic water cups into the lap of a sleeping elderly man.

"Nice one," he hears Claudia say as he flees the scene.

He lets out an audible sigh of relief at the sight of the green light glowing above the toilet cubicle, but it turns to a guttural retching noise once he's inside. As a father of two, he's seen some shit. This, however, tops even the time two-year-old Avril finger-painted on her bedroom walls with her own faeces. This is the stench of Hell.

There are green-brown patches spattering the toilet bowl and sitting in the sink is a sizeable lump of what looks suspiciously like shit. There's also a wide stripe of vomit on the inside of the cubicle door, ending in a sticky puddle that Sam has already stepped in. In his usual manner, Sam has kicked off his shoes immediately after take-off, so stands in vomit wearing only socks. The squelching sensation of someone else's vomit squeezing up between his toes is quite remarkable.

Standing on one foot, Sam carefully peels off the puke-sock and flings it into the toilet bowl. Staring fixedly at the ceiling, he then empties his full-to-bursting bladder over the mess in the toilet, closes the lid and flushes. The noise of things being sucked into space is just as terrifying as always. Upon inspection of the toilet bowl post-flush, the splatters do not appear to have moved. There is also now a puke-and-shit-stained sock glued into the middle of the whole mess. Sam carefully closes the lid, pretends to have seen nothing and exits the cubicle. Just as he reaches Claudia's seat, he hears the unmistakeable sound of someone entering the toilet cubicle and exclaiming "Jesus Fucking Christ!" at a volume usually considered inappropriate for a planeful of sleeping passengers.

Sam ducks into Claudia's spare aisle seat again, just in case the toilet swearer comes looking for the toilet culprit.

"Why is there a fucking sock in the fucking toilet?!" the unseen swearer shouts at an even higher volume.

Two flight attendants rush down the aisle in tandem to avert disaster. The sweary passenger is escorted up the plane with apologetic smiles through the curtains and into Business Class. Sam has deep and instant regrets for not having sworn loudly about the toilet himself.

"Goddammit!" he says loudly. This earns nothing more than a disapproving glare over the shoulder of one of the attendants heading off to Business Class. He turns to Claudia to complain, but she seems to have dozed off. Legs propped up on the empty seat beside her, Elizabeth Arden eye mask in place and noise-cancelling headphones blocking out all swearing, she is practically in Business Class herself. Craning his head over his shoulder, Sam can see Avril and Noah both fast asleep in their seats, heads resting on each of the unoccupied armrests of the seat he's deserted. Satisfied that they're unlikely to injure themselves too badly in his absence, Sam props his own feet up on the spare middle seat beside Claudia's feet, reclines his seat as far as it will go (despite the protesting squawk of the passenger behind him) and, finally, falls asleep.

Sam manages a good twenty minutes of sleep before the disapproving-frown attendant is back.

"Sir?" he hisses. "Excuse me, sir?"

Sam blinks awake, eyes dry and scratchy. "What?" he croaks.

"Are these your children, sir?"

Sam blinks again to bring the world into slightly better focus. Beside the disapproving attendant are Noah and Avril, both red-faced and quietly weeping.

"We thought you were gone, Daddy!" Noah says in his best anguished-orphan voice.

"You can't just leave us!" Avril says, in her more usual everybody-sucks voice.

"Jesus fucking Christ," Sam says. He still does not receive the Business Class response.

"You really can't just leave them, Sir," the attendant says, with a withering glare. "You need to be responsible for your own children."

"What about her?" Sam protests, waving vaguely in Claudia's direction. She doesn't move.

Noise-cancelling headphones or no, Sam is 99% sure that she's faking sleep so that he will have to deal with this on his own.

"Fine," he sighs, getting stiffly out of his seat and following the attendant back to the row in front of the toilet.

"Sir?" the attendant says, "Why are you only wearing one sock?"

Sam pretends to mishear and says something about family beach holidays. The attendant gives up and disappears back to wherever flight attendants hide during sleep-time.

Sam pushes the Cabin Call button. If he's going to be stuck in this seat, he's going to need at least six more vodkas.

* * *

By the time they land in Orlando, Sam has developed the worst headache of his life and his ankles seem to have swollen to double their usual size. As always, it is an absolute nightmare navigating American Customs and Immigration. Although impossible to prove, Sam is convinced that Claudia is intentionally talking at a slightly higher volume than usual, just to hurt his head. The kids are no more and no less irritating than usual, which is to say, they are extremely irritating.

The whole process takes much, much longer than seems reasonable and it's difficult to explain to children, Sam finds, something that you struggle to understand yourself.

"But *why* are we just standing here?" Avril asks after twenty minutes of fidgeting in an unmoving queue.

"They have to check everyone's stuff," Sam says vaguely.

"What stuff?" Avril asks, eyes narrowed in suspicion. "Like, if they have a bomb?"

"Shhhhhhh," Sam hisses, pointing to the nearby signs with their *All Threats Are Taken Seriously, No Jokes Please* messages.

"I wasn't making a joke," Avril says.

"You're not allowed to talk about bombs," Noah says. "Mum says, don't say bomb."

Sam smiles awkwardly at the many people now turning to glare at his family.

"Shhhhhhh," he says again.

"That's stupid," Avril says. She's not wrong.

"Who wants to get some food after this?" Sam says in a very obvious attempt at distraction. "It'll be tea time soon."

"But we just had breakfast on the plane," Noah says. "We need lunch."

"That was brunch," Claudia says smoothly. Sam is grudgingly impressed by her quick thinking.

Noah remains suspicious. "Well, why did they call it breakfast then?"

"In case people got confused," Claudia says as if this makes any sense at all. "Some people don't speak English very well."

"Oh," Noah says, apparently satisfied.

"So what do we want for tea, then?" Sam asks.

"Pizza," Avril says.

"Burger," Noah says.

Thus begins a highly emotional disagreement in the immigration line, with an awful lot of shouting and some unexpectedly colourful swear words. Claudia shuffles slightly to one side in an attempt to distance herself from this. In less than a minute, the pizza vs burger argument has escalated into actual physical violence and both children are in tears.

"Nice work," Claudia says, as Sam pushes himself between Noah and Avril, taking one small fist to the jaw and a not-insignificant kick to the balls. His headache has progressed to an audible thumping sound echoing through his skull, accompanied by agonising bursts of pain. He is wearing sunglasses to try and block out the far-too-bright lights but it doesn't seem to make any difference. As far as Sam can work out, he has now been awake for twenty-nine hours. It's not something he'd recommend.

Chapter Four

After a relatively painless run through Immigration, followed by some kind of unexplained false alarm in Customs, they emerge into the madness that is an International Airport at five o'clock on a Friday evening. There is much ducking and weaving, a minor panic when Noah is swept away with a small crowd going in the opposite direction and of course a significant amount of complaining from all parties.

Following some confusion around where to meet the Uber driver (curbside 14? What's a curbside 14?) and three toilet stops, they are in the air-conditioned, leather-seated comfort of a large Jeep that's been liberally sprayed with New Car Smell. Much to the kids' delight, there are small stockpiles of toffees stashed in various places around the vehicle.

"Help yourselves!" the driver beams. Avril and Noah stuff their faces and then begin to fill their pockets. Watching them in the rear-view mirror, the driver has obvious regrets over his own generosity, but grits his teeth into a convincing smile nonetheless.

"Where you folks from?" the driver asks, as he smoothly navigates his way through endless rows of stopped-still traffic.

"England," Avril mumbles through a mouthful of toffee.

"You don't say!" the driver says, eyes still firmly focused on the road ahead as he somehow finds tiny gaps to squeeze his enormous vehicle through. "And what's that like?"

Avril sits in stunned silence. Sam is fairly sure she has never considered this before.

"The Prime Minister lives there," Noah supplies helpfully. "And Arsenal."

"And it's cold in England," Avril says. The driver chuckles softly.

"Well, it's never cold here, honey," he risks a quick glance in the rear-view mirror before devoting himself once more to the cars around him.

"Coldest day we've had in weeks, today," he continues. "Had to put a sweater on this morning."

Sam smiles and nods politely, feeling the sweat run down the back of his neck and wondering whether he might need to vomit.

"Much to do around here?" Sam asks in an attempt at polite conversation.

The driver looks at him in surprise.

"In Orlando?" he asks, "Is there much to do in Orlando?"

Sam nods, then wishes he hasn't as the motion causes bile to rise in the back of his throat.

"Plenty!" the driver laughs. "Theme parks and water parks and shopping..."

"Is there McDonald's?" Noah asks.

"Sure is," the driver says. "One on every corner, my friend."

Noah looks out of the window with renewed interest, fast food-spotting.

"You folks going any further afield?" the driver asks. "You get yourselves a rental car, there's all kinds of things to see. Go check out Miami Beach, see the Keys, maybe the Everglades..."

He looks at Noah in the mirror again, "You might even see an alligator, if you're lucky."

Noah looks frankly terrified by this idea but gives a tentative nod. "Cool," he says in a very small voice.

Despite the driver's best efforts, they've finally come to a standstill amongst countless lanes of stopped cars, horns blaring. The driver points to an empty field at the roadside, sandwiched between two discount car dealerships.

"Fox lives there," he says. "I drive this road ten, twenty times a day. See him there most days."

"A fox?" Claudia says, as if the man had just suggested he'd seen little green men there.

"Sure," he says. "Just a little guy. Bright red. Pretty as anything."

Sam looks at the grim surroundings - factories, car dealer-ships, empty lots.

"What would he eat, around here?" Sam asks.

"Same as the rest of us, I guess," the driver says. "Leftover McDonald's! Am I right?" he looks at Noah in the mirror, but Noah is oblivious.

Lights change and the traffic begins to move again. As they move past the field, Sam could have sworn he sees the faintest flash of red far off in the bushes.

The hotel is not nice. A relic of the 1980s, it sits in between a decrepit Chinese Buffet restaurant and an abandoned movie theatre. Faded red paint peels from the doorways and window frames while the once-white stucco walls show big grey patches of mould and disturbing brown drip-stains. The large neon sign out front has lost most of its letters and now reads

"NOLGE", which Sam finds oddly cryptic. Surely there's some hidden meaning here.

"Goddammit," Claudia says. "We're paying a hundred fucking pounds a night for this place."

There's an audible intake of breath from the driver.

"That's more than a hundred bucks?" he asks.

"Yeah," Sam confirms. "Around a hundred and thirty dollars, I think."

The driver lets out a low whistle.

"You got played," he says, shaking his head sadly. "But I guess if you've already booked..."

He gets out of the car and goes around the back to start unloading their enormous suitcases.

"Tell you what," he says to Sam, who takes the suitcases from him, ferrying them one at a time onto the cracked pavement outside reception. "You like this place, then say no more. You don't like it so much, then give me a call. I know some places that'll do you a good deal, much nicer than this *establishment*." The way he says "establishment" is clearly code for "utter shithole", but Sam appreciates the gesture. The driver hands Sam a business card and climbs back up into his truck, waving them off with a cheery smile.

"At least there's a free breakfast," Sam says as he opens the door to reception, pulling a suitcase behind him.

"You'd eat anything they served in this place?" Claudia says, following him into the dingy, musty room.

The blonde girl at the counter shows no sign of having heard this. She shows no sign, in fact, of having noticed their presence at all. Instead, she continues tapping away on her phone with long, white-tipped talons. Her name tag reads *Hi!*

My name is Debbie. How can I help you?

The kids follow them through the doors and are immediately distracted by an aquarium - one of those tall, hexagonal numbers so popular in dentists' waiting rooms of thirty years ago.

"Fish!" Avril squeals, dropping her suitcase right in the doorway and skipping over to the aquarium. Then, on closer inspection, "Ewww."

There are two bloated goldfish, long dead, floating on the surface. Through the murky green water they can see another two fish, far too large for the aquarium, hovering mid-tank and staring blankly out at the world.

"Please don't tap on the glass," Debbie says mechanically, still not looking up from her phone.

"Umm... I think your fish might be dead," Noah says carefully.

"They're fine," she replies. "Just sleeping."

"They are *not* sleeping," Avril says. "This one's eyeball is hanging out."

Debbie does not seem concerned. She is clearly very busy with something on her phone.

Sam leans against the counter and gives her his most charming smile.

"Hi, Debbie," he says. She looks back at him blankly.

"Who's Debbie?" she says. Sam points at her name tag.

"Oh, right," she says. "Yeah, they just print a whole bunch of these with random names on 'em. Then it don't matter when people leave. Or, you know. Get fired."

"Right," Sam says.

"Checkin' in?" she asks, still looking at her phone.

"Yes..." Sam says. "Only, we wondered if we might change

our booking."

"To just the one night," Claudia clarifies. "Rather than ten."

Not-Debbie shrugs and taps something into the keyboard in front of her.

"Sure," she says. "It's not paid yet. Just pay for the one night and you can leave tomorrow."

Sam wonders whether this happens often.

The room has an unusual smell about it - like bleach and wet dog combined into a nauseating blend. There are two double beds crammed next to each other, leaving only a narrow pathway at the end of the beds to edge past to the bathroom.

Claudia is inspecting the pillows with a grimace, picking tiny hairs from them. The kids are ecstatic, trampolining from one side of the giant bed to the other with squeals of delight. On the one hand, Sam feels a delightful sense of relief at being temporarily ignored by everyone. On the other hand, he's fairly sure that the trampolining will end in a fight and/or serious injury within a matter of minutes.

"Anyone hungry?" he says half-heartedly. Seconds later, they're out on the street, following not-Debbie's vague directions (*I think maybe there's a place down that way, I guess?*) past a seedy attorney's office and something that looks decidedly like a crack den. Thick clouds overhead seem to be trapping the heat of the day, so that it remains midday-hot even well after six. Sam feels nasty sweat patches forming under his armpits, the wet fabric of his t-shirt clinging stickily. Claudia looks miserable. The kids look miserable.

"Chinese food?" Sam suggests.

"Absolutely," Claudia lets out a sigh of relief.

Avril and Noah burst into a chorus of whining about how

much they *hate* Chinese food and how they'd been *promised* pizza and burgers. Happily ignoring their protests, Sam almost skips back down the street to the dodgy-looking Chinese Buffet beside the hotel.

"What do you think?" he whispers to Claudia as they push through creaking doors into the restaurant. "Odds of food poisoning?"

"Extremely high," she says. "But at least it's conveniently located."

There are rows upon rows of steaming food. Prawns, vegetables, noodles, fried rice, dumplings, even a beautifully-assembled display of sushi that Sam promises himself he will not eat. At five dollars per person, it's the first good thing to happen since they arrived in this terrible country.

They eat and it's spectacular. Fresh and hot and bursting with flavour - everything it shouldn't be after hours of sitting under lights in a far-from-busy restaurant. The kids find a table of pizza and fries in the far corner and gorge themselves on the most un-Chinese of Chinese food. Sam breaks his own promise and eats fourteen pieces of the best sushi he's ever tasted. They waddle back to the hotel, full to bursting and fall into the giant bed, asleep before they have time to further inspect the state of the sheets.

Sam wakes again at three, to the sound of Noah vomiting copiously into the toilet. Claudia follows shortly after, then Avril. Sam congratulates himself on his excellent choice of sushi, then goes back to sleep.

At daybreak, Sam calls the driver from the day before. He smiles just as broadly as before, as if three of them were not deathly pale and smelling of vomit. The new hotel is a significant step up and Avril notes with a weak nod of approval that the fish in the lobby aquarium are in visibly better health this time.

Chapter Five

There are ten-year-olds in strollers. Smartphones clutched in one hand, thirty-dollar popcorn in the other, they luxuriate in their own laziness while harried adults push them from one ride queue to the next.

Avril drags on one of Sam's arms, her full body weight leaning into him. Small for her age, she's not heavy, but the constant pulling annoys him.

"Stand up straight," he hisses.

She looks up, eyes brimming with exhausted tears.

"But I'm so *tired*," she whispers.

"Don't whinge, Avril," Claudia says, on autopilot.

"This is boring," Avril says, pulling her hand back from Sam's and crossing her arms high across her chest, in a sudden swerve from distress to belligerence. "Why do people even come here?"

It's a valid question. There are no happy faces in this queue. Each of these people have paid the theme park hundreds of dollars to spend a day doing little more than waiting in line.

Waiting in front of Sam is a family of twelve (he's counted. Several times). All wear purple custom-printed t-shirts, their titles (*Aunty*; *Big Sis*; *Gran*) emblazoned across the front beneath slightly off-brand mouse ears. All wear identical grim smiles, plastered wide across sunburned faces. Nobody here is having fun, but somehow everyone is desperately trying to look like they are.

"Why is that fat boy in a pushchair?" Noah says, voice ringing out in an inopportune moment of silence. *Gran* turns to stare daggers. *Little Bro* stares fixedly at the screen in front of him, oblivious to Noah's attentions. *Mom* smiles ever wider, veering dangerously close to a maniacal grin.

Sam looks to Claudia for help, but she's typing away at her work emails, pointedly ignoring everyone around her and avoiding eye contact.

Just as Noah opens his mouth to ask another awkward question, there is movement ahead and the team-shirted family moves through the barrier and into the depths of the ride itself, *Gran* frowning back over her shoulder. Sam sighs heavily.

"Can I have a pushchair?" Noah asks. "Please?"

"No," Sam says. "You're not a toddler, for Christ's sake."

A quick glance back in the queue reveals at least two families he's offended with this comment.

"Why don't we have matching t-shirts?" Avril asks.

Sam says nothing.

"Mum?" Avril persists. "Can we get matching t-shirts?"

Claudia shakes her head, eyes still fixed on her phone as she types another email.

"No," she says. "We're not a matching t-shirts type of family."

Avril considers this. "What type of family are we, then?"

"The other kind," Claudia says. "The kind who don't wear

ridiculous shirts.*"*

The mood of the queue is becoming distinctly frosty.

A pasty teenager dressed in a mess of frothy puffery approaches, stationing herself beside the start of the ride queue.

"It's Princess Esmeralda," Noah says.

"That is *not* Princess Esmeralda," Avril says.

Hordes of children descend, the teenaged princess disappearing beneath them with an unenthusiastic royal wave.

"Can we go see?" Noah asks.

"Absolutely not," Sam says as the queue begins to move, half the families having fled for Esmeralda selfies.

"It's too hot…" Avril starts to complain, but then stops as they move into the shaded part of the queue. "Are we nearly there, then?"

"God, I hope so," Sam says, wiping sweat from his forehead with the back of one hand.

"Whose bright idea was this anyway?" Claudia says, tone deceptively jokey.

It was Sam's idea. They all know it was Sam's idea. Claudia has a special talent, Sam has always thought, for being a spiteful witch without anyone noticing.

Sam remains stonily silent.

It's another twenty minutes before they can see the end of the queue, then another ten before they find themselves lining up behind the purple t-shirted family at the final gates. Spaceship-themed ride carts rocket up the track and squeal to a sudden stop in front of the gates, riders thrown forward with some force.

"Looks like a whole lot of whiplash to me," Claudia says.

Sam assumes he's signed a waiver at some point acknowledging the risk of spinal injury.

"Hmm," he is non-committal.

Noah looks up at Sam, eyes wide in a pale face.

"We're going on the rockets?" he asks.

"Mmm," Sam nods.

"But do they go fast?"

"Sure," Sam says, still avoiding the glare of *Gran*. She knows how to hold a grudge.

"But is it *scary*?"

"Yeah, mate. Really scary. You'll love it,"

Sam realises too late that he's misjudged this, as Noah backs away, face panicked.

"Don't want to," he says shakily.

Claudia shoots her death stare at Sam.

"Dad's joking," she tells Noah, glaring at Sam over his head. "It's not scary at all. Just fun."

"Not scary?" Avril protests. "Then what's the point?"

"You think they sell beer here?" Sam jokes.

"Why?" she shoots back. "Need to get drunk already?"

"I just meant..."

Never has he wished so hard for a day to end.

The t-shirt family is whisked away and it's finally their turn to board, seated two abreast. Noah climbs aboard after some half-hearted reassurances and immediately squirms his way under Sam's arm, face pressed firmly into his father's chest. Sam pats the back of Noah's shoulders in an attempt at supportive parenting, but all he feels is irritation.

"You need to look, Noah," he says.

Twenty seconds into the ride, Noah starts to scream.

Not happy, fun screams of delight like those of the passengers behind them. No, these are the screams of a child being tortured and betrayed by those he trusted. Noah is terrified.

Thirty seconds in, Noah tries to wriggle under the lap bar and climb out of the cart. Sam physically restrains him for the rest of the ride, as they are flung around corners, centrifugal force almost throwing them out into the darkness. The carts fly along the track at impossible speeds, the ride lit so dimly that every drop comes unexpectedly, the ground disappearing from beneath them, then reappearing with all the shock of a surprise kick to the balls. They are hurled against the lap bar repeatedly as the cart races over a series of bumps. Sam hears Avril's delighted shrieks with each bump, followed by Noah's traumatised sobs.

All at once, they're back in the bright light of the boarding area, bored families lining up at the gates for their turn. The carts shudder to an abrupt stop. Sam, arms tightly secured around his sobbing son, is unable to brace himself and flies forward against the lap bar, taking the full force of impact to his groin.

Noah looks up at Sam, his face a bright red mess of snot and tears.

"I don't know why we bother," Claudia says under her breath as she climbs out of the seat in front.

"Let's not then," Sam says, feeling heat rush to his face. "We're leaving."

"Sure," Claudia says. "Perfect."

Noah breathes in hitching gasps as he wipes the last of the tears from his face.

"What do you mean?" he says. "We can't leave."

"Don't worry," Claudia says, "Dad's just joking."

"I'm bloody not," Sam says, striding down the exit with Noah in hand. "We're leaving now."

"What the fuck, Sam," Claudia stops and stares. "You can't just decide…"

"You stay here then," Sam places Noah's hand in Claudia's, knocking her phone to the ground. "I've had enough. I'm off back to the hotel."

"For a beer?" Claudia jeers.

"For ten beers, if I feel like it."

"Oh very nice, Sam," she calls after him as he emerges back into the midday heat. "Parent of the fucking year."

They are attracting disapproving stares from matching t-shirted families. They tend to be dramatically appalled by swearing in this country.

"There are *children* here," another *Mom* hisses at Claudia, hands pointedly clasped over her son's ears.

"You don't say," Claudia deadpans. "Too many bloody children if you ask me."

Sam makes it as far as the monorail before she catches up with him, Avril and Noah trailing red-faced and puffing in her wake.

Stuck in yet another queue, he fidgets with his smartwatch as the line moves impossibly slowly. Twenty thousand steps, it tells him. Seventy-three active minutes. Heart rate unusually high.

A severely sunburned woman turns to him.

"Hard to believe they even make you queue to leave the place," she says, accent like cut glass.

He chuffs out a half-hearted chuckle, then turns away as Claudia pushes her way through the queue and seizes him firmly by the arm.

"What. The. Fuck." She says, breathing heavily from the pursuit.

Sam clenches his jaw. "I said, I'm leaving. You do what you want."

One hand on either side of his face, Claudia tilts his chin up so that he's looking at her instead of glaring at his own feet.

"Sam," she says.

"Claudia," he says.

"You're right," she says, smiling an actual, genuine smile for the first time in recent memory. "This place is awful. Let's go drink by the pool while the kids try to drown each other."

He is suspicious. "Seriously?"

"Seriously," she leans heavily against him, arms wrapped around his waist. "This is the worst place I've ever been. The kids don't even like it."

"I do!" Avril protests.

"Wouldn't you rather have an ice cream by the pool, though?" Claudia suggests.

"Yes, please," Avril allows in a small voice.

"Me, too," Noah interjects, still red-faced from his roller coaster ordeal.

"I'd kill for a Mojito and a nap," Claudia says.

"Then, My Lady, you shall have it," Sam says, bowing theatrically.

As they step through the sliding doors into the ridiculously unnecessary monorail, Sam leans down to whisper into Claudia's ear.

"I'm sorry," he says. "For running away."

She laughs. "It's OK. I'll always find you."

"Creepy," he says.

"Oh, you love it," she says, waving away his protest. "You couldn't live without us."

"That's probably true," he allows. "But I'd love to give it a go."

The *Aunty Barb* sitting across the aisle is looking askance at them. No sense of humour, these Americans.

* * *

Back at the hotel, over dinner, a tentative peace is established.

They share a bottle of wine, following the usual unspoken agreement that Sam won't order any more drinks and Claudia won't comment on his drinking habits. It makes for a much more pleasant evening, this habit of brushing things under the carpet.

The kids are tired and it shows in their scratchy moods.

"Noah's *looking* at me,"

"Avril's sitting too close,"

"This bread tastes horrible,"

"I'm so hungry I might *die*"

Claudia smiles at Sam across the table, teeth clenched.

"Hey guys," Sam says, trying to keep the wheedling tone out of his voice. "Think you could maybe tone down the moaning for a minute?"

They look at him blankly, eyelids heavy. There's a beat of silence before Avril says, in a tearful voice, "I wasn't *moaning*, Daddy."

"Right," Claudia says brightly. "Who wants pizza and fizzy drinks?"

She's a smart woman, his wife. Waving the temptation of usually-forbidden food in front of them works wonders - they speak quietly and eat politely for the rest of the meal, clearly concerned that misbehaviour will result in their junk food being snatched back.

"You know I'm not good at this," she says over coffee, later, while the kids pick drowsily at half-finished sundaes. "Arguing. Compromising. Feelings..."

"You're joking," he says. "Nobody's better than you at winning an argument."

"It's not that," she says. "I have words, they're just not... never the right words, you know?"

"No," He looks at her blankly.

"It's like there are all these emotions churning around and I know that I feel something and it's not a *good* something," she stops for another sip of coffee.

"But I don't have the words to go with it, not exactly."

She laughs at his expression.

"No, honestly," she says. "Don't you ever feel like that? Like you're annoyed and frustrated and kind of sad and angry..."

"Sure," he says.

"But you can't explain exactly why. It's like something happens and it makes you feel all these emotions but then the way you explain it to someone else, it's not right. It's the closest explanation you can come up with, but what you say doesn't really match with what you feel."

"This is deep," he says, then chuckles. The wine from earlier is catching up with him.

"Don't laugh!" she says, laughing. "Look, you drink too much sometimes, right,"

"Well, I don't think…" he stiffens.

"No, no," she waves his protests away. "I'm not giving you shit. Promise."

He raises an eyebrow at her.

"OK," she allows. "Let's say that *I* think you drink too much sometimes."

"Mmm," he's still not happy with the direction this is taking.

"And I see you drinking. And you're happy. Or you seem happy."

"Right," he says.

"And it makes me so angry. But I don't know why. It's like I'm disappointed because I think you're drinking too much and also kind of disappointed in myself because you're having fun and I'm not. And then you won't listen and it's so frustrating and then I yell at you," she takes another drink.

"I yell at you but the things I'm saying are just - they're just the first thing that springs to mind. You know, like, I'm so angry because you're setting a bad example for the kids. Or, I'm disappointed because you'll be hungover tomorrow and I had plans…"

"Well yeah," he says. "That's probably fair."

"But that's why I say it," she says. "Because it sounds reasonable. Not because it's true."

"So the real reason you don't like me drinking..?"

"I don't know," she says. "Mostly I think it just reminds me that we don't have fun together any more."

"We have fun," he says.

She shakes her head at him sadly.

"Not really," she says. "Not often."

"Today was fun," he offers. She smiles.

"Today was fun," she agrees. "Let's do it more often, OK?"

Solemnly, he extends his hand across the table, takes hers and shakes it.

"Deal," he says.

Chapter Six

He wakes to the unexpected warmth of his wife nestled against his side, one arm thrown across his chest. Her hair tickles his chin, fluttering in her breath as she snores softly into the side of his neck.

It's been years since they last slept in each other's arms like this. The hair in the face; numb arms trapped under the other person's weight; the unpleasant heat of another person's body on a warm night. There were a multitude of reasons that they'd started sleeping further apart, a cool strip of empty sheet between them. It happened, he supposes, to all couples eventually - your own comfort becoming more important than the desire to embrace your partner.

But here, this morning, woken by bright sunshine streaming through sheer white curtains, it feels good.

Sam cranes his neck forward to kiss Claudia on the forehead. She blinks, looking around in confusion.

"Hey, you," she croaks in her morning-after-wine voice.

"Hey yourself," he smiles.

"I was thinking," she whispers, "Maybe we skip the theme

parks today?”

"Oh god, yes,” he says.

"Beach day?” she asks. He answers her with an open-mouthed kiss, morning breath be damned. His wife is a glorious, wonderful creature.

"I was thinking,” he says. "We should do this again some-time, without the kids.”

"Romantic getaway?” she says doubtfully.

"Absolutely,” he says, waiting for the inevitable rain on his parade.

"Sure,” she says instead. "Sounds wonderful.”

It feels like the tentative start to something better.

* * *

Following a locals tip-off from the concierge, they clamber past a construction zone to find themselves on a postcard-perfect beach with not another person in sight. The last unspoilt beach in the Keys, the concierge had said. He wasn't wrong.

By the time Sam has finished putting up the beach umbrella and laying out towels, the kids are already in the water and apparently trying to drown each other.

"Children are so sweet, aren't they?” Claudia says serenely, as Noah seizes Avril by the hair and tries to drag her under the water.

"Noah!” Sam calls in his best Grumpy Dad voice.

Both kids look at him blankly, Avril seemingly unconcerned by her brother's latest murder attempt.

"Just... be good," Sam says vaguely as Claudia snickers.

It is glorious. Lying back in sand soft as baby powder, Sam closes his eyes and focuses on the warmth of the sun on his outstretched feet and the ever-so-slight pressure of Claudia's shoulder against his. It's like a real-life version of a mindfulness relaxation exercise.

"Better than a theme park?" Claudia asks.

"So much better than a theme park," he says, but it comes out slurred. He is drunk on sunshine.

Claudia is back on her feet, bouncing from one activity to another as usual, her maximum of five minutes sitting-still time having elapsed.

Sam is vaguely aware of the splashing sounds as she joins the kids and then a series of squeals as she tries to encourage them into deeper water. There's the beginning of the thought that he should join them, but then he's asleep.

It's hard to tell how much time has passed when he wakes, mouth dry and throat parched. The sun has moved far enough in the sky that the shade from the umbrella no longer falls on his face and instead he squints up into a painfully bright midday sun. Wiping drool from his chin with the back of one hand, Sam pauses to rub at his jaw, aching from hanging open too long. Sam suspects that he has woken himself up with his own snoring. Propping himself up on his elbows, he looks out to sea and then both ways down the beach. He is alone.

The three other towels have vanished, along with everyone's shoes and Claudia's beach bag. The only sign they were ever here are the three parallel sets of shallow footprints in the sand, leading away to the far end of the beach. Squinting, he looks again down the beach but they have gone far enough to have vanished from sight.

For a moment, Sam stays where he is. He repositions the umbrella to provide at least a little shade for his already sunburned head and shoulders. He lifts his towel, shakes the sand from it and then lays it carefully back down. He sits. He stares blankly out to sea. He checks again for any sign of other people on the beach. Nothing. He checks his watch. Having already forgotten the time, he checks his watch again.

"Well, fuck it," he announces to the empty beach.

Sam stands abruptly, startling the gull that had been trawling through a tangled heap of seaweed further down the beach.

Perching awkwardly on one leg and narrowly avoiding a fall on his face, Sam peels off his shorts and throws them at the seagull. Then, starting gingerly, but rapidly picking up speed, Sam runs down the beach and into the sea where he stands, knee-deep. The water is bathwater-warm and so clear he can see the tiniest of shells beneath the tiny waves and the individual hairs on his toes waving gently in the current. An involuntary laugh bursts out, and then another; great loud guffaws of disbelief bubbling up from somewhere deep in his chest.

With a war-whoop, Sam splashes in further, high-stepping over the white-tipped crests of pint-sized waves rolling toward the shore. The heat of the sun bears down, oddly comforting against his skin despite the progressive reddening of his ridiculously pale English body. The water is lapping at his testicles and he's about to dive in when he hears them return.

"What in the actual fuck are you doing?" Claudia's voice rings out.

Sam flinches and turns, hands cupped over his genitals, ready for the first fight of the day.

"Well, I just thought..." he says. But Claudia is smiling.

"Daddy's naked!" Noah shrieks in absolute delight.

Avril has both hands clapped over her eyes and has collapsed onto the beach in mortification.

In a matter of seconds, Noah has discarded his own clothing and is skipping happily into the waves. Sam can't recall when he last saw his son grinning so widely.

"Who needs theme parks?" he shouts back to Claudia, who laughs and then holds up a six-pack of beer.

"Beer?" she says.

"This day just gets better and better," Sam says to Noah, who is dog-paddling in circles around his father.

"Right?" Noah says. "Mum let us have Coke too."

"You lucky buggers," Sam says.

"I know!" Noah says in delight, then ducks under the water in a very lopsided attempt at a somersault.

Back on the beach, skin drying and tightening in the sun, Sam raises a can of beer to his wife.

"Cheers, my love," he says.

"You're going to get sunburned balls," she says, draping a towel across his lap. Then, raising her own can and tapping it against his: "Cheers."

The kids are back in the water, playing a game that somehow involves splashing water into each other's faces and screaming a lot. Noah is still bare-arse naked.

"Should we be putting sunscreen on Noah's balls?" Sam muses.

Claudia raises her eyebrows. "I shudder to think," she says.

"Seems like they're mostly underwater," Sam says, pausing to take a long, cold sip from his beer. "That'll block out the UV, surely."

"That doesn't sound like a real thing," Claudia says. "But I'm not chasing him with the sunscreen, so we'll just cross our fingers and hope, shall we?"

Sam holds up one hand. "Parents of the year?" he says.

Claudia high-fives him. "Parents of the year," she agrees.

Just for a while, it feels like the past nine years haven't happened. Like they're still the Sam and Claudia they used to be, a team of two misfits against the world.

The last few mouthfuls in Sam's can are warm and flat, but he tries not to notice. Claudia grimaces as she finishes her can.

"American beer is godawful, isn't it?" she says.

"I don't know," Sam says. "It tasted pretty good while it was cold."

"Ah, but that's why they serve it so cold," Claudia says. "So you can't taste it."

"Want some more then?" Sam asks.

"Oh, absolutely," Claudia says, putting on her sunglasses and lying back, paperback book in hand.

Sam leans over to peck her on the forehead. It's something he hasn't done in years and they look at each other in silent acknowledgement of how much things have changed between them.

"Or a Pina Colada, if you can find one," Claudia grins.

Sam struggles back into his shorts, then digs around in that soft, white sand to find his buried sandals.

"Your wish is my command," he says.

As he struggles up the beach, feet sinking into the impossibly fine sand, Sam can hear the laughter and squealing of his children as they make half-hearted efforts at drowning one another. A shadow falls across the sand in front of him and Sam glances up to see cotton-wool clouds gathering overhead. A cool breeze blows by, ruffling his hair on the way past. Sam turns and waves back to his family but Claudia, reading, doesn't see.

Chapter Seven

It takes a while, but he finds her a pina colada.

It might be a little different to what she was expecting, Sam muses as he retraces his steps back from the petrol station, through the little town and back towards the beach. Four enormous, bright-yellow cans clink against each other in the black plastic bag hanging from his hand. Emblazoned across the front of each can is "PINA-KOLADAZ!". Intentional miss-spellings and unnecessary punctuation being two of his wife's dearest pet hates, Sam is ecstatic at this find.

He takes a wrong turn twice, but then recognises a particu-larly bedraggled palm tree marking the street that leads to the beach. A light breeze seems to sprung up out of nowhere and the tree looks less droopy with a puff of wind stirring it into life. Still, he's fairly sure it's the same tree.

By the time he sets foot on the sand, just a few minutes later, the wind has whipped up to an unexpected level of ferocity. Plastic bag dangling from his wrist, cans smacking him in the chest with every few steps, he uses both hands to hold his sunglasses on to his face. Screaming gusts of wind send up huge puffs of white sand, like snow flurries except, Sam reflects as it showers him, a lot scratchier.

He holds a half-hearted belief that the wind, having popped up out of nowhere so suddenly, might disappear just as quickly. There's a wall of dark clouds gathering out to sea at some speed and the sky has taken on a strange dark-green colour that Sam's quite sure he's never seen before. He can't stomach the thought of having to leave this beach after what feels like such a short time, but things aren't looking positive. Lounging beside the resort pool has completely lost any appeal after this morning in his little beach-front paradise.

Sam is leaning so far forward into the wind that he stumbles and falls to his knees when it disappears. It's that sudden - from screaming wind to nothing in seconds flat. He gets to his feet, brushing sand from everywhere and looking around himself in utter confusion. In the sudden absence of wind, the silence is absolute. He wonders for a moment whether he might have been struck deaf, but then he hears the gentle splash of the waves.

Nothing is moving. It's so quiet and so still that nothing seems real and Sam feels utterly removed from his surroundings, not dissimilar to the time he consumed far too much hash cake in Amsterdam and began to doubt his own existence.

Further down the beach, there's movement. He squints, brushing sand from his face with the back of a hand so sandy that it just makes the problem worse. He can make out the fuzzy shape of Claudia and the kids, huddled in the sand and waving to him. Sam lifts a hand to wave back, but then stops to squint at the large dark shape in the distance.

"What's that?" he yells to Claudia, who shrugs expansively.

He points. She turns in the direction of his finger. And that's it.

In the time it takes for her to turn her head, the vague shape from miles down the beach is upon her - a dark mass of whirling wind and airborne debris, screaming down the beach with the speed and noise of a freight train. In the centre of the churning mess of wind, there's a palm tree suspended in space, torn from the ground roots and all. It whips around in unsteady circles and Sam's family disappears beneath it.

He stares open-mouthed at that spot on the beach, now a mess of movement and screaming noise, unrecognisable shapes churning inside a funnel of white sand and dark wind. He imagines he can hear the sound of Avril's scream, but it's not possible - the noise of the wind drowns everything out, a jet-engine roar louder than anything he's ever experienced.

And then the wind is upon him and everything goes dark.

* * *

He wakes because he can't breathe.

He can't breathe because he's buried under sand.

In a blind panic, Sam flails his arms and takes a deep gasp, inhaling lungfuls of sand and choking on the dry, salty grit.

It's the coughing that saves him, in the end; he doubles over in an involuntary spasm and unexpectedly pops up out of his sandy grave. There's sand in his ears and eyes and mouth and nose; he wipes at his face over and over but can't seem to remove enough to open his eyes properly or to breathe past the mass of sand coating his tongue and sticking thickly to the roof of his mouth.

Coughing and spluttering, blind, Sam pulls himself free of the sand with some effort and stumbles down the beach in what he hopes is the direction of the water.

It's only after an extended period of spluttering and vomiting into the sea that Sam starts to think he might survive. He takes in shallow, gasping breaths of air in between retching fits. As his vision begins to clear and his racing heart rate begins to slow, he looks back up at the beach.

It's unrecognisable. Trees are snapped like twigs, jagged ends of trunks protruding from the ground like broken teeth. The shape of the beach itself has changed completely, sand piled in new places and trash strewn everywhere.

And there - right where he left them - are Claudia and Noah. Small and broken, crushed beneath that enormous palm tree, they lie huddled together with Noah held tight in his mother's arms. They are too still.

Further down the beach, face-down in the water, floats the painfully small body of his daughter. She is too still.

Sam begins to scream.

Chapter Eight

The Resort Manager is trying to tell Sam something, but he can't work out what it is.

Red-faced, with tiny beads of sweat dotting his forehead, the man is clearly uncomfortable out here poolside, away from his air-conditioning.

"I'm sorry," Sam says, not for the first time. "I don't follow."

The Manager magics a handkerchief out from somewhere on his person and dabs delicately at his sweaty forehead. Sam watches in fascination as new beads of sweat appear almost immediately.

"I mean to say, Sir," the Manager continues, then clears his throat. "That, well... that is, that you're welcome to stay as long as you need."

He makes an uncomfortable attempt at an empathetic smile.

"Of course, we understand this is a very difficult time for you," he says.

Sam drains the last mouthful from his beer, sets the can aside and opens a new one.

"Right," he says.

"And we all have our own ways of dealing with these things," the man says, intently focused on the beer can in Sam's hand. "So you just go ahead and take all the time you need."

"Thanks," Sam says, then covers his mouth with one hand to muffle a resounding belch.

"However," the Manager has found a spot directly above Sam's head to stare at. Avoidance of eye contact is probably not a good sign, as far as Sam is concerned. "However," he continues, "I understand that the..." There's a sudden flash of panic as he struggles to think of a customer-friendly alternative to *mangled corpses*. "That the bodily remains of your family are being flown home tomorrow."

Is that really tomorrow? Sam has lost a few days.

"And with your daughter already in care back in the U.K..." the handkerchief appears again. The sweat pops right back up almost as soon as it's wiped away.

Sam takes another long, cool drink and feels the pleasant drunk fuzziness return, softening all those sharp, pointy edges.

"In care," he repeats.

"Yes," the Manager continues. "So, I wondered whether you might also be leaving tomorrow, to accompany the..." another flash of panic, then, "Well, to accompany your family, I mean."

"Do you think they'll let them sit up front with me?" Sam asks.

The manager gulps and gasps like a stranded fish. "I don't... Well, I mean... I shouldn't think..."

Sam chuckles darkly.

"It was a joke," he says.

The Manager does not appreciate the humour.

"Don't worry," Sam says. "I'll be on that flight tomorrow."

"Of course, Sir," the Manager is a portrait of relief as he trots back to his air-conditioned office.

Sam opens another beer.

Sam is not on the flight tomorrow. Nor the next day.

Four days later, he stumbles off a flight at Heathrow to be met by nobody. Two hours after that, he is home.

Everything is exactly as they left it.

There are coffee cups upside-down on the benchtop, left to drip-dry after a hurried hand-washing as they were leaving. Claudia's jacket still lies abandoned on the sofa; a last-minute decision after checking the weather forecast for Florida. There's a mess of green felt-pen marking the lining of the jacket, where Noah had tried to write his name years ago. Ever-practical, Claudia was outraged at the idea of binning a perfectly good jacket *just because the inside's a bit buggered.*

The heating is turned off and it's startlingly cold. Sam's breath clouds in the air every time he exhales.

Exhausted, sore, drunk; Sam lies on the sofa and pulls Claudia's jacket over himself like a blanket. He feels a strange affinity for the jacket.

"My insides are a bit buggered too," he says to nobody in particular.

And then he cries.

* * *

In Sam's drunken absence, his wife and child have been cremated.

Sam can't quite understand why they were flown home as complete bodies, only to be burned to ashes upon arrival.

"Surely it's easier to just fly ashes?" he asks, into the silence.

The pale faces of Claudia's entire family turn to stare at him.

"Instead of bodies, I mean," he clarifies. "It must take up a lot more room to fly a whole coffin."

Claudia's father is ashen.

"Not a good look either," Sam muses. "Surely the other passengers don't like to see coffins being loaded onto their plane."

"We wanted them home," Claudia's mother says, voice unsteady. "We wanted to say goodbye."

"Yes, but that's what this memorial is for," Sam says. "To say goodbye. Otherwise why bother with all this?" he waves a hand, vaguely gesturing at the miserable group of relatives gathered in Claudia's parents' living room.

"Are you drunk?" Claudia's sister Bridget asks, clearly horrified.

He is, but less so than usual.

"Look," Claudia's father says in his well-practiced Stern Parental Figure voice. "The insurance company were happy to pay for the flights, so I can't see that it particularly matters."

He stares Sam down. Sam is the first to look away.

"Shall we carry on?" her father asks, in a voice that allows no disagreement.

Sam nods meekly.

"Why weren't you on the plane with them?" Bridget asks,

apparently not ready to let this go.

"Well they don't let them sit up front, you know," Sam says. Nobody smiles.

"I mean," Sam says, sighing heavily. "They wouldn't have known the difference, would they? Claudia, Noah - they weren't really there."

Claudia's mother reaches out and pats the back of his hand.

"No, Sam," she smiles shakily. "They were already gone."

Bridget snorts unpleasantly. "And you were far too busy getting drunk by a pool to make the flight."

This is surprisingly accurate. Sam feigns offence.

"Yes, Bridget," he says, voice heavy with sarcasm. "I was busy partying in Miami while my wife and child were being sewn back together. You know, after a tornado ripped them into tiny little pieces."

Claudia's mother snatches her patting hand back as if burned.

"That's enough," Claudia's father growls.

"And what about Avril?" Bridget continues, apparently still not done. "Have you even visited her?"

"Of course I have," Sam says.

He hasn't. He doesn't want to.

"That's *enough*," Claudia's father says again, and this time it sticks.

"So," Claudia's mother says with forced brightness, "Shall we decide on the music? I thought perhaps some Stone Roses for Claudia..."

"Area Codes," Sam's mouth says, before his brain has time to catch up. "Ludacris. It's Noah's favourite..." but then he finds himself lost for words. He remembers his son, three years old in the local playground, smiling widely and shouting *I got hoes! I got hoes!*

"Of course," Claudia's mother smiles thinly and makes a note.

Sam sees his son's face, gleeful at the thought of old people horrified by inappropriate lyrics. Noah would love it.

Sam lowers his head onto the table in front of him and sobs.

Within a few minutes, he has cleared the room.

* * *

Back at home, he tries to watch the football but can't keep his eyes away from the two jars of ashes sitting on the mantelpiece above that enormous clean-burning but ever-so-impressive fireplace Claudia had spent so much money on. He feels like they're watching him. He feels like they're judging him for mourning improperly. There are rules he should be following and everyone else seems to know what these rules are but Sam feels lost at sea.

Far too quickly, the match stops for half time and he has no idea who's winning or which teams are playing. In fact, he's struggling to remember why he was watching this in the first place. Before he's properly thought it through, Sam seizes the jars from the mantelpiece, shoves his feet back into his shoes and leaves.

He drives aimlessly for a while, the remains of his wife and child propped up on the passenger seat, seatbelt stretched around them both. Then he decides to take them to the seaside.

It's so different here. There are no endless blue skies, no impossibly white beaches, no bright-orange holidaymakers with fake boobs and tiny bikinis. It's grey and pebbly and miserable. Apart from a few determined dog walkers and a German couple picnicking bravely on the shore, he's got the place to himself.

He walks along the beach for a while, Claudia's jar in one hand and Noah's in the other. He swings them along as he walks.

They'd hate this, he knows. The cold; the sharp wind; the scabby seagulls fighting over a discarded crisp packet. It's not a beach, not really. It's a sad bloody excuse for the seaside and they'd hate it.

So, he can't explain why he does it.

They deserve something so much better.

They deserve cloudless summer skies and impossibly clear water and soft white sand. They should have stayed there, where they were happy. Or at least, somewhere close to happy.

Instead, he wades into the scummy, ice-cold water. It soaks his shoes and socks; it begins to crawl up the legs of his jeans.

He pulls the stopper from Claudia's jar and he dumps her into that disappointing grey excuse for seawater. The ashes spread murkily across the surface; it looks like someone's emptied a vacuum cleaner. He does the same with Noah's jar and stands there, the ashes of his family floating around his ankles, until they sink to the bottom to rest with the muddy pebbles and bits of rubbish.

When there's no trace of them any more, Sam leaves, stopping to fill the empty jars with handfuls of dirty beach pebbles on the way back to the car. Claudia's pebbles have a cigarette butt in them.

He could not have explained why, but it feels like something that needed to be done.

Chapter Nine

They don't play Noah's song. Sam feels unreasonably censored.

There are a lot of Claudia's songs though and just for a moment, Sam has warm feelings toward her parents for knowing their adult child so well. There's the Beatles song she always played in the car and the Stone Roses song she couldn't help singing along to. There's Amy Winehouse and the Pixies, and oddly enough even a bit of Pavarotti. It's a portrait of Claudia in song. They've decked out the place in her favourite colour (yellow) and her favourite flowers (sunflowers). God knows where they'd managed to find sunflowers in March. Sam assumes they cost a fortune.

Noah is represented too, with a small group of Spiderman figurines and his favourite Liverpool scarf. Sam wants to tell everyone that Noah doesn't really like football any more. Or Spiderman. It should be Minecraft figurines and Noah's prized Miami Heat cap.

But they can't be blamed for being a few weeks behind, really. Kids change their preferences about as quickly as they change their underwear, as far as Sam can tell.

"I never had the pleasure of meeting Claudia or Noah," the celebrant begins, in a suitably subdued tone. This seems to Sam like a terrible error in judgement. Surely she should pretend to know the people she's being paid to eulogise? Aren't they all meant to play along with that pretence? He'd thought that was how these things worked. The pastor at his own father's funeral had spoken as if he'd been a lifelong friend and nobody bothered to point out that couldn't possibly have been the case.

"But I've spoken at length with their family over the past few days," the celebrant continues, smiling sadly at Claudia's parents. Smart move, Sam thinks. She knows who's paying the bills around here.

"And I feel as if I've come to know both of them, from the perspective of those who loved them best."

It continues in that vein for quite some time and her voice fades into a steady background buzz as Sam finds himself drawn to the pictures of Claudia and Noah set up either side of the waffling woman. They are huge photos, set in large wooden frames on either side of the celebrant's little platform. Beside Noah's, there's a smaller one of Avril, shuffled slightly to the side in what Sam assumes is an attempt to imply that she's not quite dead yet, but probably will be soon. It's a shame, he thinks, to play third fiddle at your own memorial.

Claudia's photo is from their wedding day, her face enlarged to fill the big frame, Sam's face unceremoniously cropped out from beside her. It is a good picture. She looks happy; people like to think that the recently deceased were happy, Sam finds.

Noah's photo is painfully recent and Sam can't think how it came to be here. Nobody asked him for his Florida holiday snaps and yet, there it is. His son's gap-toothed smile so wide it looks almost painful, his face sun-tanned, a baby alligator cradled carefully against his chest. It was - what - three days before he died? Four days? There should be some kind of recognition in his eyes, Sam thinks. Some kind of dawning realisation that life was almost done with him. A ghostly presence over his shoulder, perhaps. Or a weird distortion in the background.

There's nothing. Just a grinning six-year-old with a baby alligator.

Abby comes in late, announcing her presence with a clatter of high heels against the wooden floor and then a series of whispered apologies as she pushes past Claudia's family to squeeze herself into the front pew beside Sam. The celebrant pauses mid-sentence for a beat, but Abby doesn't seem to notice. He supposes she's accustomed to people noticing her, so the outraged stares just bounce off.

"How are you?" she whispers, just a little too loud, as she reaches over to squeeze his thigh. Carefully manicured nails leave tiny half-moon imprints in his trousers after she takes her hand back.

He smiles, nods. Continues to stare at those over-sized photos of the same family members he dumped into the sea yesterday.

She leans so close that he can feel her breath against his ear as she whispers, "I was *so* sorry to hear what happened."

Sam glances at her blankly. He should be excited by this. The very sight of this woman from across the office used to stir him to attention but now she seems strangely irrelevant. As if she were a chair, he thinks. Or maybe a nice set of curtains.

Claudia's mother turns from her seat on the other side of

Abby to stare daggers at Sam. It doesn't seem particularly fair, considering that he didn't invite her, but he struggles to maintain the vague sense of righteous indignation.

The celebrant finishes up and Claudia's father shuffles, red-eyed to shake her hand before saying a few words himself. It is quite literally a few words, Gerald so overcome with emotion that he can't get out any more than that.

"We loved them both dearly," he says, eyes fixed on the ceiling. "There are no words for how much we miss them."

Then he returns to his seat and buries his face in the shoulder pad of his wife's elegant black suit jacket. It's not something Sam has seen before; a display of actual emotion from his parents-in-law. He watches open-mouthed in astonishment.

The celebrant invites the crowd to *share their memories* and the interminable process begins whereby people unskilled in public speaking take to the stage and ramble incoherently about his family.

Having consumed a good third of a bottle of vodka that morning and then quite a bit more from a hipflask throughout the ceremony, stumbling to the front to speak was probably a bad idea. He does it anyway.

"My family is gone," he says. He can hear his own voice, slurred and oddly emotionless. "They were there, but then they were gone and there's nothing that anyone can do..."

He pauses to take another swig from his hipflask. Claudia's mother frowns.

"I would do anything," he says. "I'd do anything to have died with them."

There's a hushed murmur from around the church. It would

seem that he shouldn't have said that.

"It's true," he continues. "And those are just pebbles. And a butt."

He means to point at the urns sat tidily beneath Claudia and Noah's pictures, but instead manages to gesture towards Claudia's weeping parents. This causes widespread confusion and significant offence, but is arguably better than if he'd been properly understood.

There is stunned silence. Sam returns to his seat, swigging again from the pretence. Abby leans away from him.

There are *refreshments* in a nearby restaurant afterwards, along with plenty of awkward conversations as Sam becomes steadily more drunk and friends try their best to avoid speaking to him. Abby is a constant presence, smiling brightly as she follows him from bar to table and back again. The more he tries to avoid her, the closer she clings to him. She's like a sexy limpet.

"Why are you…" he waves his hands at her.

"Why am I what?" she asks.

"You know," he says, slurring a little. "Doing stuff."

"Why am I doing stuff?"

"Mmmm," he says.

She leans against him, one arm around his shoulders and one breast pushed up against his arm.

"I just want to be here for you," she says with practiced earnestness. "You've always been such a good friend to me."

"When?" he says, baffled.

"You know," she says. "All those times at work."

He goes back towards the bar, but then keeps going past it to the bathrooms, desperate for some alone time.

She follows.

She pushes him up against the wall of the bathroom stall, gazing into his eyes. He burps quietly.

She slides one hand down his pants.

He starts to laugh and then he can't stop. He laughs so hard that he has to lean forward, bracing himself against his knees. He laughs until tears start falling and then it's no longer laughing but crying. He slides to the floor and sobs.

At some point Abby leaves.

At some point, Claudia's uncle hauls him to his feet and puts him into a taxi.

At home, Sam hunts around in the bathroom cabinet until he finds Claudia's bottle of sleeping pills. He takes a handful, chasing them with another swig of vodka. Then he takes another handful, for good measure.

He gets into bed and waits to die.

Chapter Ten

As it turns out, if you leave your dog at a boarding kennels for two weeks longer than originally agreed, ignoring all phone calls and emails from said kennels, they will eventually bring your dog back to your house and knock quite forcefully on your door until you answer.

This is exactly what happens to Sam twenty minutes after he's put himself to bed, full to the brim with painkillers and vodka.

Woozy and disoriented, he makes his way back down the hallway before tripping on the top stair and tumbling all the way down to sprawl bruised and battered across the hardwood floor. After so many painkillers, he's a little surprised to feel considerable pain.

The woman at the door is only encouraged by the noise of Sam's tumble and knocks with renewed vigour, while also bending to shout through the mail slot, "I know you're in there!". The dog whines and scratches half-heartedly at the door.

He knows I'm in trouble, Sam thinks. *He knows, but he doesn't particularly care.*

Lifting his face from the floor to stare daggers at the front door, Sam is dismayed to see that he's left a clear print of his own face in blood on the wood. More blood drips thickly from his throbbing nose and he's fairly sure that he can see one of his front teeth floating in the face-shaped blood puddle. It's hard to be sure though, as the world keeps flickering in and out of focus and wavering oddly around the edges.

He tries to push himself up with the arms that are tangled beneath him, but his arms don't seem to work any more.

"Fuck off!" he shouts at the door, but his mouth feels like it's someone else's and the words come out in a mushy mangle of shushes.

"What?" calls the kennel lady through the mail slot.

"I said, fuck off!" Sam repeats, but it doesn't sound like English at all.

Kennel lady is now peering through the mail slot. Somehow, she seems utterly unperturbed by the sight of a grown man smashed to pieces at the bottom of his own staircase.

"Right then," she says. "I'll just call for the ambulance, shall I?"

Then she disappears and Sam glories for a moment in the wonderful silence. All he can hear is the irregular beat of his own heart, far too loud in his head. He makes a quiet gurgling noise as his eyes close and the room around him fades.

Sam had rather expected that he would see things once his heart stopped.

He'd imagined a big bright light, maybe a stroll down a dark tunnel. A few dead relatives there to encourage him on towards the light perhaps, and then Claudia and Noah. And maybe

Avril. All waiting to welcome him with big, happy dead-people embraces.

He'd pictured rainbows and big fluffy clouds and puppies from his childhood. Endless grassy fields to frolic in. Bottomless glasses of cold beer in the sunshine. All that happy-clappy sentimental shit.

It's not like that.

There's nothing. And no-one.

Just darkness and emptiness, but then bright lights and far too many people speaking far too loudly and refusing to let him sleep.

* * *

Eventually, he wakes up in a hospital bed feeling worse than he has ever felt in his life.

Everything hurts.

He is attached to various machines making various loud-and-annoying noises. The lights overhead are so glaringly bright that he can't open his eyes properly. His face feels puffed into a decidedly unfamiliar shape. He has an incredibly unpleasant taste in his mouth; he imagines it to be a little like that of someone who's just licked a dog's testicles.

Worst of all though, is the face-slap realisation just seconds after waking that his family is dead.

* * *

Claudia's parents come to visit.

Or rather, Claudia's parents come to glare at him with disapproval and shake their heads.

He can't think of anything to say but apparently, neither can they. Sam stares blankly at the ceiling while they stare silently at him.

A nurse comes in and pushes some buttons on one of the machines, then leaves again.

Another nurse comes in and writes something on the chart at the end of his bed.

"How are we all today?" she asks in a sing-song voice, seemingly oblivious to the mood in the room.

"Wonderful, thanks," Sam slurs through a mouth that still doesn't work right. "Hardly suicidal at all today."

Claudia's father lets out a snort of disbelief. Her mother clearly struggles with a compelling urge to slap Sam across the face.

"You small, selfish, pathetic little man," Claudia's father says.

"I don't think you're meant to speak to the suicidal like that," Sam says.

"I don't care what I'm supposed to do," Claudia's father says, eyes wide and face flushed as he leans in far too close to Sam. "I will tell you exactly what I think of you."

"Well, I suppose it's good to be open and honest," Sam allows.

"Stop talking, you smarmy little shit," Claudia's father hisses. The nurse turns tail and disappears from the room.

"Did you not think about Avril?" Claudia's mother asks, voice high and wavering.

"Well," Sam begins and then trails off into silence. He hadn't. "I mean... In what way?"

"Who did you think would take care of her, Sam?" Claudia's father says. "Who did you think would pay for her care?"

"Well..." he'd assumed that Claudia's parents would take care of this with their seemingly inexhaustible piles of money, but this seems to be the wrong answer.

"That is," he says, "Insurance. All the insurance money." *Checkmate*, he thinks.

"Your life insurance won't pay out if you kill yourself," Claudia's father says flatly.

"And Avril needs her father," Claudia's mother warbles. "When she wakes up again. What would she think if..."

Claudia's father meets Sam's gaze and a clear understanding passes between them. Avril is never waking up.

He leans in so close that Sam can see the tiny red veins in his eyes and the sesame seed stuck between his front teeth.

"If you pull this shit again," he says, "I will kill you myself."

There are no other visitors. Sam sits alone, exhausted but somehow unable to sleep. He watches the clock beside the door as it ticks through the seconds.

This is what his life has become, he realises. Numbly waiting to die.

When a doctor asks whether he still feels suicidal, Sam tells her that he wants nothing more than death, but that he's willing to wait for it to happen naturally. She seems satisfied with this answer, giving Sam serious misgivings about the state of mental healthcare in this country.

"Excellent," she says, before moving on to the next patient.

It wasn't a lie. Not exactly.

In his hours of watching clock hands and pondering his sad and empty life, Sam has come to something of a resolution.

He will not kill himself.

He will let the world do it for him.

All he has to do is to make sure that he's in the right place at the right time.

Chapter Eleven

At some point in the interminable days of recovery, Sam becomes convinced that going back to work would be a good idea. A nice distraction, he thinks, from the hours and hours of absolutely pointless *life* in which he seems expected to participate. He begins to think of spreadsheets with something resembling affection and has a dream one night about his office chair in which he feels quite moved.

On an otherwise uneventful Tuesday afternoon, the en-suite toilet blocks. Refusing to accept this, Sam flushes the toilet repeatedly until the contents spill over the brim and begin oozing their way across the bathroom floor. At this point Sam fondly recalls the pristine office bathroom and phones Rogers to suggest that he return to work the following morning. In his usual overly-friendly-and-slightly-confused style, Buddy agrees that it would be "just so awesome, honestly," for Sam to come back to work, providing that Sam understands there is "no pressure. Like, literally, none. Not even a little bit."

Having secured himself the use of the office toilets for the following morning, Sam downs a bottle of wine and falls asleep on the sofa before six. An early night, he thinks, is the best possible preparation for work.

As it turns out, returning to work is not a good idea.

This becomes immediately apparent to Sam three minutes after his early-morning arrival at the office. His cubicle has been decorated with sympathy cards as if it's his birthday. As good as new, his repaired laptop sits in pride of place on his desk and there's a hastily scribbled "Welcome back, Sam!" note (featuring three kisses and a smiley face) propped up between the keys of his computer keyboard. In light of her recent tone-deaf behaviour, Sam suspects Abby.

In his absence, someone has stolen Sam's dream-worthy office chair and replaced it with one of the rubbish ones they give the new hires. He finds himself leaning forward at a strange angle, neck craning sideways to see his screen. This simply will not do, so he swaps the atrocious chair with next-desk-Jane's, assuming that his recent bereavement will give him a free pass for such behaviour.

Next-desk-Jane's chair does not cup his buttocks nor provide the excellent lumbar support he's accustomed to, but it's close enough.

He plugs in the laptop and logs on in an attempt to be deeply absorbed in work before anyone else arrives at the office. Unfortunately, IT appear to have run one of their military-style compulsory password changing offensives and he is now locked out of his own account.

Sam returns to his car, where he drinks vodka and listens to 1990s gangsta rap at a volume loud enough to shake the car while he waits for someone from IT to arrive.

Spying an ever-so-slightly off-kilter Sam from the corner of his eye, Lincoln from IT picks up his pace in an attempt to reach the front door first, thus avoiding any uncomfortable conversation. Sadly for Lincoln, this is not to be.

"Lionel!" Sam shouts, waving both arms overhead in an unmissable display. He is vaguely aware that Lionel is not the correct name, but he doesn't particularly care.

Stoop-shouldered and intentionally oblivious, Lincoln focuses on the doorway ahead of him with admirable determination.

"Lester!" Sam tries again. "Leonard!"

Lincoln is swiping his ID card with single-minded focus but manages to fumble it, dropping the card as the lock beeps in objection.

"Hey you!" Sam shouts. "IT guy!"

Unable to reasonably ignore the noise any longer, Lincoln turns to Sam with an unconvincing expression of surprise.

"Sam!" he says, almost managing to hide the irritation in his tone. "I didn't realise you were back..."

"Oh sure," Sam nods wisely, trying desperately to remember why he needed to speak to an IT person. "Got to get back to it, right?"

Lincoln swipes his card again and holds the door open for Sam, who pushes past with more of a noticeable wobble than he'd intended.

"Right," Lincoln agrees, following him through the door. "So, did you need..."

"Yes!" Sam says. "I needed an IT person."

Lincoln looks at Sam from behind over-sized glasses, head tilted in the manner of a curious puppy. "Right..." he prompts.

"An IT person," Sam repeats.

"Yes," Lincoln says. "I am an IT person."

"You sure are," Sam agrees, then continues to stare blankly.

Lincoln takes this as a signal to continue walking to his cubicle in the IT corner of the ridiculously large open-plan office.

"So..." Lincoln tries again. "You needed something for your computer..?"

"Yes!" Sam says, with a sudden flash of recognition. "A password. I need a password."

Clearly relieved that this is all that's required of him, Lincoln accompanies Sam back to his desk and performs some magic on his keyboard. Brushing invisible dust from his pants, Lincoln attempts a hasty retreat.

"Your old password will work now," he says. "Until the next update."

Sam probably would have thanked him, had he not been distracted by the realisation that next-desk-Jane had stolen her chair back.

There are 782 unread emails in his inbox. He never did set up that out-of-office message.

There is a meeting, where Sam sips from a vodka-spiked cup of coffee and says nothing. He would like to think that he's maintaining a dignified air of consideration while listening carefully to the views of his colleagues. His failure to respond to direct queries, however, coupled with a deep belch that he fails to properly muffle, quickly dispels any such impressions.

There's a minor confrontation with Next-Desk-Jane after he switches chairs again while she's in the bathroom. Apparently his recent bereavement does not excuse this behaviour. Buddy promises to order a new chair for Sam, but refuses to switch with him in the meantime.

Abby asks him out for drinks after work. He tells her that he doesn't need to wait til after work, raises his coffee cup to her and then laughs for an uncomfortably long time. Eventually, she backs away and retreats to her corner for the rest of the day.

Sam opens the half-finished report files that were due weeks ago and stares blankly at the computer screen. The numbers blur together into a meaningless mess. The words make even less sense now than they had when he'd written them. Is there even such a word as "actioned"? There's no red wiggly line under the word, but Sam is fairly sure it's not correct English. He Search-And-Replaces all incidences of the offending word, changing it to "did". This causes wiggly green lines to pop up all over the document, which pleases him greatly.

Buddy checks in with him far too many times. Everyone else avoids him like the plague.

All day, his absent family stare at him from the old photo perched on his desk. Claudia simmers with disapproval. Avril wears her usual, vaguely annoyed expression. Noah looks confused.

Eventually, he turns the photo around so that they won't see him drinking vodka and weeping silently at his desk. Even turned to the wall, he can feel their gazes on him. By mid-afternoon, he has moved the photo to the bottom of his desk drawer. He can still feel them looking up at him from beneath an assortment of ballpoint pens and bulldog clips.

Around 3pm, Buddy suggests that Sam go home and not come

back again "Until you feel like maybe you can manage a full day without so much crying, okay mate?". Buddy maintains that there is no pressure whatsoever, although the visibly pulsating vein in his forehead belies this a little.

* * *

At home, Sam finishes the rest of his vodka in front of the TV, huddled beneath Claudia's coat. The TV is unplugged, but Sam sees no real difference between an actual television show and this soothing black screen. He sits for an hour. Or possibly two. After a while, the light outside fades and the street lights flicker into life. Sam considers turning on a light but decides he prefers to sit alone in the dark.

His phone rings for a while, then stops. A few minutes later, it rings again. Sam doesn't bother checking but assumes it's Claudia's sister wanting to offload the dog. She's been begrudgingly watching him since the Overdose Incident, after which Sam was deemed incapable of caring for anything more demanding than a houseplant. The funny part of that, of course, is that he hasn't bothered to water anything in weeks, so all of the houseplants are slowly shrivelling up too.

At some point, close to midnight, Sam gets up from the couch and wanders - still huddled inside Claudia's coat - over to the end table near the front door, where his phone is plugged into the wall charger, multiple message alerts showing. He deletes everything, unread. It feels wonderful. He takes a notepad and pen from the table and carries them back to his spot on the sofa, stopping to grab three beers from the fridge on the way past.

With a singularity of focus he hasn't felt since that day in Florida, Sam sets himself to the task at hand. Pen in one hand and cellphone in the other, he Googles madly. He trawls the depths of message boards and group chats and discussion boards. He scribbles notes to himself as he navigates his way through the depressing rantings of one unbalanced person after another. He searches and reads and makes notes and drinks beer until the first pink streaks of daylight start to show in the night sky outside. As the street lights blink out again and the world outside stirs into life, Sam sits back and admires his handiwork.

There, tidily noted on the paper before him, is a list of twenty-three different ways of killing oneself. Feeling suddenly quite calm, Sam lies back on the sofa, Claudia's coat bundled up into a pillow beneath his head. And then, for the first time since Florida, he sleeps a dreamless sleep.

Chapter Twelve

By lunchtime the following day, Sam has crossed out more than half of his potential suicide options. The challenge, as far as he sees it, is that he must somehow kill himself in a way that makes it look like he *hasn't* killed himself. He prefers to think of Avril as an abstract problem, as opposed to an actual, irreparably broken child. As long as she remains an abstract problem, then the throwing of large amounts of money at her seems a tidy solution. As his father-in-law has so eloquently pointed out, death by suicide will mean no money, meaning no tidy solution to his abstract problem. He cannot have this.

He considers his options at some length, sitting in his own filth on the lounge room floor while he eats stale pizza and gets slowly drunk. There's an impressive pile of beer cans beside him, oozing brown dribble onto Claudia's expensive cream wool-blend carpet. At some point he appears to have dropped a piece of pizza, sticky-side-down and the cheesy topping has now glued itself into the very fibres of the carpet. Lucky Claude's not here to see it, he thinks for a moment before bursting into near-hysterical laughter and then back into one of his more-usual crying fits.

Having accidentally sat on the TV remote and turned it on, he's been subjected to the droning boredom of the Weather Channel for some time now. It's become little more than background noise, someone prattling about pressure levels and wind currents while he tries his very best to tune them out.

He could, of course, switch the TV off again, but that would involve moving himself enough to extract the remote from under his left buttock. He can't quite seem to summon up that much energy or willpower.

He stares blankly at the screen for some time, eyes unfocused so that the programme becomes a fuzzy mess of colour and motion. It's almost beautiful. His list is down to 9 options:

1. Fall in front of a train following very obvious tripping over shoelaces in front of multiple witnesses.

2. Go "hunting" and stumble into the path of someone else's oncoming bullets.

3. Take up some kind of dangerous extreme sport and be very bad at it (check insurance policy re exclusions).

4. Attempt to save someone from oncoming traffic, dying in the attempt (may need to push person into traffic first).

5. "Accidental" electrocution (requires further research).

6. Cut self while preparing meal, bleed to death before ambulance arrives.

7. Get gored to death in that bull running thing in Spain (google dates for bull thing).

8. Eat lots of takeaways, drink more, take up smoking, wait for inevitable heart attack.

9. Call Claudia's dad "wanker" to his face (hahahahahaha-hahaha).

None of these is quite doing it for Sam. He feels sure that the perfect answer to his little suicide problem is out there, just beyond his reach. It is taunting him.

Slowly, Sam's eyelids droop and his head begins to feel impossibly heavy. He yawns deeply and lies back on the floor, TV still blaring. And then he hears it.

"The death toll from last week's earthquake and resulting tsunami has now increased to one hundred and eighty-seven, following the release of more information from sources close to the recovery efforts."

Sam cracks one eye open and peers at the screen, showing images of enormous waves and thrashing palm trees. The presenter moves on to her next headline.

"Scientists agree that the incidence of wild weather events has increased over recent years, due to the effects of climate change. With increasing concentrations of carbon in the atmosphere, experts warn that the weather events previously known as "hundred-year storms" will continue to become ever more frequent. According to some, we could see a one-hundred-year event every year."

Sam feels like a cartoon character with a lightbulb turning on above his head. He feels as if fireworks have exploded inside his brain. He feels like Einstein with an apple falling into his bath. Or something.

Carefully, he picks up his suicide list and crosses off all 9 items. In their place, he writes one new one: DEATH BY WEATHER.

* * *

The following hours pass in a blur of frantic activity as Sam googles his way into the depths of internet weather enthusiasm. From websites to discussion groups to message boards and Facebook groups, Sam has never felt more excited about anything. It reminds him a little of his teenaged discovery of free internet porn, except that this is even more mindblowing.

He drinks cup after cup of black coffee as the first light of morning dawns outside, but it hardly seems necessary. He feels more awake than ever. He feels like he will never need to sleep again. There is so much to learn, he thinks, as he trawls through more pages of internet discussion about the increasing incidence of storm activity in Tornado Alley "outside of the traditional tornado season". He types *when is tornado season?* and *where is tornado alley?* into Google. Google tells him.

The suicide list in front of him has instead become a page covered in scribbled notes - places, times, events, people. He considers for a fleeting moment that he would've been much better at his job if he'd devoted himself to it with this level of commitment. But it hardly matters now. In a few weeks, he'll be dead anyway.

Clicking through a series of links, Sam finds himself on YouTube watching video after video recorded by stormchasers in America. He is captivated by the images of ferocious winds tearing barns and houses and buildings to confetti. He watches open-mouthed as huge trees are plucked from the earth, roots and all, to be thrown across towns as if weightless. He turns up the volume on his laptop until the speakers crackle and distort in protest, the sounds of shrieking winds and screaming film-makers echoing through his empty house.

Sam doesn't realise. In fact, if asked to qualify his current mood, Sam would say euphoric. He's unaware, but the entire time he watches these videos with a grin of wonder, his face is wet with tears.

Chapter Thirteen

This is what you wanted. Sal tells herself over and over again. *This is your passion. This is your dream.*

Knees making unpleasant popping sounds, she squats as deeply as her protesting joints will allow, then places her hands flat on the sand in front of her.

"Bakasana," says the wiry, white-haired man at the front of the room, with a wide smile. Sal notes that his knees are not making popping sounds, despite his apparent advanced age and impressively deep squat. In fact, nobody's knees are popping, except for Sal's.

She smiles through the pain and focuses on her mantra.

I am strong. I am powerful. I am at one with the universe.

It doesn't feel particularly true at this moment, as she feels a cramp starting in the sole of her left foot. But it will feel true, eventually. She hopes.

There is another audible pop, this time from Sal's elbow as she balances her knees carefully against the backs of her arms and leaning forward, tries to lift her feet from the ground. There is not a hope in hell that she can achieve anything resembling the yogi's double-jointed handstand but she makes a heartfelt attempt at her own version of a

Crow pose. It is worryingly wobbly. The twenty-something American girl with the full sleeve tattoos turns to look at Sal with an expression of concern, maintaining her own perfectly aligned crow pose.

"You okay?" she hisses.

Sal smiles even harder through the pain as her elbow starts to buckle.

"There will be no need to talk," the white-haired man says in the gentlest of sing-song voices. The American girl blushes and then frowns at Sal in a not-at-all-subtle expression of blame.

Sal gives up on the handstand idea and settles for a feet-firmly-on-the-ground version of the pose, which she suspects looks similar to the posture of a dog defecating. Trying her best to ignore the perfect crow poses around her, Sal gazes out to sea. The yogi has positioned them all on the beach this morning so that they are looking out at the sun rising over the horizon behind him. It gives him a golden halo as he stretches and balances on the fine white sand. This does not seem accidental.

They move from Crow's Pose through a series of Sun Salutations, which seem appropriate considering that they are, quite literally, saluting the sun. The sun is saluting them right back with a white-hot blast of blinding light. Despite an exaggerated squint, Sal is severely struggling to make out the shape of the yogi in front of her. She has strong regrets about losing her sunglasses.

As she peeks subtly from under her own armpit to see what everyone else is doing, the faint whirring of a vibrating cellphone can be heard. Sal rolls her eyes at the thought of these ridiculous young people, unable to live without their precious technology even at a yoga teachers' retreat.

There is a good thirty seconds of such thoughts before Sal connects the strange buzzing sensation in her pocket to the cellphone noise. Blood rushes to her face as she fumbles the phone out of her pocket to check the screen before silencing it. *Private Number.* Of course it is.

Sal feels that familiar rush of adrenaline; that same strange, fluttering feeling in her chest; the usual sense of impending doom. Even on a private beach on a Thai island at sunrise, as it turns out, debt collectors will find you. She talks herself down from the edge of panic, repeating self-affirming mantras. *This is your passion. This is your dream. This certificate will look so good on your wall.*

Phone appropriately silenced and zipped back into the pocket of her hoodie, Sal returns to a Standing Forward Fold ("*Uttanasana*" the yogi says in his irritatingly soft-spoken manner) and tries desperately to convince herself that those painful twinges up the back of both legs are a good sign. *Pain is progress*, she tells herself with a desperate, strained grin. Behind her, the American girl glances up from her Uttanasana to give Sal a withering glare. Apparently the phone call has pissed her off. You and me, both, Sal thinks, and gives the American girl a friendly, upside-down wave. This is not met with a warm response.

There is a tiny, sixty-something Scottish lady to Sal's right. Upon arrival at the retreat the previous afternoon, Sal had rejoiced in the sight of someone notably older and more fragile than herself. She had harboured short-lived visions of taking the poor dear under her wing and helping her out with some of the more difficult poses.

Looking at Deirdre now, head tucked in tightly to her ankles and spine in a perfect line, Sal is not encouraged. She pulls hard against her own ankles in an effort to bring her chest a little closer to her legs, but it would appear that Sal's body is not capable of bending in half in this way. Fucking Deirdre.

The yogi lowers himself to the ground, saying in that god-awful soft voice "*Sirsasana li Padmasana.*" This is not a pose that Sal is familiar with, so she waits to see what everyone else does. Her heart sinks as she sees Fucking Deirdre flip herself up into some kind of complicated headstand, legs crossed in an upside-down lotus position.

"Oh, for fuck's sake," she mutters to herself. Apparently supernaturally keen of hearing, the yogi is gazing at her in a clearly disapproving manner. Sal smiles benignly back. Leaning forward from the lotus position to settle the top of her head into the sand, she becomes firmly stuck. It is physically impossible for Sal to lift her body into the air but she continues to try nonetheless. Within three seconds, all of the muscles in her legs are burning. After five seconds, she has a pounding headache. Eight seconds in, she is sweating heavily. At ten seconds, something in her butt starts cramping and she collapses with a grunt.

"Every attempt is a good attempt," the yogi says. "Whatever level you're at, that's great."

It would seem that nobody else is at Sal's level because they all hold their cross-legged bloody headstand positions for another thirty seconds, until the yogi moves into yet another pose seemingly designed to torture Sal's body in particular.

An hour later, at breakfast, Fucking Deirdre sits next to Sal and pats her on the shoulder.

"How's the body?" she asks, in a lovely-old-granny voice.

"Fine," Sal says, feeling utterly depressed at the thought that she's now become Deirdre's sympathy project.

"A bit of Arnica cream'll do wonders for those aches and pains," Deirdre says.

"Mmm," Sal agrees, poking at her bowl of grey lentil mush with a spoon.

"Have you tried Devil's Claw?" Deirdre continues, shovelling her lentil mush into her mouth with great enthusiasm. "Works wonders on those ageing joints, you know." She gives Sal a little wink.

"I'm thirty-eight," Sal says in protest.

Deirdre raises an eyebrow. "Are you, dear?"

Sal looks right back, trying to stare the old lady down. Sal blinks first.

"Well, OK," she says. "Forty-two. But that's hardly *ageing*."

"We're all ageing, dear," Deirdre says, then pauses to take a sip of the atrocious, bitter tea they've been given. "It's a condition of life."

"How about you?" Sal asks, feeling belligerent. "How old are you?"

"Seventy-eight," Deirdre says with a cheery wink.

"Fucking bullshit," Sal says.

"Cross my heart," Deirdre says, looking mildly offended.

"You're a seventy-eight-year-old yoga teacher," Sal says slowly, sure that she's missed something.

"Oh, yes," Deirdre beams. "It keeps me young."

"That's funny," Sal says. "I could swear it's making me old before my time."

"Perhaps you've lost touch with your inner self," Deirdre says. "This is the perfect place for re-discovery."

Sal makes a non-committal grunt of acknowledgement.

All she can think is *seventy-eight fucking years old.*

Chapter Fourteen

Sam has always been an enthusiastic traveller. There's something about airports that has always done something to him - his pulse quickens; his mood lifts; he feels newly aware of all the wonderful possibilities of life. He likes to watch people - Claudia always found this slightly creepy, but to Sam it feels like perfectly reasonable behaviour. It's a game that he plays inside his own head, guessing where they're going and why.

Indian couple severely over-dressed for the mild weather? They've clearly just arrived on the AA206 from Calgary. Noisy group of redheads? Off to Norway for a family reunion. Sad-looking older man? Leaving on the round-the-world trip he'd planned with his wife before her untimely death. Or maybe not. No, she left him, in fact. For the pool boy.

In their younger, backpacking days, he'd always insisted on arriving at the airport hours ahead of time so that he could sit patiently in the departure hall, people-watching and slowly building higher and higher levels of excitement until he was fit to bursting by the time they were allowed to board the plane. Claudia, a reluctant traveller with a far more casual approach to timelines, was driven close to breaking point by this behaviour.

Their most heated arguments had always occurred in crowded airports, surrounded by large groups of travellers grateful for the entertainment.

Travelling with the kids had dulled his enthusiasm a little. Dragging a whining toddler through security is not fun. Spending three hours telling stories because you got to the gate far too early - it's less exciting than his guess-the-destination game. Managing meal- and toilet- and snacking- and screentime-schedules takes a lot of the shine off things. And yet, even with his family dragging behind him like an ever-complaining weight around his neck, even then he felt that same unmistakeable lift as he reached the airport. Even with the whinging and moaning and constant irritation, it was still his favourite place to be.

Now, it's different. The airport might just as well be a bus stop, the plane a commuter train to the office. There is nothing remotely exciting or uplifting about the Departure board with its list of glamorous destinations. The people swarming around him and past him and sometimes into him, they hold no mystery whatsoever. He is numb to the thrill of travel. It is, quite simply, a means to an end.

He sees things now that he wouldn't have noticed before. The red-faced, sniffling child sitting alone at the luggage carousel. The homeless man, shabby and bedraggled, pulling half-eaten sandwiches from a rubbish bin. The mascara-streaked cheeks of a tearful flight attendant, smiling so hard it feels like competitive sport.

This is not a happy place, Sam thinks as he watches a spotty adolescent girl pick her nose and wipe it on the seat beside her. This is a hub of human filth and misery.

He waits at the gate, buttocks cramping in protest at the hard plastic seat. He stares blankly into space, ignoring all of the people around him as they carry on with their normal, everyday lives in a manner that strikes him as distasteful. There is a woman on the far side of the departure lounge, who is also staring blankly into space. Somehow, over the course of a few minutes, their gazes drift until their eyes lock and panic ensues as both realise simultaneously that they are staring directly at one another. Blushing furiously, the woman opens a book and stares angrily down at its pages. Sam feels the familiar heat of awkwardness in his cheeks but is oddly disconnected from events, painfully aware that none of this means anything at all.

* * *

Her name is Cherry.
   Or Cheryl.
   Or Sherry, maybe.
   He hadn't been listening.

She is older than she'd looked under the forgiving lighting of the airport bar. Older than Sam, by at least a decade. Too old for this line of work, arguably.
   She looks up at him, wide-eyed, and tries to smile around a mouthful of his cock. Thick blue eyeshadow has run into

the tiny wrinkles around her eyes, making strange abstract patterns on loose-skinned eyelids. Her lipstick is running too, the smokers' lines around her lips filling with red and creating the impression of blood running down to her chin. He examines her face in some detail as she works away at him.

It's odd, Sam thinks, to see his own cock rock-hard in the mouth of an ageing hooker, when he feels utterly numb. She could bite right through it, he thinks, and he'd still feel nothing at all.

Cherry/Sherry/Sheryl gazes up at him as she runs a dry tongue slowly from balls to tip, making ever-so-subtle moaning sounds of faked pleasure. She's been maintaining eye contact, he realises, because she thinks he'll find it sexy.

He does not find it sexy. Nothing about this situation is sexy.

There's a dawning realisation in her expression that he is looking at her as if she were a particularly interesting bug crushed on his shoe, rather than a seductive temptress of delight. She averts her eyes and concentrates instead on the job at hand. Her face turned, he now has a perfect view of the top of her head, where a clear line of grey pushes back against the tide of too-dark black hair dye. He imagines filling in the grey bits with a felt-tip pen.

She removes his penis from her mouth and pauses to pluck an errant hair from her tongue. He stares down at himself, feeling the strangest disconnect to his own anatomy as he stands rigidly to attention, condom wrinkled and wet with saliva.

"I want you so much," she whispers, in a tone she no doubt

believes to be convincing and seductive. It's remarkably similar, he thinks, to the voice the McDonald's people use when they ask if you want fries. The thick Scouse accent is not something he'd expected to hear in this part of Spain, let alone from a wrinkled hooker with his cock in her mouth.

"Hmmm," he says, non-committal.

"How do you want me?" she asks, slipping one hand down to cup his balls tightly.

He takes her by the hips and turns her away from him, pushing her up against the motel wall.

"Oh baby," she says, as if reading lines from a script. "Oh yeah, I want it like that."

"Please stop talking now," he says. She falls silent.

She arches her back ever so slightly to make it easier for him and he slides into her.

And now, with a startling burst of sensation, he can feel something.

She is warm and welcoming and from this angle, she looks ever so slightly like Claudia. The curve of her hips. The tiny dimples above her buttocks. The surprisingly perky breasts crushed against the wall.

"Claude," he chokes out. She remains blessedly silent.

Slowly, gently, he pushes all of the way inside her and it is glorious. It is beautiful and wholesome and loving. For a moment, he forgets that he's fucking a whore in a cheap motel.

He kisses the back of her neck as he thrusts into her, holding her hips firmly in both hands and pushing against them again and again.

She makes a small noise that's so different to her earlier

play-acting, he starts to sincerely believe she's enjoying it.

He pulls out and leads her to the bed, switching off the light on the way past. He lies her down gently against the pillows and then rests himself carefully on top of her, savouring the sensation of warm, bare skin against skin. Sam feels at home.

He pushes into her again and she lets out a small gasp. He kisses her shoulders and chest and then takes a nipple into his mouth, biting down on it ever so gently in the way that always made Claudia moan. She does not moan, but she doesn't pull away either. She squirms against him and all at once he is thrusting hard into her body and she is pushing back equally hard. He pulls out again and lies beside her and she climbs on top of him with remarkable agility.

She rides him like a cowgirl, pushing hard against his cock, hands braced against the headboard behind him. She thrusts harder and faster and an unstoppable heat builds in his balls, so that he can no longer make any sounds at all. But she is making enough noise for both of them, her voice rising through a series of shrieks into a high, wavering scream as she pushes hard against him and shudders. He feels it.

He feels the muscles inside her tightening against his cock and that's all it takes for him to explode into an orgasm so all-encompassing he sees stars.

He lies flat on his back, breathing hard, as the room spins around him. There is a deafening ringing sound resounding in his skull.

In the seconds it takes for Sam to regain a basic understanding of his surroundings, she has gone. She has taken his wallet with her.

* * *

Next morning, Sam wakes to the noise of cheap windows, rattling loose in their frames under the onslaught of a strong wind.

There's a moment of panicked disorientation as he tries to make sense of the room around him. Deep cracks across a sagging textured ceiling; strange brown stains splashed across the wall; a rogue spring pressing into his thigh from the mattress beneath him. Then he sees the condom, puddled stickily on the bald orange carpet beside the bed and it all comes back to him in a jarring smack of understanding.

He examines the underside of his testicles with an oddly disconnected sense of scientific curiosity, unsure of the odds of contracting a venereal disease from a one-off encounter with an ageing prostitute. Taking into account the lack of questions asked, her complete disinterest in his personal hygiene and the theft of his wallet, he weighs up his chances of infection at fair-to-middling.

There's another rattle from the windows, then a loud creak of protest from the window frames. Sam looks over at the crooked curtains with renewed interest.

It doesn't sound like the Storm Of The Century promised on the Weather Channel. Not yet. But it could have the makings of something quite impressive, he thinks.

Taking care to avoid stepping on the condom, he picks his way barefoot across threadbare carpet to the windows, then holds his breath as he draws back the curtain. And then he smiles.

Outside, the world is utterly changed from the sticky warmth of last night. There's not a soul to be seen in any direction. The neighbourhood is deserted, but everything is moving.

The street is a river, twisting currents of muddy grey water streaming past at high speed, bobbing sticks and bits of rubbish rocketing along atop dirty waves. The cars parked outside the motel stand axle-deep, a particularly tiny Suzuki alarmingly close to floating off downstream as it rocks dramatically in the wash of the floodwaters.

Rain falls spasmodically in thick sheets, as if thrown from buckets. The dry, dead grass near the kerb is transformed to sludgy mud, peppered with the pink bloated bodies of drowned worms.

And the wind.

It's like nothing Sam has ever seen. Even that day in Florida, it wasn't like this.

The wind is *alive*. It's full of aggressive intent, howling and screaming with all the rage of the demoniacally possessed. The sheer noise of it has Sam staring open-mouthed as he watches thick trees bend like twigs under its force. There's a pained groan from outside and then a loud fracturing as an enormous limb is torn free from the tree directly in front of the window. It crashes to the muddy ground in a splintering of branches and the newly limbless tree swoons drunkenly after it. Heavy roots tear themselves from the ground on one side and a thick spray of mud spatters across the window. Sam flinches.

On the other side of the street, beyond a dense grove of bedraggled alder trees, there's a river. A real river. From where

Sam stands, the river is hidden by the trees and the scrubby bushes that grow between them, but he knows it's there.

He feels something warm swell inside his chest at the thought of those river banks crumbling into the floodwaters. There is a sudden certainty within him, an indisputable understanding that he is exactly where he needs to be and that all will soon be right with the world.

With all the giddy excitement of a child on Christmas morning, Sam dresses in last night's clothes, having conveniently discarded them on the floor several hours earlier. He stops for a moment to consider finding a jacket, then waves the idea away.

Moments later, Sam strides through the motel lobby in a wildly inappropriate outfit of shorts and a Hawaiian-print shirt, both liberally splattered with a greenish substance that looks suspiciously like dried vomit. He finds himself grinning at the desk attendant in a manner that she seems to find deeply unnerving. The lobby is full of staff and guests but the flurry of agitation stops dead as Sam passes through. There is silence in his wake as he pushes through the front doors and out into the storm.

* * *

The moment he steps outside, the storm slams into him and tears the breath from his lungs. Doubled over, winded, he braces himself with both hands against his knees and sucks hard for air. Icy rain smashes itself against all the exposed parts of his body, so cold it burns. He holds a hand up to stop the torrents of water hitting his eyes and he squints into the gloom. Out here, it's like another world. A shrieking, throbbing, assault on all senses. Glancing back at the motel, he sees the faces of strangers gazing out at him open-mouthed. He gives a cheery wave and attempts a friendly grin, but it's difficult to move his face properly when it feels frozen solid.

Peering out at the world through a narrow gap between his fingers, Sam starts out across the sodden motel lawn towards the street. With every step, his trainers sink deep beneath the grass and into thick mud beneath. Every time, it's an effort to pull his foot free and then place it in front of him, without falling. He feels precariously balanced, at the mercy of buffeting winds that attack from all sides. He is shaking; his whole body wracked by involuntary shudders. He's never before been so cold and so uncomfortable, yet somehow, he still wears the mindless grin of the redeemed.

It takes longer than it should to reach the road. Just a few metres, really, but he's heaving and sweating as if he just ran a marathon. With a pained groan, he steps down into the street and starts splashing his way through the dirty brown torrents. His feet have lost all sensation and it feels oddly as if his body ends at the knees; as if he has lumps of meat tied to each leg that he's dragging numbly through the icy water. He stumbles several times, tripping over unseen obstacles that leave bruises and gashes he can't feel. He falls forward and lands hard on both knees, floodwater drenching him from the shoulders down. There's a moment - just a few seconds - where he feels the full force of the current pressing against him, and one knee lifts from the road surface and his whole body sways. There's a very clear image in his mind of a large ship tipping heavily to one side before disappearing beneath the waves.

But then his knee finds contact again and he is no longer in danger of slipping away.

And then he's reached the far side of the street and scrambles up the scraggy hill, limbs flapping loosely as filthy water squelches from his shoes with each step. There's a scrawny dog sheltered beneath one of the trees and she growls a warning at Sam, hackles raised. He waves at her as he passes, moronic grin still plastered across his face.

Keeping a safe distance, tail tucked between her legs and body close to the ground, she follows.

The trees are thicker than he remembers and it feels as if he's been walking for hours. High above his head, the branches thrash around with a desperate kind of violence, but he can't help thinking that their enthusiasm is waning. Surely the rain was heavier than this, when he was crossing the flooded street? Wasn't the wind stronger?

He flexes his fingers experimentally, bunching his hands into fists and then popping them open again. It occurs to Sam that he can *feel* his fingers again. At the same time, a deep ache begins to throb behind both kneecaps and he glances down to see thick ribbons of dark red trailing down his shins. Both knees are mashed into a mess of blood and skin, dotted with sticky clumps of leg hair. They look like mincemeat. No wonder that skinny dog is following him.

For the first time since waking, he feels his mood begin to

dim and his smile falters, ever so slightly. Lightning flashes overhead, illuminating the forest around him. There's a booming clap of thunder, but it sounds much further away now. Sam's smile fades a little more.

He picks his way more carefully up a small slope, wet trainers sliding in the mud. After a long, dry summer followed by an unseasonably warm winter, this part of Spain is near mummified. There's no grass anywhere outside of the motel's artificially irrigated lawns. There's nothing green anywhere, really - even the leaves on the alder trees have crisped in the sun to a dusty brown. So now, there's nothing holding this hill together. It's a mess of churned mud and it's like ice under Sam's shoes so he slides back three steps back for every one he takes forward.

Taking a new approach, he kicks the toe of one trainer as hard as he can into the hill and then balances on that foot while he finds a toe-hold further up with the other shoe. It's a frustratingly slow process but eventually, he stands victorious atop the small hill and sees, just a few steps away, the storm-churned waters of the river. He feels a pang of happiness so deep and complete that his fixed grin is replaced all at once by a soft smile of genuine satisfaction. His eyes are wet already, streaming in the biting wind, but he feels a new warmth as real tears brim. It feels like coming home.

He stumbles down the other side of the hill and sits on the riverbank, legs hanging over the edge.

The river is high and it's angry. It thrashes itself against the bank where Sam sits, showering him in an icy-cold mess of watery filth. The water is thick with floating objects - broken branches bob along on its surface, but so do crisp packets and plastic bags and a broken lawn chair; an assorted mess of life leftovers, swept away at startling speed.

He has thought the plan through to this point, but no further.

He knows that he's in the right place. He knows that this is where it will happen. He's just not sure quite how.

He takes a slow look around at the world gone mad. It's a swirling, shrieking grey mess of cloud and mud and rain and... is that hail? Lightning flashes again overhead and he glances back to see the same skinny dog silhouetted at the top of the hill. She shrinks back, eyes wide and teeth bared as she presses herself into the muddy ground. Then the thunder comes, a roar so loud and so sudden that the dog startles and flinches away. And then she starts to slide.

Paws scrabbling in urgency, she tries to stop the slide with teeth and paws and claws, but it's hopeless. Sam feels pangs of sympathy in his own battered hands and feet, recalling that sensation of the ground sliding away from beneath him as if it were an ice rink. He watches it happen, feeling oddly removed from the situation as a wild-eyed, gnashing ball of teeth and fur slides down the hill at increasing speed towards him.

It's not until she's snapping distance from him that Sam's thought processes kick into action.

"Oh shit," he hears himself say, as the dog slams into him. She manages to seize his arm firmly between sharp teeth, drawing blood with a nauseating crunch in the seconds before they both topple over the edge and into the river.

Chapter Fifteen

It hadn't been a complete failure, Sam reflected. He wasn't dead, so results had been far from ideal. On the flip side though, he'd saved someone's miserable fucking dog from a watery grave. So, there was that.

He was fairly sure it hadn't been the *very* worst moment of his life; blinking back to consciousness sprawled across the bank of a dirty river with a mangy dog licking his face. Not the worst. But certainly in the top ten.

He'd flirted with the idea of throwing himself back into the river to be swept away to sweet oblivion, but then he'd noticed the terribly excited Spanish family standing around him with blankets and warm smiles. There was a painfully cute child wrapped around the neck of the mangy dog, small face buried in the flea-infested ruff of fur under her chin. A small, stooped grandmother held out a blanket. Sam had felt that suicide at this point might seem rude, so instead he'd taken the blanket with a slightly panicked smile.

Now, miles above the clouds in a stinking, overheated budget airliner, he watches tiny white-caps on the ocean far below and wishes with all his might that the plane would plummet into the water. There's a small child in the seat behind him, wheezing snottily and slamming tiny feet into the back of Sam's chair. He closes his eyes and leans back in the seat, adjusting his posture ever so slightly until the pounding feet line up nicely with the stiff and aching places along the left side of his spine. Just like a massage. Almost.

After several failed attempts to flag down a passing flight attendant, Sam persists in making eye contact with a particularly anxious-looking red-head with smudged mascara. In the instant that she realises it's too late to look away, he sees panic cross her features before she plasters a polite customer-service smile back into place. Following the misadventures of the previous day, Sam sports a remarkably puffy black eye, a dark mess of bruises across the opposite cheek and a nasty gash up the side of his neck, ending in a torn earlobe. Coupled with the patchy salt-and-pepper almost-beard and hair recently doused in a muddy river, he can imagine that this presents something of a wild-eyed hobo image.

"Sir..?" the flight attendant makes a show of craning her head in Sam's direction but manages to stay well outside of grabbing distance. Probably wise, Sam considers.

"Vodka," he rasps through still-tender vocal cords. This sets off a thick, rattling coughing fit that seems to spread disquiet throughout his fellow passengers.

"You'd like to make a purchase from our in-flight bar service?" the redhead asks, a confident smile belied by the tremble in her voice.

Sam, now struggling through a particularly hacking fit of coughing, waves vaguely at the flight attendant with a thumbs-up and a smile, though tears are streaming down his battered cheeks.

"Any... um, mixer with that?" she asks, looking quite concerned for his health.

Sam shakes his head, holding up a hand with three fingers while continuing to struggle for breath.

"You'd like three vodkas?" she asks. "On the rocks?"

He smiles weakly through the coughing that just won't stop. The flight attendant backs away and disappears behind a curtain.

The elderly woman seated in front of Sam turns to give him a disapproving glare. He shrugs and coughs a little harder in her direction.

On the bright side, the kicking seems to have stopped.

The flight attendant reappears with three tiny bottles of cheap vodka and a plastic cup full of ice cubes. Sam forks over the princely sum of twenty euros, uncaps the first bottle and throws it back. The cough disappears as quickly as it started and, clear-voiced again, Sam orders another three bottles.

By the time his flight lands amidst a nasty grey drizzle, Sam has the beginnings of a nice glow on. He can hardly feel the bruises any more and the shooting pains in his chest have dampened down into the range of irritating as opposed to crippling.

The long wait at customs is mind-numbing. He stares blankly at his own shoes for a good twenty minutes, replaying the previous night over and over in his mind, each time throwing himself back into that freezing river with gleeful abandon, despite the friendly Spanish grandmother.

* * *

There's nobody and nothing to welcome him home. The house is dark and cold, its emptiness so immediately apparent that Sam is mildly surprised to see that he's not been robbed. The mail slot in the door is stuffed full, junk-mail protruding like a tongue.

With the optimism of the suicidal, Sam had paid no attention to the location of his house keys and stashed them into the nearest available spot when he'd left for the airport the previous week. Now, he sheds layers of clothing, checking every pocket without success, then emptying the contents of his suitcase across the doorstep. He's considering dossing down outside for the night when the keys tumble out of an upturned shoe.

Indoors is no more welcoming. There's even more mail heaped in a pile on the lounge side of the mail slot, large words in primary colours screaming up at Sam about sales and clearances and amazing-once-in-a-lifetime-savings. Leaving the contents of his suitcase strewn across the doorstep, he pushes hard against the front door, slowly nudging the mail pile to one side and squeezing his way inside. Claudia's jacket is still on the sofa where he left it. Sam takes a half-full bottle of vodka from the fridge and settles in for a night of staring blankly at the TV, Claudia's jacket spread across his lap like a blanket.

It might be an hour later. It might be six. The only indication that time has passed at all is the empty vodka bottle on the floor and the pitch-black night outside. There's a high-pitched fizzing sound from the television followed by an unnerving pop as the screen blinks out. Sam feels a vague pang of disappointment, but quickly shakes it off and continues to stare at the blank screen instead. It doesn't feel much different.

Eventually, Sam rises unsteadily to his feet in search of another drink. On his way to the kitchen, his socks slide in the pile of junk mail and he narrowly avoids falling face-first into the door, arms windmilling as he struggles to regain his balance before toppling slowly to the floor in something resembling a controlled descent. Right at eye level, in amongst that pile of cheap, shiny paper, there's a white envelope. Actual, addressed mail. Addressed, in fact, to Sam. With a big blue Life Insurance logo on the front.

It doesn't change anything, not like he'd expected. It's a big number. A number so big they'd joked about it - Sam pretending to throw Claudia down the stairs; Claudia waving a steak knife in the air.

He can see her now, knife in one hand and a half-full wine glass in the other, shouting "Watch yourself, Dickhole!" and slashing at the air around her with gleeful abandon. "You'll be six feet under and I'll be a millionaire in Mexico!"

It should feel good, to know that he need never work again. Or it should feel bad, trading something so common as money for the woman who once called him Dickhole and made him laugh until he couldn't breathe.

But it didn't feel like anything. Just numbers on a ridiculous letter from faceless bureaucrats who were apparently deeply sorry for his loss.

He sits on the lounge floor, surrounded by junk mail and discarded food wrappers, staring blankly at the letter in his hand and wondering how much vodka he might get for eight hundred thousand pounds.

Probably not enough, he decides. It's never enough.

Chapter Sixteen

It's morning. He can tell because he's just been rudely awoken by that unique combination of smashing and crunching and wet thuds that signifies the rubbish truck emptying bins outside. The arrival of new leaflets thrust through the mail-slot to land on his face is another giveaway and the godawful piercing brightness of sunlight right in his eyes is the final touch. It's definitely morning.

He rises carefully to his feet, stretching his arms out tentatively in front of him. He's rewarded with a series of pops and creaks from his joints and a dull ache down one side of his neck. The skin on his chin feels oddly dry and papery; he picks at it carefully for some time before realising that it's just a night's drool, dried into a stiff mess in his stubble.

There's nothing noticeably different about this particular day. He feels the same pointless numbness that he feels every morning. He wants nothing more than to curl up under Claudia's coat with a new bottle of vodka.

But for some reason, he wanders blearily into the kitchen instead and boils the jug.

He sits at the table and drinks black coffee. He eats stale, dry toast until his tongue sticks to the roof of his mouth. Then he washes it down with more coffee.

Three coffees and a half loaf of bread later, Sam realises that he can feel something.

He's not sure what it is; not exactly.

It's not happiness. It's nowhere near happiness. It's not contentment or mild pleasure or even acceptance. He still feels as if there is a gaping emptiness around him into which everything good has vanished forever. He still feels sad and angry beyond anything he'd ever realised he was possible of feeling. The world is still a dark and nasty and meaningless place.

And yet, he feels as if maybe there's something he needs to do. And that maybe, if he does that thing, then he might feel marginally less shit.

So he does.

He stands under a steaming shower for so long that the water runs cold, gazing in fascination at the unending streams of river mud, twigs and leaves disappearing down the drain. There's a fleeting moment of sympathy for the other passengers on the plane as Sam realises just how filthy he must have been on that plane and just how much he must've stunk. *Like Worzel Gummidge, but scummier*, Claudia used to say of his tendency to avoid showering until visibly filthy. Just for a second, he smiles and it feels so unfamiliar that he touches his face in wonder.

But then it's gone and he's still just a sad, bruised man standing under a cold shower.

Showered and shivering, he stands in front of the mirror with razor in hand for some time before deciding that he's not ready. He needs that patchy, grey cover. It's just who he is now.

Hobo chic Claudia would say, slapping him on the arse and leering at him in the mirror. He's startled to see another small smile flash across his face; he turns away from the mirror to vomit copiously into the toilet.

Instead of shaving, he makes do with using one of Claudia's makeup wipes to pick the bits of puke from in between his stubbly bits of beard.

Noah's booster seat is still strapped into the car, sticky with spilled juice and covered in crumbs. At the sight of it, Sam feels something cold twist in his gut and he has to stop, leaning heavily against the side of the car, breathing deeply. On Avril's side of the backseat, there's an empty crisp packet and a mysterious purple stain. *It's a good thing we have that rule about no food or drinks in the car* Claudia says, somehow inside his head again. Of all the times he imagined Claudia gone, Sam reflects, he never once expected to miss her snarkiness. Her hugs, yes. Her boobs, absolutely. That peanut chicken noodle thing she cooks occasionally, for sure.

With a final deep breath, he opens the door and gets into the car, shoving the driver's seat forward because it's still set in Claudia's far-too-far-back position. *You drive lying down* Sam tells her. *It can't possibly be safe.* There's no answer.

Her empty coffee cup in the console; her radio station tuned into the stereo; her bracelet hanging from the gearstick - it's so clearly her car that he feels like he's intruding. But he grits his teeth and drives, Led Zeppelin blasting from the speakers at a ludicrous volume.

Not concerned about damaging the children's hearing then? He asks her.

Just trying to damage my own so I can't hear the whining she whispers back.

At the shops, he feels zero guilt for parking in the Parents With Young Children spot right outside the entrance. A woman in a giant people-mover raises her eyebrows at him as she drives on to less premium parking. With a wide smile, he presents his middle finger.

Shopping has never really been his forte. It was one of the first things he and Claudia had bonded over - their shared distaste for shopping malls and clothing stores and home-wares. Shopping, they agreed, was a task best approached with a military attitude: commence only when truly necessary; identify objectives in advance; get in and get out as quickly as humanly possible.

Today though, he wanders. He strolls aimlessly from one shop to another, piling items into trolleys and baskets with no clear idea of why he needs them. He stops off at the car every now and then, piling the boot to overflowing with boxes and bags and packages. It might well be a car so heavily possessed by his wife and children that it's physically painful to be around, but it also has an impressive amount of storage space.

He stops at the coffee place and orders one of the white-chocolate-caramel-vanilla-butterscotch lattes that Claudia has always frowned upon with such disdain. To compensate for all the syrup, he asks the teenager on the counter to add three extra shots of espresso.

Quite frankly, he finds, it's delightful. So sugary his teeth ache; a frothy mess of confection and caffeine that clogs his chin-stubble with milky nastiness and leaves him feeling like an over-stimulated toddler. There's a gentle humming noise reverberating inside his head and the world around him seems somehow brighter, as if he's just snorted a decent noseful of cocaine. It seems quite possible at this stage that he might never sleep again.

When he gets home, it helps that he's ridiculously over-caffeinated and high on sugar. Armful after armful of assorted purchases leaves the car to be dumped into an ever-growing pile beside the sofa. He spends the afternoon setting up the new TV (having thrown the old one into the neighbour's skip with some pleasure), assembling an over-sized desk and office chair, setting up the new super-computer he appears to have purchased and covering every inch of wall space with charts and maps. The caffeine-and-sugar high begins to wane just as he blue-tacks the last weather chart to the last free spot of wall and then collapses onto the sofa, exhausted.

For a moment, he sits and stares at the room that used to be a lounge. It's very similar, he thinks, to the dodgy hideaways they always find in cop movies - where the serial killer's been hiding out and planning his crimes while jacking off over the random pieces of dead bodies he's kept as trophies.

He does wonder for a moment whether it might be a little excessive to have created such a fabulous monument when he's really just planning on killing himself.

Still, if you're going to do something, you may as well do it properly. Surely, he thinks, surely now he can find exactly the right place to be at exactly the right time. It seems outrageously unlikely to Sam that his death will result in seeing Claudia again, but it does seem certain to end this unbearable feeling of being in a world without her nasty, sarcastic, wonderful presence. It's enough to make him smile again.

Sam settles back into the couch cushions, the caffeine having seemingly fled his body all at once and left him in a swooning puddle of yawns. He pulls Claudia's jacket over himself and rests his head against the arm of the couch.

Within seconds, he's asleep.

Just before he closes his eyes though, the last thing he hears is Claudia's voice low in his ear: *But what about Avril?*

Chapter Seventeen

It's a new experience for Sam, learning for the sake of learning.

Never the strongest of students, Sam's school days had consisted mainly of football practice, smoking and copying test answers from Spotty Murchison at the next desk. University was much of the same, except with less football and more drinking. As far as Sam was concerned, study was purely for the purpose of scraping through exams at the last minute. All-night study sessions the night before an exam; paying some brilliant seventeen-year-old to write his essays; staring at textbook pages in the desperate hope that something might stick; it was only ever the bare minimum, only ever so that he could get that stupid piece of paper and find the job that's been driving him slowly mad ever since.

This is different though. This is no *Introduction to Commerce* textbook. This is absolutely fascinating and Sam finds himself paging through thick Meteorology volumes as if they were Stephen King novels. He is a voracious consumer of information. He can't wait to get to the next chapter and find out what happens next. Claudia wouldn't recognise him.

He spends hours every day with the textbooks on the couch, highlighting passages, dog-earing pages and writing notes in the margins. He only stops reading to check the computer or to Google things he's found in the books. It's like a whole new world has opened up right in front of him, with all the answers he needs right there for the taking.

Sam has signed up to every weather group he could find and posted in every discussion board; a vague intro post as an enthusiastic newbie wanting help:

Hi! My name's Sam and I live in the south of England. Very new to all this storm-chasing stuff, but I saw some crazy weather on a recent trip to Florida and it's made me really want to find out more! Went to Spain a few days ago because I heard there was going to be a huge storm but no dice :(Any tips for a newbie would be much appreciated!

Help has come very quickly. Response after response from welcoming, excited and knowledgeable strangers of questionable sanity. They write stream-of-consciousness tirades about storms and weather patterns and pressure systems that made little sense to Sam initially, but are slowly starting to mean something to him. After all these years, Sam has finally found his community: storm chasers.

He is cursing himself already for his stupidity in flying to Spain on the basis of a newspaper headline anticipating the "storm of a century". Of course it wasn't, as St0rmcha5er27 so helpfully points out, because it involved a warm front. *"Warm fronts only ever cause pussy-ass storms"*, as it turns out. *"You need a good cold front to get a real storm brewin."*

Sam knows exactly what he needs to do this time. He will research and research and research until he can research no more. He will pick the brains of these incredibly knowl-edgeable weather weirdos. He will find the Next Big Storm before anyone else knows it's coming and he will plant himself squarely in its path.

He will feel the sound and the vibrations and the white-knuckle terror these people tell him about and he will love every last second of it, because he'll know that he's exactly where he's meant to be and doing exactly what he should've done six weeks ago when the weather smashed his family into little pieces but forgot him.

* * *

There's a series of dings as the alerts on his mobile phone, the computer and the smart speaker all echo one another. Sam flings the book to the floor and dashes over to the computer, where the browser is open to multiple different message boards on multiple different tabs. It's him. The Weatherman has posted something. Sam hears himself giggling in delight and wonders - not for the first time - whether he might be losing it.

Nobody seems to know where The Weatherman came from. He's been on the message board for as long as the message boards have existed - for as long as the internet has existed, it seems. He's an ex-weather presenter, or a Professor of Meteorology from some prestigious university, or possibly the survivor of a terrible natural disaster, with a taste for chasing down the storms that took his home... There are a hundred different stories about where he's based and who he is, but ultimately it doesn't matter. He's the king of this strange little world; the undisputed authority on anything and everything to do with storms.

Every thread on every message board seems to have some kind of contribution from him. Always insightful; always enlightening; usually sharply cynical and devastating to anyone stupid enough to disagree. He posts at every hour of the day, leaving no clue as to his location. He often disappears completely for weeks at a time, catching up in a flurry of posts and responses once he's back. He writes always in well-researched, academic sentences so different to the garbled excitement of most posts on these boards. There are never anecdotes or personal stories in The Weatherman's posts. It's pure science and his hundreds of virtual disciples love him for it.

Now, he's doing what he does best - crushing an overly-enthusiastic newbie beneath the weight of data and reason.

No such thing as global warming! writes the cringingly-named GoTrumpGo: *Colder than ever down here this winter - snowstorms like you wouldn't believe. I wish we had some of that climate change goin on so I didn't have to dig out the driveway every morning.*

There are a few excited responses from a small echo-chamber of climate-change-deniers, along with some half-hearted responses from those opposed. They're clearly waiting for someone else to come in and do his thing - and now he has.

Welcome newbie! He writes. *We appreciate your interest and quite honestly, we were all stupid once.*

Sam laugh-snorts, black coffee burning the insides of his nose.

There follows a bullet-pointed list of accepted evidence of climate change within the scientific community, alongside colourful charts, graphs and figures. There are photos of weather events and detailed flow charts explaining the effects of atmospheric carbon dioxide levels on weather patterns. There's a timeline of recent weather events, detailing the disturbing increase in frequency of devastating storm events.

It is an exhaustive presentation.

Yeah, but my Grandpa says it snowed more back when he was young bleats GoTrumpGo

Four weather enthusiasts jump on this at once.

StOrmcha5er27: *The plural of anecdote is not data*

Tornado_Allie: *The plural of anecdote is not data*

HiPressureSystm: *The plural of anecdote is not data*

Cyclone_Sal: *The plural of anecdote is not data*

They've been well trained.

There's another series of dings and Sam feels blood rush to his head as he realises that The Weatherman has replied to Sam's post. Heart racing, he clicks through to the post.

I'm sorry for your loss it reads *I'm sure we all remember reading about the freak storm that took your family and these things are a sobering reminder that this weather we find so fascinating can also have terrible consequences for real people.* Sam stares blankly and breathes: "What the actual fuck?". His post had said nothing about Claudia and the kids.

He scrolls back up the page to re-read his own message, in case he's remembering it wrong. He's not remembering it wrong.

Suddenly, his post is hot property. Response after response appears under The Weatherman's post:

OMG that was you? How awful!

Wow man, what was that like? Were you there?

I'm so sorry, @Frosty_Snowman. Are you OK?

Shiiiiiiiiiiit that's some heavy shit

So unlucky, Florida at that time of year's usually fine

Well actually, I think you'll find that there have been some significant events in Florida even in winter. What about the Kissimmee tornadoes back in '98?

Or 2019, that tornado ripped apart an army base down there – think it was December? January? Nowhere near storm season anyways

It continues in this vein for some time. Sam watches comment after comment go by, with no idea of how to respond.

Eventually, he clicks out of the post and goes hunting for information on storm-chasing tours instead. There's the expected derisive comments – they're ridiculous; they're over-priced; they'll never get you close enough to the action because they don't want to get sued; it's all fake; it's just for tourists...

The Weatherman is conspicuously silent on all of these posts, apart from one comment urging aspiring storm-chasers to research all companies and ensuring they're properly licensed before handing over any money.

There's a steady thread through all of these messages though – don't go on a storm-chasing tour. But if you do...

It's the same company, grudgingly recommended over and over as the *least* fake, the *least* over-priced, the *least* touristy.

So, Sam finds the website and books a tour for the following week, when Tornado_Allie has promised him there will be "some crazy good storm systems in town".

For the first time since Florida, Sam sleeps in his own bed, tangled in dirty sheets with his head on Claudia's pillow, breathing the ever-so-subtle smell of her shampoo all night.

* * *

His plane lands in Dallas under a slate-grey sky and a gentle rain. As he sits, waiting for the signal to disembark, he watches from the window as patches of dark cloud are lit from within by flashes of lightning. The other passengers are conducting the landing-time ritual of standing immediately (despite the usual request to remain seated) and crowding the aisle for no clear reason. He can hear three separate conversations, all variations of the same complaint about the weather.

"We came all the way from Birmingham for this!" a bright-orange woman on tottering heels repeats over and over. "Birmingham!"

He wonders for a moment - appalled at the thought - whether the Birmingham family might be planning to join his storm-chasing tour, but then he spots the Dallas Cowboys t-shirts on the two weepy children sandwiched either side of orange woman and decides he's probably safe.

There's a hold-up at the luggage carousel somehow caused by the orange woman from Birmingham, necessitating a sprint through the airport for Sam to make his connecting flight. By the time Sam's at the gate, ready to board his flight to Oklahoma City, he's covered in a fine layer of sticky, smelly stress sweat. This stale sweatiness, together with his still-unshaven face and slept-on hair makes him a singularly unattractive seat mate, so he gets three seats to himself. Prior to this whole life-falling-apart situation, he really hadn't understood the many benefits of poor personal hygiene.

Running on pure adrenaline, Sam has somehow survived thirteen hours of international travel without any alcohol. Upon realising this, he orders a vodka on the rocks. The one-hour flight goes by quite swimmingly and Sam arrives in Oklahoma City in a pleasantly warm bubble of general well-being. Ever so slightly inebriated, he shakes hands with a number of people at the hotel, immediately forgetting all of their names. He eats an enormous dinner of over-sized hamburger and thousands of chips at an oddly cowboy-themed restaurant with these same people. As far as Sam can tell, he's an absolute delight - full of entertaining stories and fascinating weather-related titbits. It is possible that his viewpoint has become slightly warped by alcohol however, as he is cut off at the bar very early on before being asked to leave so politely that he's already in bed at the hotel before he realises they've kicked him out.

Nonetheless, he counts it as a successful day and sleeps the contented sleep of someone whose fondest dreams are about to come true.

* * *

The next morning, sitting on a rock-hard plastic chair in an interminable briefing meeting at an ungodly hour, Sam has some regrets.

He's wearing the same bright-yellow t-shirt as everyone else in the room, emblazoned with "Storm Chase OKC" across the front and "April 24 Crew" across the back. He's not sure that he likes the idea of being part of a crew.

There is a man at the front of the room, speaking very loudly and very enthusiastically into a microphone. Loud enough without amplification, his voice through the speakers is skull-shattering. At least, it seems that way to Sam. Nobody else seems particularly bothered by it.

"Now it's pretty early in the season for storm activity," Loud Man says. "But there've been some pretty darn good signs in these last few days that we might have something pretty big coming."

There's a murmur of excitement throughout the group. Sam nods sagely. Tornado_Allie has not put him wrong.

"Y'all might be wondering," he says, "what you're in for this week…" he squints out at his captive audience from beneath a battered cowboy hat, channelling Dirty Harry. There's a theatrical pause.

"Is it storms?" Sam deadpans. "Are we in for storms, by chance?"

Harry fixes Sam with an ever-so-slightly pissed off stare.

"Yeah," he drawls. "Yeah, I guess you might say we're in for storms."

There follows a long and detailed explanation of exactly what's expected of the Crew over the next eight days. Sam finds that the briefing focuses more heavily than expected on the dining plan. This does, in fact, seem to be the single most important component of the schedule. There is much consternation about the idea that everyone should purchase their own snacks to take in the jeeps.

A woman with a towering beehive hairdo in a startling shade of pink is concerned that someone might bring peanuts onboard.

"Any y'all allergic to nuts?" Harry asks, in a tone that strongly suggests nobody admit to this weakness of character. There is silence.

"Good enough for ya, Sugar?" Harry asks. Again, it's not a question.

Sam is not at all sure whether this is a term of endearment, or whether the woman's name is, in fact, Sugar. Stranger things have happened.

Conversation continues for a good twenty minutes on the subject of food, with Harry providing repeated assurances that the group will be fed at least three times per day and that nobody will starve. By the time they're loaded into the bright yellow jeeps, it's well into mid-morning and Sam is itching to be underway. As the engines start and they roll away from the curb, Sam feels an irresistible sense of giddiness rising in his chest. It's like he's eight years old again on Christmas morning, that enormous 1980s computer wrapped and waiting underneath the tree.

The sky overhead is an unremarkable shade of washed-out blue, wispy bits of white cloud drifting innocuously. In the distance though, there's a darker shadow where a wall of purple-grey stormclouds gather on the far horizon. Sam watches with fascination as their jeep makes frustratingly slow progress towards those clouds. He can't wait.

Chapter Eighteen

This never happens, according to Dirty Harry. In thirty years of storm chases, they've never before had an eight-day trip "with such promising storm signs" end in precisely zero storm activity.

Sam finds himself grumbling things like "fucking typical" at regular intervals throughout this last day of half-arsed chasing, as the convoy of bright-yellow jeeps roam aimlessly around countryside basking happily beneath unseasonably bright sunshine and clear blue skies.

"It's been a great adventure though, hasn't it?" enthuses the tiny, bright-eyed, sixty-something woman seated behind Sam.

"Not really," Sam says. "Waste of fucking time, really."

He leans back in the admittedly very comfortable seat and takes a sizeable swig from the plastic Coke bottle in his hand. He no longer cares whether his fellow chasers can tell that his carry-on Coke bottles contain significant proportions of vodka. He no longer cares about much, if he's honest.

The small woman leans forward in her seat and tries again, "Where're you from, Sam?" she asks. Her breath smells of the milky tea she carries in an enormous orange thermos flask.

"England," he mutters, with zero enthusiasm.

"Well, yes," she says, one eyebrow raised. "I realise that, dear."

After seven and a half days of sharing a jeep with this woman, it's only now that Sam realises she has a fairly strong Welsh accent.

"Surrey," he says. "Small town, you wouldn't know it."

He tips his "Stormchasers OKC" baseball cap forward over his face in what he hopes is a clear signal that he'd prefer to sleep, rather than carry on this conversation. She does not take the hint.

"Lovely," she beams.

"Not really," he mutters to himself.

"Your wife will be looking forward to having you back, no doubt," she says.

"No wife," Sam says.

"Wedding ring's a strange choice for an unmarried man," she observes.

"Why are you here anyway?" Sam says. He means, why is she leaning forward into his seat space in this particular moment, but she takes the question more broadly.

"Well dear," she says. "I was married for forty years to my Clive..."

Under cover of the hat, Sam rolls his eyes. He can see where this dreary fucking story is going. *We always said that one day we'd do this together...*

"And Clive passed," she says in a small voice. "And do you know, it was the most wonderful thing to ever happen to me."

"The forty years of marriage?" Sam asks, feeling that he should contribute to the conversation in some way. She snorts.

"Absolutely not!" her voice drops to a hoarse whisper. "The

day that boring old bastard died; that was the first day of the rest of my life, love."

Sam lifts the cap from his face to see whether she's being genuine. Her eyes shine with something close to the religious mania of the recently reborn.

"Every fucking day of my life with that man - constant bloody whinging."

"Well," Sam feels an inexplicable need to defend the recently-passed Clive. "Maybe he had some stressful things going on..."

She snorts again.

"Bollocks to that," she declares. "Forty years, we never went anywhere. Never did anything. I wasted forty years of my life listening to that miserable bloody man whinge and moan about all the dangers of the world."

Sam makes a vague noise of confusion. He's not sure what he's meant to say in this situation.

"I spent forty years stuck in that dreary little cottage in that dreary little town with that dreary little man," she fixes Sam with a sardonic smile. "Choked on a pickled onion sandwich in the end."

Sam makes a surprised face. It seems appropriate.

"I know!" she chuckles. "All those terrorists and natural disasters and mass murderers he used to tell me about. All those reasons we couldn't ever go anywhere or do anything..."

"Worried about the wrong things," Sam says wisely.

"Well, exactly," she says. "Didn't see that scary bloody sandwich coming, did he?" she chortles to herself for long enough that Sam begins to suspect her tea might have a similar percent-proof to his vodka-spiked Coke.

"Nothing would've bothered him more, you know," she

confides. "That miserable bugger is rolling in his grave while I spend all the life insurance money on wild and crazy adventures."

"Same," Sam says, startling himself with his own honesty. "Life insurance money."

"Mmm?"

"My family's dead," Sam says, amazed by the way that his voice chokes up even after all the times he's said this. "All dead."

It's not strictly true, but it's close enough. The woman nods slowly, eyes fixed on his face with a steely gaze.

"And I want to be dead too," he says. "But I can't do it myself. Because..." he swallows, "It doesn't matter why, but I can't."

"You do realise we're unlikely to die on this trip?" she seems concerned.

"Well, yes," he sighs. "I know, there's all the health and safety things..."

"It's America," she says. "Not a chance they'll do anything they could get sued for."

"I sort of thought," he waves a hand vaguely, takes another swig of spiked Coke. "Maybe we'd get close enough that I could just... run off. Towards the storm, I mean."

She nods, apparently unconvinced.

"I think they'd just chase after you."

"No," he is sure of this. "It's in the disclaimer. They're not responsible if you ignore directions."

She is quiet for a moment, then sits back in her seat. She opens her thermos flask on the little plastic table in front of her and pours tea into a plastic cup, passing it forward to Sam.

He takes a large gulp and coughs. There is much more alcohol than he'd suspected.

She sips delicately at her own plastic teacup.

"You need a decoy," she says. "I shall spill hot tea all over myself and shriek wildly."

"Well," he says, "I'm not sure that…"

"I shan't take no for an answer," she says. "You give me a signal. Say something English and I'll throw the tea and then you make a run for it."

"They all speak English," Sam says.

"No, no no," she rolls her eyes at his idiocy. "Something ridiculously English. You know, the things they think English people say. Toodle pip, old chum. Like that."

"There's no storms though," Sam points out.

"You just wait," she says, eyes flashing with a maniacal kind of excitement. "I've got a good feeling about today."

* * *

The good feeling does not pay off.

"Sorry it didn't work out," she says, as they wait at the departure gate twelve hours later.

"S'alright," he says.

She pours another two cups of spiked tea from the thermos she's somehow managed to smuggle through security.

It occurs to Sam that he's never asked her name. It seems too late to ask, now.

He downs the tea in a series of chugging gulps, then closes his eyes as his head swims pleasantly.

"That's not tea," he says.

"Well, it's not exactly whiskey either, love," she smiles.

"Somewhere in between, I'd say."

They sit in silence for some time, watching people come and go with no real interest.

"What next, then?" she says eventually. "Back to real life?"

He shakes his head slowly, sipping at a fresh cup of whiskey-tea.

"Not that," he says. "I don't think real life is really for me."

She nods. They go back to sitting in silence.

* * *

Four months after the accident, Sam goes to his daughter's hospital. He hasn't quite made it as far as Avril's ward, but he counts it as something of a small triumph to have entered the building.

There are three doctors in the meeting he's been called to - each a little younger and a little more earnest than the last.

The amusingly named Doctor Foster is an alarmingly tall woman who appears to be eighteen years old and wears jeans and pink Converse with her regulation doctor coat. Somehow, she seems to be in charge.

"There's no easy way to say this, Mr Frost," she begins.

Propping her elbows on the desk in front of her, she leans towards Sam with an expression she must surely have practiced in a mirror - equal parts concerned, caring and understanding, with a side order of medical wisdom.

"We're doing all we can for Avril and you should know that she's in no discomfort," she says.

Sam nods. He's fairly sure that he's supposed to say something, but he can't think what that might be.

The acne-spotted youth sitting next to Doctor Foster clears his throat uncomfortably. According to his name tag, he's called Doctor Khan.

"Like Imran," Sam says thoughtfully. Doctor Khan appears panic-stricken under Sam's thoughtful gaze. Doctor Khan makes an odd gurgling noise, eyes darting about the room like a cornered rabbit.

Unperturbed, Doctor Foster continues: "I'm afraid that Avril's condition has not responded to treatment in the way we'd hoped it might."

Sam blinks at her.

They've been monitoring Avril's brain activity, Doctor Foster explains. And there's none.

She suggests, in words very carefully considered, that it might be time to think about switching off the machines.

Switching her off at the wall, Sam thinks. Like a TV.

"Absolutely not." Claudia's father is predictably firm. Claudia's mother weeps silently into a lace handkerchief.

"Of course, your feelings are absolutely understandable," Doctor Foster smiles patiently. "And these decisions should be made as a family group."

"Well, then…" Claudia's father seems unimpressed by the team of white-coated youngsters on the other side of the desk.

"But the decision must ultimately be made by Avril's legal guardian," she says.

As if choreographed, all heads in the room turn as one to stare at Sam. He begins to regret his choice of vodka shooters for breakfast.

"Right," he says, then clears his throat dramatically. "Well, I think it's quite…"

"You're not switching those machines off," Claudia's father says.

"She can hear me!" Claudia's mother says. At least, Sam's fairly sure that's what she means; the wet lace handkerchief is clutched to her face, muffling her voice into incoherence.

"Sorry?" Doctor Foster says.

"She can hear me!" Claudia's mother repeats, removing the handkerchief to reveal red-rimmed eyes and flushed cheeks. "When I read to her. I've seen her smile. I've *seen* it."

Doctor Foster looks slightly thrown by this.

"It can be difficult to acknowledge..."

"She's not brain dead!" Claudia's mother shrieks.

"Shall we just leave the machines, then?" Sam goes for a jaunty tone, but may have misjudged. "Like, for now. See how it goes..."

"That's not really how it works..." Doctor Khan begins, apparently taking himself by surprise as he trails off into red-faced silence.

"We could look at moving Avril to another part of the facility," Doctor Foster says. "For more *palliative* care."

"She'd be kept comfortable," interrupts Doctor Ross, the small Australian woman seated between the other two doctors. "She'd be cared for and her condition would still be monitored, of course, but..."

"But I feel that we need to be very clear about her prognosis," Doctor Foster says, pausing to take a deep breath. "Avril will not recover from this."

Claudia's mother lets out a squeak of indignation.

"Avril will always need machines to breathe for her. It is extremely unlikely that she will ever regain even very basic brain function..."

"But you never know," Claudia's mother begins. "Miracles can happen!"

"It is extremely unlikely," Doctor Foster repeats. "When the human brain is damaged this severely, it's just not possible for any kind of higher-level function to return..."

"You should not expect that Avril will improve," Doctor Ross says, voice flat and devoid of emotion. "Avril's brain has been damaged beyond any ability to work as a brain should."

"I prefer to have hope," Claudia's mother says, eye bright with angry tears.

"That little girl could spend decades like this," Doctor Ross says. "And eventually, her body will give up and she will die. Is that what you think Avril would want? Is that what her mother would've wanted?"

All of this in that same oddly flat voice.

Claudia's mother gasps as if she's been slapped.

"What Doctor Ross means," Doctor Foster interjects, all sympathetic smiles and pink shoes. "What she means, is that we want you to have all the information you need to make this decision."

"Avril's organs could save lives." Doctor Ross adds helpfully.

"Well, that's positive," Sam says. Claudia's father stares daggers.

There's silence. After thirty seconds or so, Doctor Khan begins to fidget.

Apropos of nothing, Sam gets to his feet.

"Right, you can all sort this whole thing..." he says, waving one hand vaguely to indicate his comatose daughter's current medical situation. "I'm off to see Avril."

"I really don't think..." Claudia's father blusters.

"Whatever you decide is fine," Sam says as he leaves the room, the drama of his exit ever so slightly marred by the minor wobble to his gait.

For reasons he'd find impossible to explain, Sam really does go to see her.

He sits in a wobbly plastic chair beside her bed, holding one of her small, bony hands between his own. He watches her face and tries to see any sign of the life his mother-in-law is so sure about. He doesn't see it.

There is a child in the hospital bed. She's the right age to be Avril and the right build. She's wearing Avril's Wonder Woman pyjamas and the tufts of hair sprouting from her shorn scalp are roughly the right colour.

It feels like a clever copy. Like a robot wearing his daughter's face.

There are faint, white scars across her cheeks and he marvels for a moment at the thought of her damaged body repairing itself, even in the absence of a working mind.

He reaches out a trembling hand to brush a loose eyelash from her cheek and then pulls back as if scalded.

Her face feels wrong; the skin loose and slack and cool.

He leans forward so that his lips are almost touching her ear. Something deep inside him clenches tight at the sight of the tiny unicorn hanging from the small hoop earring she'd bought in Florida.

"Avril," he whispers hoarsely. Then louder: "Avril!"

Then, somehow, he is standing and the plastic chair has clattered loudly to the ground. He is leaning over his daughter, one hand on each shoulder and shouting her name.

She doesn't flinch.

He stands upright, brushing carefully at the shoulders of her pyjamas to remove the dirty marks where his hands had rested. As a nurse slips tentatively into the room, one wary eye on Sam, he rights the fallen chair and brushes dust from the seat. He smiles politely at the nurse and leaves without looking back.

In the lift on the way down to the lobby, Sam phones Buddy and quits his job.

Buddy is audibly relieved.

Chapter Nineteen

Two weeks in, Sam is finding that unemployment suits him quite nicely.

He usually wakes around noon, peeling his face from the pillow with increasing effort each day, occasionally stopping to shower before his first drink.

Early afternoon is his drinking time, spent sprawled on the couch under Claudia's jacket with the radio turned up loud enough to shake the windows, eliciting fairly regular noise complaints from the neighbours. He usually finishes a box of beers by nightfall, when he orders pizza and downs three or four espressos in short order while the computer wakes itself up. Then, he settles in for a red-eyed, caffeine-fuelled evening of virtual weather-chasing from the comfort of his own lounge room.

This particular Thursday morning gets off to a slightly different start.

Sam is thrown head-first into consciousness with all the subtlety of a punch to the face, Claudia's father leaning over the bed to yell, "Get the fuck out of bed, you pathetic little bastard!" at a volume Sam considers quite impolite.

He blinks, heavy eyelids scraping across eyes dry and gritty with what feels like a severe lack of sleep.

"Morning," he manages.

"Good morning, Sam," Claudia's mother says, her manners apparently so ingrained that she must always respond politely.

Leaning up on one elbow, Sam peers across the room to see her perched awkwardly on the chair beside the door. There's at least a week's worth of dirty laundry piled onto that chair, but she's managed to find a tiny corner to balance herself on.

Sam clears his throat and takes a deep gulp from the glass of flat beer beside the bed.

"Well, I must say," he says. "This is an unexpected pleasure."Claudia's mother averts her eyes.

"Get dressed," Claudia's father says. "Get downstairs. There are things that need saying."

He spins on his heel and leaves the room, Claudia's mother close behind him.

Sam finishes the rest of the beer, pauses briefly in the bathroom to vomit up said beer and then pulls on Claudia's old purple dressing gown before following her parents downstairs.

There's a group of people gathered in his house. Some of them sit uncomfortably on the couches, having moved piles of paperwork and unwashed socks out of the way. A few of them sit around the dining table, pointedly ignoring the stacks of old pizza boxes in front of them. A few more stand around, looking a little lost amongst the mess of fast food packaging, empty bottles and dirty laundry that has taken over Sam's house. He's most surprised to see Buddy standing in a corner, examining one of Sam's weather maps in apparent fascination.

"Should've said," Sam mutters, taking a beer from the fridge

"I would've made hors d'ouevres."

There is a room full of people staring at him.

"Any takers?" he asks, waving the beer.

"Love one, mate!" Buddy chirps, seemingly unaware of the effect this has on Claudia's father.

Sam pitches a bottle across the room in Buddy's general direction and is grudgingly impressed by his boss's agility in snatching it from the air and popping it open in one smooth move.

"Sit. Down. Now." Claudia's father says through gritted teeth, face flushed an unhealthy-looking shade of puce.

Sam flops onto the carpet, back propped against the wall beside Buddy, who sinks down to sit too.

"Cheers!" he says, clinking bottles. "Office is not the same without you, Sam." Buddy looks a little misty-eyed at this.

"Appreciate that," Sam mutters.

"This. Is. Not. A. Party." Claudia's father's face has flushed a shade of purple not often seen in nature.

"Well, of course not," Sam squints up at him. "This'd be a completely inappropriate time for a party, I'd say."

Buddy nods sagely, then takes another long swallow of beer.

"We are here to tell you," Claudia's father continues, "That you've gone off the rails."

Sam considers this for a moment.

"You're probably not wrong," he says, "But I'd say it's not unusual to have a period of adjustment, following the catastrophic deaths of one's family."

Buddy nods again. "Perfectly understandable," he says.

Claudia's father has clear regrets about inviting Sam's ex-boss to this event.

"You're a drunk," he spits out, lips curled in disdain. "You're drunk right now."

"I prefer "problem drinker"," Sam says. "And this is my first beer of the day."

He's sure that the half-glass of flat beer he drank upon waking doesn't count, considering that it mostly ended up in the toilet.

"Perfectly reasonable," Buddy says agreeably. "Almost noon."

There's a noticeable wave of discomfort spreading through the crowd in Sam's living room.

He can see Claudia's brother-in-law shuffling slowly towards the back door with all the care and subtlety of Inspector Clouseau. Andy Evans from Number 10 is staring fixedly at his socks, while Noah's schoolteacher is quite clearly searching for the nearest exit.

"What would Claudia think if she could see you now?" Claudia's father roars at something close to the volume of a jumbo jet taking off. Mrs Stanton from Number 12 looks mortified.

"I'd like to think she'd be right here with me," Sam says softly. "I can't imagine she'd be back in the office, bright-eyed and bushy-tailed."

"She was not a drunk!" Claudia's father roars again.

"No," Sam says, "She was a good Mum. This would've broken her."

He doesn't realise that he's crying again until the tears start dripping off his chin and Buddy passes him a box of tissues.

There's a quiet, embarrassed exodus from the room until it's just Sam, Buddy and Claudia's parents.

"You do realise we're English," Sam says to Claudia's father. "We don't really *do* interventions."

"Never going to work," Buddy agrees. "Nice try though, mate." He beams up at Claudia's father.

"Right, then," Claudia's father says. "Rot in your own filth, for all I care."

He spins on his heel and leaves the house, apparently forgetting about his wife and almost catching her face in the door as he dramatically slams it behind himself.

"Look after yourself, love," she can't help muttering as she slips out behind him.

Sam and Buddy sit in companionable silence for a good five minutes before Buddy drains his beer and leaps to his feet with an agility Sam shouldn't find surprising considering all those hours at the gym.

"Another beer, mate?" he calls back over his shoulder as he heads for the fridge.

"Sure," Sam says, settling back against the wall and rearranging the folds of his purple dressing gown around himself. It still smells like Claudia.

"Hey, Buddy?" he calls. Sam has genuinely forgotten his boss's actual name.

"Hmm?" Buddy calls back, balancing four beers in the crook of his elbow.

"If I die," Sam says.

"You're not going to..."

"No," Sam interrupts the platitudes. "I said, if I die."

"Right..." Buddy returns to the living room and slides down the wall to sit beside Sam, carefully moving a bit of purple dressing gown out of his way.

"You will look after Avril," Sam continues. It's not a question.

"Ummm," Buddy says. Sam realises what he's about to say a second before it comes out of his mouth. "Avril's the dog, yeah?"

Sam smiles through tears. This could not be more perfect. Nothing would enrage Claudia's father more than dealing with this idiot savant for the rest of his life.

"Avril is my daughter," Sam says. "She's brain-dead. Pretty low maintenance."

Buddy looks lost.

"I just need you to be her legal guardian, OK?" Sam says slowly. "Just sign papers and agree not to unplug her. Things like that."

Buddy shrugs. "Sure," he says. "Why not."

"Why not, indeed," Sam says, raising his bottle in a toast.

"To April!" Buddy says.

"Avril," Sam corrects.

"To Avril!" Buddy says.

Good enough, Sam thinks.

Chapter Twenty

There's a distinct smell of swamp steaming up from the murky water of the spa pool. It's reminiscent of the rotting mess in the bottom of Avril's school-bag, that time that she left three sandwiches and an apple in there for a full term - musty and ripe and very, very wrong. Clearly, this is why Claudia insisted on sprinkling chlorine into the spa at regular intervals

.

Buddy doesn't seem to notice the smell.

"This is the life, mate!" he says, eyes closed in apparent ecstasy as the stagnant water bubbles and churns around his shoulders.

Sam makes a non-committal grunt and takes another long gulp of cold beer.

"Do you ever wonder," Buddy says, eyes still closed, "how many people in the world have ever fucked a chicken?"

Sam chokes on his beer, a stream of froth spurting out of his nose and into the pool.

Buddy cracks one eye open. "That a weird question?"

Sam considers this for a moment. "Not by your standards, Buddy."

"So..?" Buddy squints at Sam. "How many?"

"Is it even possible?" Sam says. "Physically?"

"Sure!" Buddy smiles widely. "You can fuck anything, if you really want to."

Sam feels slightly queasy at this.

"And if they consent." Buddy says with some sincerity.

"How would a chicken consent?" Sam asks.

Buddy considers this for some time. Just when Sam thinks the conversation is over, he says, "Body language."

There's an insistent, high-pitched trilling noise from inside and Sam gets out of the pool, splashing swampy water all over the floor as he stumbles back into the house. There's a close call in the kitchen as he slides precariously on a patch of wet lino, but he makes it to the computer relatively unharmed. The screen is flashing. Sam clicks the mouse to stop the alarm and scrolls down the page.

He hears Buddy come into the house, slipping on the same patch of lino and just catching himself with wildly windmilling arms.

"What's happened?" he says breathlessly. "Is it April?"

"Avril," Sam corrects automatically.

"Right," Buddy says. "Avril."

Sam clicks from post to post, scanning for key information as his heart begins to race.

"So..." Buddy says.

"Not Avril," Sam says. "I'm going to Mexico."

Buddy nods. "That's your Mexico alarm?"

"Something like that," Sam says.

Apparently satisfied, Buddy takes a fresh beer from the fridge and returns to the spa pool. Sam stretches his hands in front of him, fingers interlaced and is rewarded by a series of unhealthy popping sounds.

"Gettin' too old fer this shit," he says in his best grizzled cowboy voice.

"You say something?" Buddy shouts back from the patio.

"Keep an eye on the house for me?" Sam calls, as he opens three different flight booking websites in three different windows. "For a week or so?"

"Absolutely!" Buddy sounds excited beyond all reason. "Won't let you down, Sam!"

* * *

Claudia always wanted to go to Mexico.

Dia de Muertos in Mexico City, specifically - tequila shots and sombreros and parades through the city streets. Sam had pointed out with class-swot smarminess that the parade was about as authentic as movie-theatre nachos, having been invented for a James Bond movie in the 70s. This earned him two days' silence and an extended period of cold-shouldering, after which they both chose to forget that the conversation had ever taken place, while Claudia continued to make vague plans for a trip in November of some unspecified future year.

It was odd then, to be here without her.

Crammed into a train carriage full of humanity, sweating and panting in the unseasonable heat, Sam wonders absently whether Claudia would've been disappointed in this heaving, sweating mass of people. Somehow, he thinks she would have loved every stinking second of it.

He gets off near the centre of town, shoving his way past

three elderly ladies and a group of schoolchildren in his panic to get through the doors before they slide closed again. He mumbles heart-felt apologies in broken Spanish over his shoulder, but is fairly sure that one of the ladies has placed some kind of curse upon his very soul.

Joke's on her, he thought - life can't possibly get any worse than this.

As he drags his far-too-heavy suitcase up a flight of stairs and out of the station, the wheels break off with a comical popping sound and bounce all the way back down the stairs behind him and onto the train tracks. Fucking karma, he thinks.

The hotel he's booked is conveniently located two minutes' walk from the train station, but the rain is so heavy that thick streams of dirty water are cascading down his face by the time he reaches the lobby. His clothes are plastered to his body and his feet swim inside his shoes. The hotel staff seem wholly unimpressed at the state of him.

The tall, painfully thin receptionist raises one perfectly-shaped eyebrow in Sam's direction and says something in very fast, very pointed Spanish.

"Ahh yes," Sam says. "Buenos dias."

The receptionist smiles so widely and with so little real emotion that it looks physically painful.

"You speak English, sir?" he says through gritted teeth.

"Hablo un poco de Espanol," Sam says, with what he hopes will be a winningly modest smile The receptionist is unmoved.

"Do you have a reservation, Sir?" he asks, without appearing to move his mouth at all.

"Si!" Sam grins. "Si. Me llamo Sam Frost."

The receptionist continues to act as if Sam's torturous garbling of the Spanish language has not happened. He taps away at the computer in front of him for a few seconds, then holds out a hand towards Sam, eyes still fixed firmly on the screen in front of him. Sam takes the proffered hand and slowly shakes it, not quite sure what's happening.

"Mucho gusto!" Sam says.

The receptionist lifts his eyes from the screen and directs an expression at Sam as if he were a giant cockroach. He pulls his hand out of Sam's grasp, wiping it (not at all discreetly) on his uniform trousers.

"Your credit card, Sir?" he says. "For the deposit."

"Ahh, si!" Sam says.

Following the unpacking of his entire suitcase across the lobby floor and several minutes of fumbling through every pocket of his clothing, Sam remembers the nasty-looking beige pouch strapped to his chest (subject of many a withering glare from Claudia on previous trips) and produces a somewhat misshapen credit card. He hands it to the receptionist with a flourish and can't help but smile at the frown of revulsion crossing the man's face when he realises the card is warm from Sam's body heat.

"What do you think of these things?" Sam asks, lifting his shirt to show off the chest pouch.

It is clear that the receptionist shares Claudia's opinion.

"Yeah," Sam says. "The wife always said it looked like an adult incontinence product."

"Quite, sir," the receptionist says.

After retrieving all of his belongings from the floor - apologising all the while to the much-more-presentably-dressed guests tiptoeing around him - and taking the key-card and wifi password from the receptionist, Sam stumbles his way over to the elevator and up to his room. This hotel is significantly fancier than expected. Retrieving the crumpled credit card receipt from his pocket, he squints at the figure in deep concentration. Ten thousand pesos can't be much, surely? Some quick mental arithmetic assures him that ten thousand pesos can in fact be quite a bit of money.

He's prepared for the shittiest of hotel rooms, assuming that the receptionist has down-graded his booking to the worst possible room on the property. As he swipes the key-card and the door swings open with a satisfying swish, he wonders whether the receptionist may instead have upgraded him in an attempt to hear nothing further from the annoying English tourist. An entire wall of floor-to-ceiling windows looks out across the square from a ball-dropping height. The bed is some kind of ultra-wide, super-long behemoth, King size-plus-plus, topped by a monstrous tower of pillows and cushions, four towels carefully rolled into an origami-style tower at the other end of the bed.

Through a door he spies a bathtub larger than his spa pool at home and a shower with four heads. What on earth would you need, he wonders, with four...

There's a sharp series of knocks on the door.

Shit, Sam thinks. He's in the wrong room.

Opening the door with some reluctance, Sam decides to play up the confused foreigner angle.

"Si..?" he says, blinking slowly and affecting a blankly idiotic expression.

There is a young woman at his door, dressed in the same

hotel uniform as the receptionist. She is, however, much more skilled than the receptionist at hiding her distaste at Sam's bedraggled appearance.

"Mister Frost?" she asks smoothly, flashing a quite spectacular set of straight, white teeth.

"Si..?" Sam repeats.

"I trust everything is to your liking, Sir," she smiles again.

"Si," he says again.

"I do apologise for the interruption," she continues, with the slightest trace of an accent. "But you seem to have left some belongings at the reception."

Awkwardly, she holds out a strange assortment of objects. There's a tourist guide for Mexico City, the credit card he distinctly remembers taking back from the receptionist, his cellphone and a pair of his deceased wife's lacy underwear.

"Ahh, si!" he exclaims brightly, taking his possessions back from her. Sam feels an unfamiliar heat in his cheeks and realises with detached amusement that he's blushing. For the life of him, Sam cannot remember the last time he felt embarrassed. He waves the underwear in the woman's direction and is impressed again at her unflinching professionalism as her smile remains fixed in place.

"My wife's," he says in a conversational tone, "She's dead, you know."

The woman's professional smile slips ever so slightly towards a concerned frown.

"Hurricane," he continues mildly, in tones usually reserved for discussing less extreme weather, "Tore her to pieces, you see."

The smile is gone. She looks horrified.

"I'm so sorry to hear that, Sir," she says, eyes firmly fixed on the underwear he continues to wave around.

She begins to back away slowly.

"I'll leave you in peace, Sir," she says as she flees back down the corridor.

Tucking the underwear into a pocket, Sam closes the door and takes a running jump onto the largest, softest bed he's ever experienced in his life.

Gathering the contents of the mini bar around him, Sam settles back into the enormous pile of ridiculous pillows and begins to drink his way through the afternoon, gazing out across the Zocalo square at the dark clouds slowly gathering over the city.

* * *

Three days later, well showered and better rested than ever before in his life, Sam stands on a deserted Mexican beach as a freezing rain pelts down like ice-cold bullets all around him. Freshly-shaven face turned up to the sky, Sam glories in the pain of each rain drop as they strike his skin with unreasonable force. Eyes closed, he hears the wind whistling and howling all around him as it whips his clothing in all directions away from and then against his body. He feels a slow, contented smile spread across his quickly numbing face.

Behind him, he hears the frantic scuffle of resort workers as they stack sun loungers into tall piles of plastic and attempt to secure them beneath beachfront sun shelters already swaying and buckling beneath the wind. They seem to be fighting a losing battle, as far as Sam can tell. He expects that the resort behind him is packed full of nervous tourists, gathered in groups behind their high security walls and peering through triple-glazed sheet windows out at the dangerous world beyond.

There are thick piles of snot-green seaweed strewn widely across the beach. One morning of missed seaweed patrol and the resort's spotless white sand beach is returned to normality, Sam thinks, covered in nature and real life instead of sheltered tourists and ice-cream carts. Even the smells are different – all salt and fish and cold rain on hot sand. It's quite glorious, as far as Sam is concerned, but he doubts the tourists inside would be quite so impressed.

It's not yet gone 10 o'clock in the morning, but it's as dark as evening already. Occasional flashes of lightning flare overhead, bringing bright daylight back for mere seconds at a time. A large fish appears to have been stranded by a rogue wave on the sand near Sam and lies flapping weakly, gasping wide-eyed at impending death. Sam's tempted to pick it up and throw it back in the sea, but then thinks that perhaps its here on purpose. If anyone threw Sam back into the ocean right now, he would be most unimpressed.

Time passes. Sam stands on the beach absorbing the glorious fury of nature all around him. He glances down at the fish to see that it is no longer flapping or gasping. It stares blankly at nothing. Sam likes to think there's a certain serenity in its expression but then again, he's not sure that fish really *do* expressions.

It feels like a sign, so Sam begins to undress. One foot at a time, he removes sandy shoes and peels off sodden socks, discarding them carelessly on the sand. He steps out of jeans so rain-soaked they fall to the ground unaided, then pulls windbreaker and t-shirt over his head, throwing them far up the beach in the direction of the resort.

The pounding of the weather against his naked skin is exhilarating. He's never felt quite so alive as he does right now, in the moments before his death.

With a shout of triumph that seems to come from nowhere, Sam runs into the pounding grey-green surf. He dives under, surfaces, begins to head out in a jerky breaststroke towards the lighting bursting over the horizon. Everything feels right. Everything is as it should be.

That's the precise moment when an elderly fisherman seizes Sam by the armpits and pulls him back to shore, with quietly murmured reassurances in Spanish that everything will be alright.

Sam can't tell whether his face is wet from rain or seawater or tears, but he suspects it's a mixture of them all.

Chapter Twenty-One

Sam has always hated England in the springtime.

Rain-soaked, grey and miserable, it's a season with no redeeming qualities as far as he can see. A few bloody daffodils and a bit of apple blossom is hardly anything to get excited about.

Sitting on his unmade bed, staring out at the soggy park next door while a Converse-wearing doctor blathers on at him through the phone, Sam doesn't bother to disguise a loud yawn.

"I'm sorry," Doctor Foster says, sounding moderately pissed off. "Am I boring you?"

"Just a wee bit," Sam mumbles.

"I'm sorry?" she repeats, the pitch of her voice rising into the realm of severely pissed off.

"Never mind," Sam says. "Carry on."

"I was finished," she says. "I was waiting for your questions."

"Well," Sam says thoughtfully. "I mean, I wasn't *completely* paying attention last time we spoke."

There's a sigh of extreme frustration from Dr Foster.

"You don't say," she deadpans.

"Well, you can hardly blame me," Sam objects. "Distress and grief and jetlag and whatnot."

She remains silent.

"Anyway," Sam continues,"I distinctly remember you telling me that Avril was hopelessly brain-dead."

"Well, I'm not sure that's entirely.."

"A vegetable, you said."

"I absolutely did not!" she is indignant.

"No hope at all, let's pull the plug. Or am I remembering that bit wrong?"

"The thing is, Mr Frost, that in cases like Avril's there is no..."

"Did you or did you not advise me to turn off life support to my daughter?" Sam demands, an unexpected flash of anger leaving him clear-headed in a way he hasn't felt for months.

"Well... yes." Dr Foster's voice is small. She sounds exactly like the adolescent, pink Converse-clad child that she is. "We did in fact advise that might be the appropriate decision."

"I don't think you understand how much it pains me," Sam sighs, "to think that my Mother-in-law was right about this."

There is silence on the line.

"That is what you're telling me, right?" he asks. "That she was right and Avril's not brain-dead after all?"

"Not exactly," she says and sighs again. "It would really be much easier if you would just agree to come into the clinic and.."

"No."

"Right. Well then, I need to make it very clear that Avril is still extremely unlikely ever to recover anything close to her previous levels of mental function."

Sam makes a vague noise of encouragement.

"It is likely that she will always be severely challenged."

"But not as bad as you thought?"

"No," she agrees. "Not as badly as we'd first expected."

As it turns out, his daughter can breathe unassisted. He can't help but wonder whether someone accidentally knocking out the life support plug has given Avril's doctors this new understanding of her condition, but apparently it's irrelevant. She doesn't need the machines any more.

What she does still need is 24/7 care and monitoring at a facility costing more per night than the Mexico City hotel, which has become something of a bone of contention for the insurance company currently funding her debaucherous lifestyle. Sam disconnects his call with Dr Foster to see that he's missed another three calls from the insurance company.

Deciding to make this a Future Sam problem, Sam turns his phone off and goes back to sleep.

* * *

The Weatherman has posted a new video. On every one of Sam's online chaser forums, people are absolutely losing their shit over it.

It's been up for forty minutes and has been viewed more than 10,000 times. The view counter is ticking over faster than Sam's eyes can follow, a blur of fast-changing numbers as the chasing community gorge themselves on video footage with gleeful abandon. He's watched it three times already and is settling in for a fourth viewing when Buddy lets himself into the house, announcing his arrival in the usual fashion with a resounding belch.

"You don't even bother knocking these days?" Sam asks without turning around.

The recliner creaks in protest as Buddy throws himself into it. There's the sound of a can opening.

"Cheers, Sam," Buddy says, then swallows loudly.

Sam doesn't reply. He's captivated.

Sam's seen thousands of chase videos in the past few months. He's seen shouty, over-excited Americans pant and sweat at the camera as they run from twisters. He's heard countless voices repeating the same tired lines about how crazy these storms are, how unreal, how completely fucking insane. There's a lot of profanity in these videos, which Sam finds surprising coming from Americans who seem most reluctant to say anything impolite in the course of everyday life. He's seen tornadoes and hurricanes and typhoons and tropical storms. He's seen the disappointment of an anticlimactic fizzle and the white-faced terror of an unexpectedly destructive twister. When it comes to chasing, Sam has seen everything. But he's never seen anything quite like this.

There's no talking in the Weatherman's video. There's sound - a riotous calamity of crashing and screaming and roaring nature - but there's no talking. It's almost as if the camera's been left outside, alone in a deserted street while the tornado whips itself into chaotic frenzy around it. And yet, there *must* be someone there. There's that tell-tale wiggle as the camera pans, those micro movements unique to a hand-held shot. The calm of the person holding the camera - the calm of *the Weatherman!* Sam thinks with excitement bordering on hysteria - is evident, the camera moving slowly in a full 360 degree spin as devastation unfolds all around. At one point, four minutes and fifty-three seconds into the video, the viewpoint makes a smooth but quick shift a good two feet to the left just as a large mailbox whips past, spinning end-over-end around a post still rooted deep into a lump of concrete. At seven minutes and thirty-two seconds, there's a shift back to the right and a white picket fencepost shoots past as if thrown like a javelin.

He is standing in a suburban street. The Weatherman is standing alone in the middle of a street in a tornado, filming the neighbourhood as if nothing unusual is happening. The Weatherman, Sam reflects, must have balls the size of watermelons.

The footage lasts for nine minutes and forty-eight seconds. Just after the nine-minute mark, there's a change in the sound and strength of the tornado. The trees lining the street begin to right themselves, the wind that had blasted them to near-horizontal slowly easing. The screaming noise of the tornado dies back to a shriek and then a murmur. A black cat emerges from beneath a shrub, wide-eyed with ears flattened against its head. Belly close to the ground and tail twitching, it crawls across the nearest house's front lawn then streaks up the front stairs and through a cat door. The door swings in its wake. One swing, two swings and then nothing, the video cutting to black with no fanfare.

"What in the actual fuck are you watching, mate?" Buddy says.

Sam turns to see him leaning forward in the recliner, beer can paused halfway to his mouth. He has never seen Buddy look quite so startled.

"Storm chase," Sam says, turning back to the screen and restarting the video.

"But nobody was chasing shit," Buddy says. "They were just *standing* there."

"Yep," Sam agrees, watching again as the winds whipped themselves up from nothing.

"What kind of crazy fucker stands in the middle of a hurricane?"

Sam glances over his shoulder. Buddy is staring open-mouthed, beer still nowhere near his mouth. Sam has never seen Buddy hang on to an open can of beer for quite this long before.

"Tornado," Sam corrects. "It's a tornado."

"It's a big fucking storm, mate," Buddy says. "Even I can see that."

Sam is struggling to tell whether Buddy is entranced or horrified.

"Want to come storm chasing with me next time?" he asks.

"Oh fuck, yes," Buddy breathes in an awed tone. "I thought you'd never bloody ask."

They watch it four more times. Buddy's beer remains unfinished, discarded on the coffee table where it's fallen over and sits in a sticky brown pool of spilled beer.

* * *

Before they even leave the airport, Sam knows that he's made a mistake. This is neither the time nor the place for Buddy.

He's like a big, dumb puppy watching the world go past with a complete lack of understanding. His brain does not work in the way that a normal adult brain is supposed to work. The world around him is a constant source of fascination to Buddy and the answers to every problem are inside a pub.

Following Sam's most recent outburst in the middle of the Duty Free shop (in response to Buddy's repeated claims that he "invented Duty Free") and the previous one at Passport Control (in response to Buddy's repeated attempts to swap passports "for shits and giggles"), Buddy has gone unusually quiet. They sit silently at the gate, awaiting any sign of the boarding that was scheduled to happen twenty minutes earlier.

Sam is comparing weather forecasts across four different apps on his phone. Buddy appears to be swiping left and right on an app he has previously decreed to be much like Tinder but better in unspecified ways.

"So imagine," Buddy says, still swiping. "Imagine if vaginas were detachable, right?"

Sam stares, certain he's misheard.

"And like, they could just jump off and you know, go out for a night on their own."

Sam blinks slowly.

"So then the woman, she could just have a nice quiet night in, you know? Spot of telly. Do her nails, whatever. Get some beauty sleep."

"And then you'd have these packs of vaginas just rampaging around the town. Causing havoc. Burning the place down."

Buddy smiles serenely as if he's just created a lovely image.

"What do you even..." Sam is interrupted by the long-overdue boarding call and decides it's better not to discuss this any further.

While their plane is still on the runway, the weather warnings are downgraded.

By the time they land, the forecasts are for blue skies and sunshine.

It's four days of drunken debauchery with Buddy before they return home. It's the biggest waste of time Sam's ever experienced but Buddy has had the time of his life.

Chapter Twenty-Two

Jaw clenched, Sal is staring at a large inspirational print behind the front desk. It's emblazoned with the words "All good things are wild and free."

"Fucking hypocrites," she hisses under her breath.

The receptionist smiles at Sal as if she hasn't heard.

"I do apologise for the inconvenience," she says. "If you could possibly provide another card then I'm sure we can…"

"What about "All you need is love"?" Sal says.

"I believe that was The Beatles," the receptionist says. "We are quite clear on the fees associated with our courses."

"What if I worked in your kitchen and…"

"Do you have another card, Ms Abaroa?"

Sal thrusts her credit card back at the woman.

"Try it again," she says through gritted teeth.

Again, it declines.

"What about helping those less fortunate?" Sal tries. "I mean, what would the Dalai Lama think of your mindless pursuit of material wealth?"

"Perhaps it might be best…" the receptionist begins.

"Oh get fucked," Sal says. "I'll go."

It's probably for the best, considering the shooting pains up both legs and her newfound inability to turn her head to the left.

She leaves the retreat, limping and hunched under an overloaded backpack where she's stashed two loaves of wholegrain bread from the communal kitchen, some artisanal hemp shampoo from the bathroom and three stolen yoga mats. On her way out, she passes Deirdre, returning from her early-morning 20km run and glowing with good health.

Deirdre stops to embrace Sal in one of her ridiculous grandmotherly hugs. She's not even sweating. Fucking Deirdre.

"Where are you off to?" Deirdre asks. Eyes fixed on Sal, she seizes one foot in both hands and swings it above her head. Her lovely-old-woman smile doesn't waver for a second.

Sal stares.

"Sorry, love," Deirdre says as she drops that foot and seizes the other. "Just stretching out those adductors."

Sal makes a non-committal murmur. Deirdre is still waiting for an answer.

"Had enough," Sal says. "Need to go somewhere and find myself, you know."

"Mmm," Deirdre nods sagely. "Of course."

Deirdre spends another twenty minutes giving Sal detailed directions to the many mountaintop trails and jungle hikes of the area. She seems certain that Sal will find herself in one of these not-very-accessible spots, which Sal hopes is not the case. She strongly suspects that a cocktail bar on the beach might be a more likely spot for the new and improved Sal to be hiding out, but it seems rude to disagree so she listens through an apparently interminable explanation from Deirdre before sloping off in the direction of the beachfront backpackers' accommodation.

She does have other cards, of course. Four of them, all very close to maxed-out and all on Final Notice status from the bank, but that is a problem for another day. A quick trip to the ATM returns a sizeable wad of cash from one of the Final Four and she's soon happily ensconced in a grotty dorm room amongst unkempt backpackers, munching through her first loaf of stolen yoga retreat bread. By nightfall she's found exactly the kind of beachfront cocktail bar she'd hoped for and is quite confident of rediscovering herself after a few more rounds of shots.

Chapter Twenty-Three

Some time the following week, Sam awakes to find Claudia in bed beside him. His wife. Living and breathing. Claudia.

He blinks away the fogginess of sleep but she's still there – back toward him, dark hair across her face, one bare shoulder exposed where the duvet's slipped down.

He reaches out a hand to rest his fingertips ever so carefully against the skin of her shoulder and it's all still real. It's soft and warm and the skin dimples beneath his fingers when he pushes harder.

She lets out a small snore, blowing the hair away from her face and it's still her.

It's still his wife, asleep on her side of the bed, one pillow clutched against her chest in the way she's always slept. Snoring like a pig.

There are tears in his eyes and his face is wet. He's making odd, desperate little gasping noises like a child sobbing hard.

This whole thing – this whole awful experience – he realises now that none of it has been real.

"Dream," he says, the word tearing free from his throat in a pained moan. "All just dreams."

He looks at the clock on Claudia's side of the bed to see that it's 11:27am.

It's odd, he thinks, that they've slept so late. Claude's alarm should've gone off at 6:25.

It must be a weekend. Or jetlag. Of course, they've just got back from Florida and those melatonin tablets have clearly played havoc with their sleep patterns. No wonder, he thinks. No wonder he's had the worst, strangest, most devastating dreams of his life.

He sits up in bed and feels the unmistakeable rock-in-the-guts nausea and disorienting head-spin of a bad hangover. Bloody pills.

On the table on his side of the bed, there's an empty vodka bottle. Duty free, he thinks. Then, inexplicably: *Buddy thinks he invented Duty Free.*

On the bedroom floor there are two empty gin bottles and three used condoms.

He sits, staring. He blinks slowly. This doesn't compute.

"Oh fuck," says Claudia, rubbing her face in her hands. "What in the fucking..."

"Right?" Sam says, turning towards her. "No idea what happened but I had the weirdest bloody..."

It's Bridget.

Claudia's sister Bridget is naked in Sam's bed.

The weight of it all falls on him in one awful moment. The grief is a fresh wound all over again. It is unbearable.

* * *

Later, when the tears have passed, there is some unpleasantness with Bridget.

It seemed only right to offer her a cup of tea and a biscuit, but there's no milk in the house and his already-opened packet of Digestives has ants in it. He suggests they pop down to the cafe on the corner instead. She agrees that this is a good idea. As it turns out, this is not a good idea.

For starters, she orders something called "smashed avocado". It costs twelve pounds. This strikes Sam as ridiculous.

"Sure you wouldn't rather bacon and eggs?" he double-checks.

"No."

She's always been a woman of few words.

"Or an omelette? Claudia always liked the..."

"No."

"So just an avocado then. A squished avocado."

"Smashed."

"Right," he nods sagely. "Better be a fucking fabulous avocado, is all I'm saying."

"I can pay for my own breakfast, Sam." She rolls her eyes at him, arms folded tight across her chest.

"No, no," he waves a hand vaguely in the air. "It's on me. Least I can do."

She raises her eyebrows at him.

"What's that supposed to mean?"

He excuses himself and hides in the bathroom until the food arrives.

On reflection, the avocado looks decent.

They eat in awkward silence. She is intently focused on her phone and ignoring him completely.

"So," he says. She does not look up.

"I mean," he tries again. There is no response.

"D'you think," he says. This time she looks up.

"Do I think we made a horrible mistake? Do I think my sister is turning in her grave? Do I think you're a disgusting excuse for a human being? Yes. Yes to all of those."

"So, we did have sex then?" Sam asks. This is not the right thing to ask.

"For fuck's sake, Sam," she says, lip curling in revulsion. "You don't even remember?"

He chuckles darkly.

"Don't remember much these days," he says.

Face-down on the table, Sam's phone starts to ring. He flips it over, sees that it's the insurance company and declines the call.

"You need to talk to them," Bridget says.

"Don't really want to," Sam says.

"Avril's getting better, Sam," she says. "You'll need to sort things…"

"I think better is a relative term in this case," Sam says.

"Better is always a relative term," she says. "That's basically the definition of the fucking word."

"Touché," he says.

"They'll have questions. You'll need to fill in forms and sign things and whatever else," she says, attention back on her phone. "They could cut you off if you don't talk to them."

"Don't care," he says, although a lack of money would present him with certain challenges.

"It's not about you though, is it?" she says, eyes flashing. "Your daughter is in hospital and someone needs to pay to keep those machines on!"

"Apparently she doesn't need the machines," Sam says. "That's the problem."

"It's not a problem," she says. "It's a fucking miracle!"

He excuses himself again and leaves out the back door. She can pay for her own fucking avocado.

Chapter Twenty-Four

It's like nowhere else Sam has ever been.

He'd guess that it's like nowhere else on earth, but this is well outside his realm of expertise so it's hard to know for sure.

There's steam rising from the ground and brilliant, unnatural colours everywhere and the smell is god-awful. It's not exactly what he'd been after following the spur-of-the-moment purchase of a flight to the other side of the world, but his plans to throw himself into an active volcano have been somewhat curtailed by the discovery that said volcano is no longer open to tourists, having recently exploded onto a group of them.

It had been a decent plan, he thought. His infamous clumsiness coupled with his recent descent into full-blown alcoholism would provide a perfectly reasonable explanation for his slipping and falling into the crater. According to Google, a volcano would provide a foolproof method. Chances were good that sulphur dioxide gases would stop Sam's breathing on the way down. If that didn't take care of things, then the fall itself was quite likely to kill him due to terror-induced heart attack. Then there was the ultimate back-up of a crater full of lava hot enough to melt the flesh from his bones.

The thing that Sam finds particularly appealing about the volcano method is the all-or-nothing nature of it. Once he's toppled over the edge, his demise is 100% assured one way or another with no going back and no helpful Mexican fishermen jumping in to rescue him. Lava, apparently, sits somewhere around 1800 degrees Fahrenheit and while Sam can't quite figure out how to convert this into normal country measurements, it seems hot enough to the do the job. He has read, in fact, that standing too close to lava will have the uncomfortable effect of drying out one's eyeballs as all of the fluids steam off into the air.

Unfortunately, the unforeseen closure of said volcano island has left Sam at something of a loose end. A very confused woman at the airport information desk suggested he might enjoy venturing to the top of an intermittently active volcano a few hours south, where the waters of the crater lake are currently at the temperature of a warm bath. This did not sound like quite the flaming death-hole Sam had envisaged.

It took far longer than it should have done for her to mention the vibrant centre of thermal activity bubbling away a little over two hours' drive away. It's not a *volcano*, per se, but dear god is it spectacular.

Sam gapes open-mouthed as he follows gravel paths and wooden boardwalks across bubbling mudpools and sulphurous vents in the earth, steam hissing out as if from a natural tea-kettle. There's a winter chill in the air and the other tourists are wrapped in puffy jackets, but the heat rising from the land all around keeps Sam perfectly warm in his poorly-planned outfit of shorts and t-shirt.

There are signs all around pointing out the potentially fatal consequences of leaving the marked paths and guardrails to prevent tourists tumbling into geysers. Sam is very pleased to find that there does not appear to have been a great deal of thought put into the prevention of fully intentional throwing of oneself into the steamy depths.

He tests this theory for a moment by leaning out over a guardrail, hanging over at waist level so that his face is directly above a bubbling pool of stinking mud at the base of a cliff a few metres down from the path. He can't quite tell whether his eyeballs are drying out but the immediate flush of sweat breaking out across his forehead seems a promising sign. It's certainly hotter than a warm bath, but it's difficult to judge whether a tumble into the mud would result in a quick and painless death or whether it would simply result in incredibly painful, non-fatal injuries of the sort he'd rather avoid.

Sam hangs over the mudpools for a good two minutes, watching bubbles open like yawning mouths and then disappear into the mud again. Sweat drips steadily from his face into the mud and trickles back down his neck. Nobody seems to care in the slightest. This is an excellent sign.

Sam slowly tips himself back until he's standing upright once more, eyes streaming and face flushed. There's a pounding pressure inside his head but this seems related less to any toxic effects of the mudpool vapours and more to hanging upside-down for an extended period of time because the throbbing fades as he blinks his way back to a feeling of relative normality. The icy breeze against his hot face is heavenly.

Slowly, the throb in his head receding, he follows a group of Japanese tourists down the path past more bubbling mudpools towards the enormous cloud of steam gushing from a geyser in the distance. As they round a corner, a vista opens up before him with a shallow pond made up of colours so vibrant they can't possibly be real. Sam shuffles over to the barrier and leans out again, over steaming water that smells like boiled eggs. There is a murky pond of dark khaki green, surrounded by bright sunshine-yellow mud fading into orange, then white and then red. Sam had not previously realised that mud came in such colours. It seems unfair that his home country has been lumped with such a limited palette of uninspiring browns.

Thick white steam wafts across the colours in front of him, moving in random bursts as icy gusts of winter wind blow over the water's surface. It smells awful, but it looks spectacular. It's unclear whether he's affected more by the sights around him or more by hanging upside down over a mudpool, but either way Sam is not entirely himself and spends a good three hours wandering aimlessly in something of a stunned daze before he remembers that he is supposed to be throwing himself into the volcanic earth, rather than standing around admiring it. In a sudden burst of determination, Sam throws one leg over the barrier and clambers over towards his fiery doom.

Or at least, that's what he tries to do.

With one foot on the crumbly hot earth on the far side and the wood of the barrier wedged uncomfortably into his crotch, Sam comes to an unexpected halt. There is a very large tattooed man in a black t-shirt holding him firmly by the foot.

"What the fuck d'you think you're doing?" the man asks, one eyebrow raised in a remarkably casual expression.

"Well," Sam says, but then can't think of anything to follow up with.

The man continues to stare at Sam. Sam begins to lose his balance and is forced to make little shuffling half-hop movements on the foot that's not currently in the grip of a scary looking local.

"That is," he continues, "I was just..."

"You can't swim in there," the man deadpans. "It's not a spa pool."

"Oh no," Sam smiles. "I wasn't planning on surviving the experience."

This does not improve the man's mood.

"You're going to throw yourself in?" he asks.

Sam nods enthusiastically.

"No, you fucking won't," the man says.

Sam wobbles again, smacking one testicle against the barrier with some force.

"This is a special place,"the man says very slowly. Sam nods. "It is not for you to desecrate with your miserable little corpse," the man continues.

The large, apparently quite angry man leans back and Sam's weight begins to shift away from the steaming depths and back towards the safety of the path.

"I only meant..." Sam stutters.

"You thought my children should have to look at your pasty English body dissolving into that water?" the man smiles but it is not a friendly smile.

"Well, I hadn't really..." Sam frowns at the mental image.

"You thought you'd just pollute this place with your remains and fuck the consequences?"

"I mean, not exactly..." Sam's foot lifts from the volcanic

ground and he lands heavily back on the path. His other foot is still in the grip of a man who looks even larger from this angle.

"You know what they have to do if that happens?" the man asks, releasing Sam's foot and wiping his hands on his black jeans with obvious distaste. Sam shakes his head.

"You know what a rahui is?"

The man chuckles coldly at Sam's blank expression.

"Absolutely fucking oblivious, aren't you?"

Sam gets tentatively to his feet, brushing dust from his knees and making a garbled attempt at an apology.

Behind the man, there's a small girl dressed in an immaculate pink dress and fairy wings, plastic Disney Princess tiara nestled amongst her curls. She wraps her small arms around the man's leg.

"Hey darling," the man says, as if butter wouldn't melt. He sweeps her up and nestles her against a hip.

He flashes a shark-toothed smile at Sam.

"Off home now, aren't you mate?"

Sam nods, but evidently shows insufficient enthusiasm because the man continues.

"Off back to your own country where you can do what you damn well please, right?"

The Disney Princess slaps a small hand across the man's mouth.

"No swearing, Daddy," she frowns.

The man nods to Sam, one eyebrow raised in a way that somehow conveys quite clear malicious intent. Sam limps back to the car park and then checks into a nondescript motel on the outskirts of town where he sleeps like the dead.

* * *

Sam wakes twelve hours later and decides, with a burst of renewed enthusiasm, that the middle of the night is probably a much better time to tumble to his fire-and-brimstone death, unobserved. Wearing the motel dressing gown and slippers, Sam doesn't bother locking the door behind him as he sneaks across the car park in the dark. He can see the shape of his rental hatchback on the far side of the parking area, cast in a small pool of light from the street-light nearby. He heads towards the light, slippers making little plastic scuffling noises in the night.

There's a quick flare of light beside the building just a few feet away and Sam screams a little. Even in the dim light from the car park, he knows it's the man from the geysers. It takes Sam a moment to realise that the man has no cigarettes and has flared the lighter simply for dramatic effect.

"Going somewhere?" the man asks, voice low and threatening.

"Oh just... You know. Forgot something." Sam says. "In the car."

He does wonder for a fleeting moment why he feels the need to explain his movements to a complete stranger who appears to have been stalking him.

"That right?" the man doesn't move. Sam doesn't move either. They both stand in an empty car park at 3am for a good five minutes, each waiting for the other to do or say something.

"Right then," Sam says eventually and saunters over to his rental car in what he hopes is a convincingly casual manner.

The man doesn't move. Sam rustles about in the car, looking desperately for anything that might seem a reasonable reason to go to his car at 3am. Eventually, he emerges with a handful of pamphlets and waves them in the general direction of the man standing beside the building. He heads back towards the building and the relative safety of his motel room.

Moving with all the stealth and silence of a ninja, the man is suddenly right beside Sam and snatches the paperwork from his hand. He holds it up to the glow of a small security light beside the door.

"Hobbiton, eh?" he growls.

"Oh absolutely," Sam says. "Love those hobbits."

"Love them so much you needed to find out more at three in the morning?"

"Had to check the schedule," Sam said, pleased to hear that his voice was hardly shaking at all. "Don't want to miss the breakfast buffet."

"Bit of a drive from here," the man observes.

"Exactly, mate," Sam agrees. "Got to get an early start."

"You know, *mate*," the man says, "I'd recommend you go straight to the airport from there."

Sam makes a non-committal noise of consideration.

"And get right back on that plane and bugger off back where you came from," the man continues.

"Think that'd be best for everyone, don't you?"

Sam does not feel that he's in a position to disagree. Back in the saggy bed in the uninspiring motel room, he lies awake for three hours and then quietly dresses, picks up his Hobbiton leaflets again and returns to the rental car. There is no longer a tall, scary man standing outside his room. He takes this as a very encouraging sign and heads off in the opposite direction to Hobbiton.

On the passenger seat, scribbled in ballpoint pen on the back of some rental car paperwork, is a hand-drawn map provided by the German backpacker who gave him the keys at the airport. The scale of said map is far from accurate and the road names are almost all incorrect, but it worked for finding the potential death geysers yesterday so he decides to follow it again in search of "hot creek in bush" this morning.

As it turns out, she meant something more along the lines of "smelly tepid bathtub in the forest" and Sam finds the creek already crowded at this early hour of the morning with hungover backpackers and irritatingly noisy children. Sam is quite certain that both the backpackers and the children are peeing freely into the water. Nonetheless, he settles himself into a quiet corner and tries his best to feel some kind of serenity amongst the rainforest. There are leafy ferns growing on the banks of the creek and trees towering above, birdsong echoing while steam rises gently from the slowly moving water of the creek. It all seems like it should be quite lovely, but it's not quite the fiery doomsday experience Sam was after.

He rests his head on the mossy bank and closes his eyes for a moment, listening to the birds and concentrating on the sensation of warm water flowing over his body. It's almost peaceful for a minute before he hears the unmistakable sound of a very large man clearing his throat nearby. Sam's eyelids spring open at great speed. The very large, uncommonly scary man sits beside him in the creek, showing a multitude of tattoos in his shirtlessness.

"Thought you were off to Hobbit breakfast?" he asks in a deceptively mild tone of voice.

CHAPTER TWENTY-FOUR

"Yep," Sam agrees. "Hobbits."

The man makes a show of checking his watch and confirms that it is in fact almost eight o'clock.

"You might miss breakfast, mate," he says.

Sam is back at his rental car within two minutes, dripping still-steaming creek water all over the car seat.

Even on the plane over the Pacific Ocean a few hours later, Sam can't quite shake the feeling that he's being watched. It's only after three double vodkas and a handful of sleeping pills that he dozes off, face smushed against the window and airline blanket clutched against his chin for protection.

Chapter Twenty-Five

Five times in the following week, Sam is sure he senses the enormous scary man watching him.

It doesn't matter that Sam is back at home and the enormous scary man is presumably still somewhere in the South Pacific. Nonetheless, Sam sees the man *everywhere*.

He's at the supermarket, lurking behind cans of vegetables. He's in a white van, parked for a suspiciously long time at the kerb outside Sam's house. He's in the shadows outside Sam's window, vanishing into the nearby bushes whenever he turns on the outdoor lights.

While it could be argued that Sam's mental health has not been in the best state of repair for several months now, this feels like the final prod that might just push him over the edge into utter insanity.

The following Wednesday morning, Sam sits in a kitchen chair that he's pulled over to the front door and positioned so that he can see through the blinds without anyone outside seeing him. He has been observing the neighbourhood for three hours when Buddy unexpectedly arrives on the doorstep and opens the door with enough force to upend the chair and dump Sam onto the floor.

He looks up to see Buddy looking down at him with what appears to be more disappointment than confusion.

"What's up, Sam?" he asks, closing the door carefully behind himself.

"There's a man," Sam says, getting slowly to his feet and peering out the window. "A crazy man."

There certainly is, Claudia's voice whispers unexpectedly inside his head. Sam screams.

Taking this all in stride, Buddy puts down the carton of beers he's brought with him and goes to retrieve a chair from the kitchen. He places it beside Sam's and hands him a can.

"Right," he says, pausing to open his own can and take a swig. "What does this man look like?"

By noon, Buddy has clearly tired of the surveillance activity and his attention has shifted from the street outside to the book about volcanoes that he found discarded on Sam's living room floor. Nonetheless, he remains committed to sitting in the doorway and drinking beer while Sam surveils the neighbourhood, which feels remarkably supportive. Sam feels a little less unbalanced when in non-judgemental company.

By early afternoon, Sam's buttocks have gone completely numb. In the absence of any sightings of Enormous Scary Man, or of anything else of interest, they elect to move to the comfort of the couch and watch football for the afternoon while finishing off Buddy's beers.

At one point, in a completely out-of-character display of fastidiousness, Buddy goes to the kitchen to find a damp cloth and then prods at a small red stain on the arm of the couch.

"Wine," Sam says. "Very old wine. Won't come out."

Remember what happened? Claudia's voice hisses inside his head again. Of course he remembers.

They'd sat right there, on the couch in front of the TV with three empty bottles of wine on the coffee table and a picked-over cheeseboard slowly melting in the warm room. It was their anniversary. The kids were with Claudia's parents to allow for a fancy romantic evening out in the city, but at the last minute they'd decided to stay in, drinking wine and listening to music as if they were still young and child-free.

It had been a nice evening.

Nothing special. Not the extravagant event that ten years no doubt deserved, but a night of eating and drinking the things that they liked and watching music videos from their youth in the warmth of their own home while it was freezing bloody cold outside.

They were both drunk at this point, of course. Not *drunk* drunk. There was no danger of vomiting or passing out but they were both flushed and relaxed, swaying gently in their seats, bursting into fits of childish giggles and then forgetting what they were laughing about.

Every few minutes, Sam would press the wrong button on the remote and search for songs on Netflix while Claudia laughed at him. Every time she had to explain that he was on the wrong app. They both agreed that someone needed to drunk-proof the television.

And then something changed. Looking back, he could never remember anything really happening but as the night wore on, Claudia's mood soured. He consciously played up his drunken buffoonery, clowning for her in an attempt to bring back the giggles of earlier in the evening but the things she'd found hilarious an hour ago now seemed to be irritating her beyond all reason.

"You're sexy," he said to her at one point. "You're still so fucking sexy."

She'd snorted and backed away from him.

"Bullshit,"she'd said. "I'm old and fat and sat here wearing pyjamas on a Friday night."

"Still sexy," he'd insisted and leaned in for a kiss.

He wasn't sure exactly what had happened but somehow she'd scooted out from underneath him and red wine was soaking the front of his shirt; burning his eyes; dripping from his chin.

She'd stood there looking at him uneasily, empty wineglass in hand.

He'd shaken his head, little wine droplets flying everywhere and it should've been funny really but it wasn't. It really, really wasn't funny and he'd been filled with a frustrated, offended rage and it felt a lot like a dam breaking under an insistent weight that just goes on and on and on without ever stopping.

"What the *fuck*?" he'd said and he'd meant it as a question but it came out as an animal roar. "Why the *fuck* would you throw a drink in my face?"

She shook her head and backed away further and she was saying something but it didn't make any sense and all he could think was that this was the last straw and that he was so disrespected in his own home that his own wife would throw wine at him as if he was *nothing.*

He reached out and seized the front of her stupid pyjamas and pulled her in close until their faces were kissing distance apart. But he didn't kiss her. He screamed at her and all of the frustrations of the past ten years came tumbling out in a hateful torrent of foul language and savage insults and somehow he couldn't stop himself even though he could see her shrinking inside her own skin and he could see flecks of saliva spattering across her face and he thought *good*. He thought that she deserved to feel every bit as disregarded and disrespected as he had and then he spat in her face.

And everything stopped.

He stared at her in disbelief as the spittle slid from her cheek towards her chin and she stared back at him in utter horror and neither of them said anything at all.

She hadn't wiped it off. She'd just stared at him as it moved down her face and then dripped off her jaw onto the pyjama top. Then she'd turned and walked away, head held high, saying nothing. She'd gone upstairs and he'd sat back down on the couch, numb and then it was the next morning and her parents were dropping the kids off so they all sat around the kitchen table drinking coffee and eating biscuits as if everything were completely normal and nothing out of the ordinary had happened.

"I never hit her," he says to Buddy and he is crying again. "I never laid a hand on her."

"Of course not, mate," Buddy says, patting him awkwardly on the back. "You're not a violent man."

Well, Claudia whispered inside his head again. *That depends on your perspective, doesn't it?*

* * *

It seems to Sam that, at last, the gods have smiled upon him.

His latest letter has arrived from the insurance company, emblazoned with DON'T IGNORE in an enormous red font.

He picks up the morning's stack of mail and takes it to the table where he sits down to a well-balanced breakfast of ant-infested Digestive biscuits and lager.

He is about to open the letter. It's the closest he's come. It is in his hands but then he sees the newspaper beneath it.

It seems only fair that he should finish his beer and flick through the paper before dealing with this insurance thing, so he sets the letter aside.

There appears to be absolutely nothing of note to report in the front section. The sports pages are interesting only for their detailed analysis of exactly why Sam's team has had their worst football season ever and who should take responsibility for their inevitable relegation. Someone is having a sale on beds. Someone else is clearing out last season's stock of televisions. None of this provides quite the escapism that Sam was after.

But then he comes to the international section and it feels like all the stars have aligned in this one magical moment.

HEAVIEST MONSOON IN FIFTY YEARS ARRIVES THIS WEEK.

Sam leans back in his chair, feet on the table and raises his beer in a toast to himself.

"Fucking spectacular," he says.

Such promising news seems worthy of celebration, so he drinks the other seven beers in the fridge before booking the next flight to Bangkok.

Three hours later, he realises that he's booked for the wrong week, so spends an hour on the phone to someone in a call centre getting the dates changed again. For unspecified reasons, this costs an ungodly amount of money. In light of the potential impending loss of all his insurance funds though, Sam figures he may as well spend as much as possible, as quickly as possible. He tries to tip the call centre person over the phone, but apparently this is not logistically possible. They do seem very pleased by the question though and Sam is momentarily filled with the joys of making someone else feel good.

He finds his passport at the bottom of the bedroom wardrobe, where he'd thrown it in panic upon his return from the South Pacific.

The passport goes into his shoulder bag, along with his wallet and an old paperback he found under the bed. Digging around in the search for his much-maligned flesh-toned wallet holder, Sam finds a small plastic figurine of a Minecraft zombie. One leg has snapped off. He sits on the filthy carpet and cries for a while, before blowing his nose and returning to packing.

Sam wonders for a moment whether this might be how it is for the remainder of his life. Perhaps he could sleepwalk through another twenty or thirty years like this - realistically, his liver won't last any longer than that. He could sit around this house doing nothing, living off insurance money and drinking with Buddy. Eventually he supposes he'd just get used to these random occurrences of uncontrollable sobbing. He could start carrying a handkerchief maybe. He's found it's not so much the tears that make people uncomfortable as the snot that goes along with them.

He wonders how many people do this. He suspects that Claudia's parents are doing something similar - just going through the motions until death puts them out of their misery.

"Not for me, mate," he says to his reflection in the bathroom mirror, angry pink streaks around his eyes and snot dried around one nostril.

Better to go out with a bang than a whimper, he thinks.

At the back of his mind, there's a tiny but very insistent voice saying something. He can't make out quite what it's saying but the voice itself sounds an awful lot like Avril's.

He opens a new bottle of vodka to drown it out.

Chapter Twenty-Six

Sam's been to Bangkok before.

Twice before in fact, in the cliched style of thousands of his countrymen on lads' holidays. Fifteen and twenty years later, both trips are memorable only as a blur of bright lights, noise, alcohol and breasts.

He is moderately ashamed of the fact that neither of these trips involved venturing further afield than Bangkok itself. To be fair, on the second trip they hadn't even left the hotel until it was time to go back to the airport. It had been a nice hotel though. With a rooftop pool and several bars and a helpful concierge supplying hookers and absolute fucktonnes of cocaine.

The vibe is a little different this time around.

The plane touches down and Sam is only in Bangkok long enough to transfer to his next flight.

Island-bound, he seems to be the only actual adult on a plane full of grubby and intoxicated backpackers. It's unpleasant not least for the ripe aroma of feet and unwashed hair, although Sam is equally upset by the fact that all of these people seem so ridiculously content. Full of the joys of life, they have years of frustration and failure ahead of them, but they don't know it yet. Sam is deeply jealous of this mild stupidity.

There is much raucousness, so that Sam feels a lot like the parent helper on a school bus trip. There are a ridiculous number of different nationalities on the plane but the lack of a common tongue doesn't seem to have put a damper on things. Instead, they have taken with great gusto to the shared language of music and treated Sam to the absolute worst performance he has even heard of Total Eclipse of the Heart, followed by an appalling rendition of Bohemian Rhapsody. His head is pounding. He's close to snapping and shouting at them all to just shut the fuck up, but the image of himself as a grouchy old man is something he can't quite stomach.

At one point, the sunburnt German child in the next seat turns to Sam with a slightly drugged-looking smile and says, "Life is great, yes?".

"Oh yes," Sam says. "Life ripped my wife and children into tiny pieces and threw them about like confetti."

This goes down surprisingly well and he receives a fist-bump of apparent support.

Sam does not understand the youth of today.

The most satisfying part of Sam's day is just before landing, when thunderclouds appear out of nowhere and hard rain starts drumming against the windows. The sense of a hundred excited holiday dreams deflating all at once is quite intoxicating. There is no more singing after that.

The flight lands at noon. By 12:30, Sam has found himself a very comfortable seat at a very cheap bar on the beach and is nursing his first beer of the day. It will not be his last.

There's a fine drizzle in the air and it's colder than anyone had expected. Backpackers sit forlornly at the bar, shivering in wet t-shirts and shorts, rubbing their hands together for warmth. Sam shouldn't get any pleasure from the sight of their sad and confused faces, but he does.

In the absence of anything much else to do, Sam is intently focused on drinking himself, slowly and steadily, into a stupor. Four warm and watery beers in, he's starting to feel a mild buzz alongside an uncomfortably full bladder and a churning unpleasantness somewhere deep in his digestive system. The pig's ear in his left hand has become strangely goopy after repeated gnawing and is leaking an angry red ooze across his knuckles. As far as Sam can tell, it's a mixture of dribble, sweat and the hottest spice mix known to man. He lifts the ear to his mouth and grips the sodden edge between his teeth, feeling that familiar sensation of chilli so hot his eyeballs seem to be sweating. A piece of ear comes loose and he's swallowed it before he's even noticed it's there. Chili and offal slide their way down his throat, setting off fireworks all the way down.

Sam downs a fifth beer.

"That's a bit revolting," someone says in a tone of mild approval.

Sam looks around to see an ageing blonde woman perched awkwardly on the stool beside him.

"What are you doing?" he says, then "Sorry," an impressive belch having escaped him unexpectedly.

"Drinking?" she says, making it sound like a question. She is Australian. Historically, Sam is not fond of Australians.

"With your feet," Sam says, gesturing at the bartender for another beer. "Why are your feet like that?"

For a moment she looks at him in stunned silence and it occurs to Sam that she may in fact have some kind of terrible deformity of the feet.

"I mean…"he says.

She laughs and unfolds her legs from a ridiculous upside-down tangle into something more closely resembling usual human posture.

"Yoga?" she says. "Good for the core, you know?"

"Yoga?"Sam says, then tears another chunk from his pig's ear and chokes a little as it flames its way down his throat.

"You don't have to say it like that," she says. "Yoga has clinically proven benefits for physical and psychological well-being?"

It takes Sam a few seconds to realise that this is not a question, but merely an irritatingly Australian way of speaking.

"I'm Sal?"she says.

"I don't really care if you are or not,"Sam says, delighted to see that his next beer has arrived.

"And you are?"

There's another awkward pause as Sam realises that this was indeed a question.

"Sam," he says.

"Cheers, Sam?" she says, raising an almost-empty glass of some indeterminate beige liquor.

"Cheers?" he says, sounding remarkably Australian himself.

With some effort, he focuses on his beer clearly enough to make contact with the Australian woman's glass before downing it in what feels like quite a heroic series of gulps. Another belch escapes.

"Another round?" she says. This time it's a genuine question but clearly rhetorical. The barman is already there with a new pint. The Australian woman smiles at the barman in what Sam suspects is intended as a charming manner. Sam does not find this charming and neither, evidently, does the barman.

"You got money this time?" he asks flatly, one eyebrow raised in a display of facial agility Sam finds most impressive.

"My new friend here..."the Australian woman begins.

"Not your friend." Sam interrupts.

"No money; get out of my bar," the barman says with a flick of his wrist in the general direction of the Australian woman. She hesitates.

"Out!" he says again, much louder this time. The Australian woman slinks away.

Her barstool is quickly taken by a young and sunburned German.

"Funny man from airplane!" the German shouts in delight, grinning so widely his pink skin seems in danger of splitting open. "Confetti made of wife, yes?"

"Yes," Sam says, the pig ear back in his mouth. "Confetti."

The German child buys six Jagermeister shots and deposits three in front of Sam.

"Drink, funny man!" he shouts.

Sam remembers nothing after this.

Chapter Twenty-Seven

Sam wakes in a gutter. To be fair, it's hardly the first time this has happened, but he is accustomed to a more upmarket type of gutter. Sam's usual gutters tend to be full of dirty rainwater and the odd crisp packet, often with a subtle hint of stale urine. This gutter is more of a full-noise blast to the senses. There's rotting food and seaweed and every imaginable bodily fluid and some kind of toxic waste and dog shit and old socks and the smell of unwashed hair all mixed up in a riot of such intense unpleasantness that Sam lets out an involuntary squeak of panicked revulsion.

He blinks fast and hard but the world remains a bleary mess of colour and light. The gutter stench, it seems, is burning his eyeballs.

Tentatively, Sam lifts his head. His left cheek peels away from the concrete, leaving an unmistakeable face-print in the sticky pool of vomit that's spread around him.

The German is asleep beside him, lying face-up across three black rubbish bags. A beatific smile is spread across his sleeping face and he is completely naked. The sunburn, Sam notes, covers every inch of skin. Clearly the German has passed out in similar circumstances previously. Sam lifts himself into a sitting position, managing not to vomit despite the lurching gurgles in his gut. He is pleased to see that he remains fully clothed.

The sky is dark purple-grey, heavy with the rain that seems likely to fall any second. The air is warm but damp, sticky with a humidity that Sam's brain struggles to comprehend. Is he breathing air or water? He is damp and sweaty and queasy. It's not a pleasant feeling.

For a minute, Sam contemplates waking the German so that they might continue to the next bar, but the insistent pounding in his temples convinces him that perhaps a nap at the hotel is called for. At least, he thinks as he wanders off, the German won't get sunburned today.

He can't remember exactly where his hotel is, or what it's called. Something about beach views, he thinks. Or ocean views, possibly. Or ocean breezes. Certainly something water-related. He wanders the waterfront unsteadily for two hours before finding the Exotic Dragonfly Inn, where he has apparently booked himself a tiny, sweaty single room with no window and a broken ceiling fan.

"Lovely," he says to a very short, remarkably hairy man in the shared bathroom as they step into adjoining showers.

"No rats," the man says, in what Sam takes for agreement.

The shower is a rust-coloured trickle of water of such a precisely lukewarm temperature that it leaves Sam feeling just as sweaty and dirty afterwards as he had done beforehand.

"Lovely," he says again, keeping one eye on the large black spider hanging just above the shower head.

Damp from the shower, Sam flops heavily across the grubby

bedspread in his room and passes out before his head hits the pillow.

He's awoken several hours later by a clap of thunder so near it shakes the building. Heavy rain lashes the tin ceiling and drips through the wiring of the broken ceiling fan, leaving a puddle in the threadbare carpet. The air is thick with humidity, beads of moisture covering Sam from head to toe. Despite the lack of windows, it's fairly clear to Sam that the monsoon has begun. In a burst of excitement, his hangover vanishes and he is filled with an energy he hasn't felt in months.

It's time, he thinks, for a trip to the beach.

* * *

Even in a town as mad as this one, packed full of young backpackers with a sense of adventure and minimal thought for self-preservation, the beach is not a popular location in this weather. Small groups of wild dogs shelter under the trees but show no interest in Sam as he passes. Otherwise, the beachfront is deserted. Even the seagulls have disappeared to somewhere a little more hospitable - it's just Sam, alone on the wide strip of sand with only the shrieking wind and the slamming waves for company. It's quite lovely, he thinks.

The wind whips his hair in front of his face and stings his eyes, so there's little point in trying to see where he's going. Instead he navigates mostly by sound, heading towards the crashing noise of the surf, which is only *just* audible over the backing scream of the storm.

Sam is stopped by a sudden, breathtaking pain in his left foot. He screams but the sound is whipped away on the wind.

He collapses into the sand and examines the sole of his foot, squinting to make out the damage through watering eyes and whipping gusts of sand. There is an awful lot of blood. It covers the base of his foot as if he's stepped in red paint and a steady stream drips from his heel into the dirty sand below. There is something sticking out from the soft, fleshy part of his instep.

Sam tries to grab it and flinches back, fingers now bleeding freely as well.

"Fuck!" he shouts. Even at the top of his lungs, he can feel his mouth forming the word but he can't hear anything. Despite vast quantities of his blood splashing themselves all over the beach and throbbing pain in both foot and hand, Sam grins. This storm is absolutely spectacular.

Wrapping his fingers in the hem of his t-shirt, he tries again and removes half a broken beer bottle from the sole of his foot. This causes a renewed flood of bleeding and Sam feels suddenly very light-headed. Tiny little dots appear all around him and he wonders what kind of exotic monsoon phenomenon this could be, before realising that this is what people mean when they talk about seeing stars. He giggles and then promptly passes out, smacking his head on the abandoned beer bottle and gashing his forehead.

When he wakes, Sam's not sure whether it's minutes or hours later but there is now a deep throbbing pain in his face as well as his left foot and right hand. This is, of course, in addition to the familiar hangover headache he's been nursing all day and the remains of several spicy pigs' ears churning around in his stomach. It hasn't been the best of days but, upon reflection, he's probably closer to death than he has been in quite some time. From that perspective, he supposes that things are going very well indeed.

Hoping that the other half of the beer bottle is not in the near vicinity, Sam begins to crawl towards the sea. Wet sand sticks to his skin and grit blows into his face, but he keeps smiling and inches his way slowly towards the waterline, narrowly avoiding a dog turd and a used condom along the way. By the time he reaches the waterline, his knees are grazed and his bottled foot is bleeding anew. He sits for a moment and enjoys the feeling of being alone on a beach in a monsoon. There is nothing but the wind and the rain and the raging storm. And Sam.

Small and human and fragile. Bleeding and damaged. Already broken.

There is something incredibly calming about the thought that he has come to the place of his death; that if he only waits here patiently then the storm will do to him what it promised months ago in Florida. He takes a deep breath.

Sam twists himself around so that he's facing back up the beach, waves crashing behind him. He likes the idea that a particularly large wave might smash him from behind and drag him out to sea. The optics, he thinks, would be perfect.

That's when he sees that bloody Australian woman a little further up the beach, sitting cross-legged beneath thrashing palm trees.

Sam shifts around a little further so that she disappears from his line of vision and goes back to contemplating his own mortality.

It's no good. The vibe is all wrong with that woman here.

With a sigh that he can't hear but can feel with every fibre of his being, Sam crawls back in the direction of the Australian woman.

She opens her eyes and smiles when he stops beside her, but somehow seems unsurprised to see him.

"What are you doing here?" he shouts, over-emphasising the words in the hope that she'll read his lips.

She shrugs and gestures vaguely at the storm around them, smiling that same ridiculous yoga smile.

"It's dangerous," he says. "You're a moron."

She shrugs and closes her eyes again.

"The names come from a list, you know," he shouts to be heard over screaming wind and the chopper-loud noise of branches smacked together by the gale.

"Well, six lists. One a year for six years and then they start again." White sand is flicked up violently from around his knees and thrown into his face, burning his eyes and the inside of his nose.

"A to Z. Male and female. Like, Annie, Bruce, Carol..." He says.

Waves smash themselves against the sand in chaotic frenzy. Salt spray clouds everything, fuzzing out even the vaguest outlines so that it all looks like a dream. A wet, painful, terrifying dream.

She's not listening. Face turned away from him and into the howling wind, he's not sure she can even hear him.

"The storms that kill people. The big ones," he shouts louder. "They retire those names. Nobody wants to be reminded, I suppose."

She nods, clearly distracted. He's sure now that she can't hear him. She just wants him to stop talking.

"This one's Larry. It'll be the last Larry, for sure." Screaming winds, handfuls of sand thrown violently into the air, rain bucketing down so hard it's like drowning: it doesn't *feel* like a Larry.

It's exactly right, he thinks. It's everything he wanted. Arms thrown out wide; chest bared to the thrashing bursts of wind and the hard rain; eyes closed tight.

This is it. He waits for the moment.

He sees it coming from miles away and just like that he's back in Florida, objects whipping along the beach like weapons. It's a palm tree, he thinks. Or at least, it used to be before it was ripped from the ground and battered about for a while. It tumbles end over end towards them and he stares, unmoving.

The tree moves like it's been hurled by a giant, headlong toward Sam with all the unstoppable force of a freight train. It feels like fate.

But then something changes and he realises that the tree is going to crush the stupid Australian woman to death. Much as this shouldn't particularly bother Sam, it doesn't sit right.

He doesn't think about it. Not really. There's no particular moment where he decides to do something heroic; it's more that his body starts doing its own thing despite his mind screaming at it to stop. Sam rolls across the sand in an awkward flurry of thrashing arms and tangled legs. He hits the

Australian woman with a grunting thud, bowling her across the sand and throwing her up against a large rock much harder than he'd intended.

There's a whipping, scraping, shrieking noise as the tree spins past, hurling bucketfuls of sand at them with such force it tears skin. A sizeable chunk of thrown seashell lodges itself in the flesh above Sam's elbow and dark blood pools around it.

The Australian woman stares at him with the same stunned expression people in movies use to show that they've just been shot. Her eyes are wide and bloodshot. She doesn't blink. She doesn't move at all.

"Oh fuck,"Sam says. "Are you dead?"

Then she blinks. And smiles widely.

"Fucking hell, mate,"she says. "You saved my life?"

Sam is not sure why, but his stomach lurches with a definite feeling of impending doom.

Chapter Twenty-Eight

Sam had been under the impression that the past few months had been the worst of his life. There'd been a certain reassurance in knowing he'd hit rock bottom and there'd be only pain until he finally stumbled his way into the glorious release of death. There was something quite nice about knowing that things couldn't get any worse.

That was before he saved the life of literally the worst person he'd ever met.

He'd then spent three days in a Thai hospital, in the very next bed to that same awful woman while she prattled endlessly and kept him up all night with her resonant snoring.

He'd wanted to die before. Now, it takes every ounce of self-control he possesses to stop himself seizing a ballpoint pen from a passing nurse and stabbing himself in the eyeball.

On the morning of the fourth day, Sam wakes to the looming face of the Australian woman mere inches from him. Naturally, he screams.

She claps a grubby hand to his mouth and shakes her head

vigorously.

"Shhh!" she hisses, glancing over her shoulder.

With a wink that seems to involve half of her face, she presses something into his hand. It's the hand he sliced on the beach, trying to pull glass out of his foot. There's a blinding flash of pain but then he sees what she's given him and shuts up very quickly.

There's a bottle of indeterminate liquor in his bandaged hand.

Presumably, it's full of methanol and likely to cause him long-term organ damage, but he could not be more pleased.

The Australian woman returns to her own bed, extracts an identical bottle from under her pillows and holds it up in an unmistakable *Cheers* salute. Sam returns the gesture.

They begin to drink, sipping at their clandestine bottles under cover of hospital blankets.

Sam's not completely convinced that the nursing staff would give much of a shit anyway, but it certainly adds a certain edge of excitement to think they might get in trouble at any moment.

An hour later, Sam is certain that the nurses don't give a shit.

"So then," the Australian woman says at very high volume. "So then, I've said *Fuck you buddy* and he's gone and called me some really fucking nasty names..." she stops for another swig from the bottle.

"And I'm like, you know, that's really uncalled for?"

Sam is not following.

"So apparently, they reckon you can't do that but I've said

well, you know, who fucking says so? You know?"

Sam does not know, but nods sagely nonetheless.

"So you do know?"

Apparently he will no longer get away with feigning under-standing.

"I do not know," he admits. He takes another sip of fiery devil liquid from the dirty plastic bottle and continues.

"You have given me great insight into the mentality of your people," he says.

"You what?" she squints at him. He suspects she's having the same difficulties with double-vision he's currently experi-encing.

"It's quite unique to the Australian people," he says. "This very odd use of the present imperfect tense."

To be fair, this was always a pet hate of Claudia's. He'd never quite understood what she meant until this precise moment.

"He's said?" he continues. "I've gone?"

She looks blank.

"It's not really English though, is it?"he says. "More a mangled mash-up of noises."

She blinks slowly.

"*You're* English," she says.

"Yes," he says. "Yes, I am."

"You sure are," she says, voice thick with some kind of drunken emotion.

There is a series of phlegmy snuffling noises from her bed and with a dawning horror, Sam realises she's crying.

"I'm sorry," he hisses. "You talk fine."

"It's just so..." she starts, then breaks off to blow her nose with a startlingly loud honking. "Just so crazy, you know?"

Sam is loath to admit that he does not know.

"Like, I'm there on the beach you know, communing with nature and shit," she sniffs.

"That's why you were on the beach?" Sam is surprised afresh by this woman's idiocy.

"Yeah, like letting the Earth speak, you know?"

Again, Sam does not know.

"No," he says, "I really don't know."

"It's like this thing that Deirdre from the yoga place says," she says with an intense earnest that Sam finds deeply uncomfortable. "Nature has *messages* right, but nobody is listening?"

"Nature has messages." Sam repeats, trying out the words. They sound just as moronic, it turns out, without the ridiculous accent.

"Yes."She nods enthusiastically.

"Could you tell me, then," Sam begins, "Could you tell me what the message was when Nature smashed my family into tiny little pieces?"

She looks confused.

"You have a family?"

It feels a lot like talking to a toddler.

"I had a family," he says slowly. "But then Nature decided to give me a message, you see. And the message was something along the lines of *Go fuck yourself.*"

She nods slowly.

"Nature picked them up and spun them round and dumped them back in the dirt, ripped into tiny little pieces," he continues. "And I can't help but think that perhaps you're right. And the *message*, as you say, was that I should've been there and I am meant to be dead too."

She blinks very fast. He can almost hear the sound of her brain ticking away frantically.

"No,"she says. "No, I don't think that's..."

"That is, in fact, what I was doing last night," he says, pausing to take another sip of devil fire water.

"I was putting myself squarely in the path of nature, so that all of this," he gestures vaguely at the hospital around them, "All of this would be over and there would just be a wonderful, final, silence,"

"But," she stares at him. "But, you'd be dead?"

"I would indeed," he agrees. "I imagine it's nice and quiet."

"That's not the message, though," she says.

"That's not the message?" Somehow they're reversed roles and he's the one talking in questions.

"The message is *redemption*," she whispers, wide-eyed. "The message is, stop thinking about yourself and think about how you can help other people. You know?"

"So..." he takes another long swig. It burns all the way down in a way that signals lingering ill effects on his gastrointestinal health.

"You saved my life,"she interrupts. "So now we share a very deep connection?"

"No," he says with such urgency he spits a mouthful of devil liquor halfway across the room. "No, we absolutely do not."

"And now," she smiles dreamily, "Now it's *my* job to save *your* life."

"No, thank you, "he says. "Not necessary."

She smiles at him as if he were something small and cute. A puppy, perhaps. Or a particularly fluffy gerbil.

"It's my job now to be your protector," she says. "Any time you start thinking dark thoughts, I'll be right there to save you."

He is, in fact, thinking very dark thoughts right now, but she doesn't seem to notice.

* * *

The next morning, Sam wakes to an empty bed beside him.

The Australian woman has apparently absconded in the night, without bothering to leave any contact details or pay her bill. It would also appear that she owes the princely sum of five American dollars to the janitor for two bottles of his finest moonshine.

He is so relieved to have shaken her that he gives the janitor a handful of colourful local notes without looking too closely. The man's slightly startled grin and immediate disappearance seem to indicate that Sam has overpaid significantly, but he could not care less. He lies back and glories in the wonderful silence of an empty room.

In the absence of the Australian woman, the nursing staff have become significantly more attentive to Sam and his admittedly not-particularly-serious medical needs. His bandages are changed by a tiny woman with a voice so soft he can decipher nothing of what she says to him. The janitor returns twice. The first time, he comes bearing a rumpled stack of English-language newspapers that appear to have been rescued from a rubbish bin. The second time, he brings a TV with a tiny screen and an enormous body, the bulbous shape of which Sam has not seen since the early 1990s. The janitor balances this carefully atop a hospital trolley and wheels it to the end of Sam's bed, setting an ancient set of rabbit ears on top and plugging it into a power point presumably intended more for life-saving medical equipment than thirty-year-old televisions. The power cord snakes across the ward in a clear and obvious trip hazard and the TV trolley blocks access to the room such that even the tiny nurse has to visibly suck in her belly and crab-walk sideways to get past it.

Nobody seems to mind.

At one point, a different nurse brings a tray of unidentifiable gloop with a spoon. Sam picks at it suspiciously. It tastes better than it looks.

Shortly afterwards, the janitor returns for a third time bearing a steaming box of fried chicken. Sam weeps a little while handing over fistfuls of cash and the janitor seems sufficiently frightened that Sam doubts he'll return.

Sam watches fuzzy reruns of the Simpsons for several hours, wallowing in his own sweaty filth while a rusty ceiling fan turns in lazy circles above him. As the daylight outside begins to fade, another nurse brings him more gloop. Despite being identical in appearance to the previous gloop, it tastes completely different.

"Pudding gloop!" Sam says to the nurse.

Looking alarmed, she crab-scuttles past the TV at an impressive pace, avoiding eye contact.

The gelatinous, lumpy texture of pudding gloop does not lend itself well to eating in bed. Ten minutes later, Sam is spattered liberally with a brownish mess that he attempts to clean up with a wad of newspaper. It's not particularly successful but does leave him smeared rather than spattered, which seems like a marginal improvement. It's only as he's aiming the filthy newspaper at a nearby bin that he sees the weather page, a map of Thailand looking up at him in a glorious tangle of closely-packed isobars.

It's today's newspaper.

There's more terrible weather on its way.

On the little TV screen, Mr Burns tents his yellow cartoon fingers and smiles ghoulishly. "Excellent," he says. Sam could not agree more.

Chapter Twenty-Nine

Sam's self-discharge against medical advice causes quite the stir. It seems disproportionate to the extent of Sam's injuries - now that his foot and hand wounds have been tidily stitched and bandaged, there are just a few bruises, a couple of superficial grazes, a suspected sprained ankle and a knee that keeps making strange popping noises.

There is a very polite, softly-spoken doctor who keeps following Sam through the hospital with a plaintive request to *please just wait a moment, sir?* The doctor appears to be around twelve years old and Sam feels a twinge of guilt in ignoring him, but at the same time he fails to see any need for further medical attention to his playground-level scrapes and bruises.

As Sam approaches the main doors, the tiny doctor attempts to place himself in front of the entrance but he makes for a very small physical blockage and Sam just walks around him.

It's only once he's waiting at a bus stop several blocks away that Sam realises the doctor was concerned about his *mental* health, rather than his physical health. Upon consideration, it's quite sweet. And also quite perceptive for a child.

On his way out of the hospital, one of the nurses handed Sam a scruffy brown paper bag. He had expected it to contain the few possessions he'd had with him upon admission (and, he assumes, the nurse had thought something similar). It is with a sense of increasing delight, then, that he sits at a bus stop pulling out the strangest assortment of items he's never seen before. He removes these things one by one and lays them out on the wooden bench beside him.

There's a stack of battered old tarot cards, held together with a rubber band stretched almost to breaking point. A beaded purse with a broken zip gets Sam quite excited for a brief moment, but turns out to be empty aside from a movie ticket stub and a watch battery. There's half a bag of peanuts; they're stale and dotted liberally with ants but Sam's not in a position to be fussy, so he takes a handful and chews.

He pulls out a pair of purple tie-dyed tights and an orange hoodie stamped across the front with the logo for a local yoga school.

These are definitely not Sam's possessions. These clearly belong to the mad Australian woman. The mad Australian woman is likely now the proud owner of his sunglasses, flip flops and a small stack of cash.

Sam packs everything back into the paper bag and takes it with him on the bus back to his hotel. You never know when you might need a random assortment of shit, he thinks.

As he makes his way clumsily onto the bus and collapses into a seat, a small figure darts up the steps behind him and slumps in a seat at the very back, hood pulled low to shadow their face. If Sam were a more suspicious person, he would think he was being followed. If the figure were twice as tall and much wider, he would be having panicky flashbacks about tattooed stalkers from New Zealand.

As it stands, Sam doesn't really have the mental energy required for this level of suspicion so instead he falls asleep and wakes to find that the bus has continued on several kilometres past his stop. Paper bag clutched under one arm, Sam slowly makes his way back towards his hotel. A few metres back and not particularly well hidden, a small hooded figure follows along behind.

The man at the front desk is remarkably unconcerned by the sight of Sam. Having been missing for several days, Sam is visibly scratched and bruised and is wearing a bright orange hoodie several sizes too small for him. Front desk man takes this in stride.

"Having a pleasant stay, Sir?" he says with a smile so enthusiastic it almost seems genuine.

"To be honest, mate," Sam says, "I've had worse holidays."

Taking this as positive feedback, Front Desk Man's smile widens even further.

"But I lost my key. In a monsoon. With the rain and the wind and so on," Sam continues. "So I'd kind of hoped that..."

Front Desk Man holds up a hand.

"Say no more, my friend," he says, before rummaging around in a drawer and handing Sam a key on a string. Either this man has a remarkable memory for the room numbers of his guests, or the same key opens every door. Sam suspects it's the latter.

The charge for the replacement key, of course, is more than the cost of a night's accommodation. Sam scribbles an illegible version of his own signature on a scrap of paper and hopes it's all a little more above board than it seems.

It takes Sam less than two minutes to retrieve his belongings from the room, check his phone (eight missed calls and three emails from the insurance company), cram everything back into his bag and return to the front desk, where Front Desk Man looks ever so slightly bewildered by the return of his key. In seconds, his unflappable demeanour is back in place but Sam is sure that he saw it crack for a moment there.

The weather page, torn from the newspaper, is folded in the front pocket of Sam's new orange hoodie and he pulls it out repeatedly in the taxi, superstitious that it might somehow have changed. It hasn't.

The taxi driver confirms that Sam is headed for the right place and that he's on time for the right ferry to get him there. This communication, however, takes place through a combination of grunts, wild gestures and pointing to a torn newspaper page as neither man speaks the other's language. It could be a beautiful illustration of the shared human experience, Sam thinks. Or it could be a wrong ferry.

It's the wrong ferry. Or rather, the wrong time for the right ferry.

Sam settles in to wait for three hours on a uncomfortable bench, watched warily by four skinny dogs.

There is a person on the next bench also waiting. They have a hood pulled low over their face.

It occurs to Sam that he never did return any of those calls, emails or letters from the insurance company. He wonders fleetingly whether a large multinational insurance company might employ a small-time Thai gangster to follow a recently bereaved client on his suspicious trips around the world. It seems unlikely, but Sam can't think of anyone else who'd want to keep an eye on him. Apart from Claudia's parents of course. Or Bridget. Or maybe Avril's medical team. Or possibly the bank, in light of the number of mortgage payments he's forgotten to make of late.

On balance, it seems best to simply accept that somebody is following him and think no more about it.

It's an uneventful ferry ride, followed by an uneventful train journey on a crowded train in the stinking heat. Too many hours later, Sam disembarks at a small town where dark clouds hang heavy overhead and small currents of wind whip up rubbish in the streets. More skinny dogs watch him as he passes.

He walks to the beach and settles himself under a palm tree, his backpack nestled under his head as a makeshift pillow and the orange hoodie snuggled over him like a blanket.

Then he falls asleep.

A few metres down the beach under another palm tree, a small hooded figure also sleeps.

Two days later, a disappointed Sam is back on the ferry. The man at the hotel desk remains unperturbed when he asks to check back in.

Chapter Thirty

Sal wakes to a faceful of bright morning sunshine. She is alone on the beach. She sits and stretches in a pale imitation of the Sun Salute she was once quite enthusiastic about. Her eyes hurt, her mouth is dry and her hair is matted into a knotted, sandy mess but she smiles nonetheless.

The sun is shining, the sky is blue and she's a on a beach in Thailand. For extra bonus points, she's *alive* following a close call with a tree in a monsoon and this seems well worth celebrating.

Sal shuffles herself into a cross-legged sitting position and gazes out to sea, slowly repeating her mantras and rejoicing in the gentle heat of the sun on her face. All is good. All is peaceful. All is well.

Something is vibrating.

She pulls her cellphone from her pocket to see the familiar "Private Number" message. She declines the call. Immediately, the phone starts to vibrate again. She declines the call again. Three seconds of peace and it starts again. Sal switches the phone off and glories in the delightful silence.

Her stomach grumbles and she feels a sudden pang of hunger.

Sal gets to her feet and shrugs into her backpack, then humming under her breath, she heads off in search of food. There is a large wad of banknotes in Sal's shoe. It was Destiny that gave her the wrong bag at the hospital and she intends to respect the universe's gift by spending every bit of it on things that bring joy. Starting with a decent Pad Thai.

Chapter Thirty-One

Starbucks is the same in every country.

Usually Sam thinks this is a bad thing.

In this case, he is embracing the sanitised corporate familiarity.

He sits at a booth in the darkest corner with his laptop, feet up on the seat opposite and some kind of unpronounceable abomination rapidly cooling in a mug in front of him. It has whipped cream. Also, rainbow sprinkles. It seems designed for six-year-olds, but has a significant enough caffeine content that his hands are shaking after drinking less than half. Sam feels very awake.

It's been far too long since he last dipped a toe in the waters of the online storm-chasing community and he is making up for it now with great enthusiasm.

His mood has fluctuated wildly over the past few minutes from ecstatic excitement to crushing disappointment as he scrolls through feed after feed. He sees photos of storm-wrought devastation; photos taken less than an hour's drive from where he sits. He finds video footage of the very beach he was at a few days earlier, the same trees uprooted and whipped past the camera with unbelievable force.

He came so close.

The beach; the storm; the tree. All the makings of the perfect ending, perfectly wasted by an idiotic Australian woman.

His phone vibrates on the table, skittering its way across the shiny surface.

The call is from Avril's doctor.

Sam declines the call.

Seconds later, the screen lights up again and the vibration begins anew.

Private number.

Sam declines again.

There is a small hooded figure sitting a few tables away, a newspaper raised in front of their face in the manner of a particularly conspicuous spy from children's television. The only part missing is the eyeholes cut out of the front page. It's such a ridiculous image that Sam immediately writes it off as an innocent coincidence. Surely any proper henchman worth their salt would avoid such a cliched approach to following someone.

But when he returns to the table after a two-minute bathroom interlude, his laptop has been moved and his bag rifled through. The hooded figure is in exactly the same spot, newspaper in place.

Sam drains his mug of the questionable sugary concoction and returns to the counter to order another. His card declines. So does the other one. He fishes out the only-for-emergencies-joint-savings-account card. That one declines too. Sam suspects that he might be fucked.

218

Chapter Thirty-Two

When Sam met Claudia, it hadn't been love at first sight.

Set up by mutual friends, they'd met at a painfully hip cocktail bar in the city and made awkward, stilted small talk about things that didn't matter.

Sam could see exactly where his football mate Jonno had been coming from (*Jonno's just like a puppy*, Claudia said much later, *a little bit stupid but so fucking cute that you can't get mad when he shits on the rug*). She was, of course, beautiful and possessed of a set of boobs so magnificent that Sam struggled to direct his gaze anywhere else. She was tall and elegantly dressed and spoke with such obvious intelligence that Sam found himself struggling for words.

When she asked what he did for work, he couldn't really explain it.

When she told him about her future ambitions, he had to admit that he didn't really have any.

When she wondered what he liked to do for fun, he told her that he liked to drink.

She was stunning and classy and clever. She was everything he was meant to want in a woman and yet the sight of her left him cold. She seemed like a cardboard cut-out of a perfect woman; warm and welcoming on the outside but ice-cold and shrill beneath.

Sam remembered looking at that beautiful, uninteresting face (slightly blurry at the edges due to excessive cocktail consumption) and trying desperately to think of an excuse to leave before his soul fled his body completely.

And then she belched.

Not a little, ladylike burp covered demurely with a napkin. Not the burp of a classy adult in polite company.

This was an unapologetic release of gas, forced out through a wide-open mouth in such a way that it echoed, clearly audible above the subtle soft jazz playing through the bar. Heads turned. Mouths dropped open.

"It's a bit fucking uptight in here, isn't it?" Claudia had said, eyes sparkling.

And it was at that precise moment that Sam fell in love.

* * *

Twelve years later, they came back for anniversary drinks with a side of nostalgia. The bar was exactly the same; pretentious, industrial chic with drink prices so high you'd assume they were joking (they weren't joking). The bar was the same. Sam and Claudia were not.

"You're nothing." She said to him after a few gins. He rolled his eyes.

"No, seriously," she said, "It's like you're just an empty

space where a person should be. A vacuum."

He'd thrown back another jager bomb, ignoring the twinge where his soul used to be.

"What is the *point* of you?" she'd continued. "You don't do anything. You don't think about anything. You don't believe anything."

"You don't even like anything," she said. "You have no interests and no hobbies and just nothing. You are an empty space inside of a body that just sits and vegetates and does *nothing*."

He'd smiled without humour and pulled her face in towards his.

"I don't want to be with you, Claudia" he'd hissed through his teeth. "You are cold and bitter and *old*. I haven't fancied you in years."

It was intentional cruelty; twisting the knife into an increasingly fragile self-image.

It was something he'd learned about beautiful people like Claudia; their looks meant nothing to them until they started to fade. Then, all of a sudden, they meant everything. There was a moment when he saw something in her eyes; something inside her crumpled and bent. But then the moment was over and the same tough-as-nails Claudia stared him down.

"You think I want this?" she sneered. "You think this is all my dreams come true?"

She leaned in even closer, so that their noses almost touched. He felt the fine mist of spittle on his face as she spat the words at him.

"You are a sad little excuse for a man and I wish that I was anywhere other than in this pathetic marriage with you."

Then she'd turned to the barman with a wide-eyed smile and ordered another dirty Martini.

"Fuck you, Sam," she said as she threw it back.

Chapter Thirty-Three

There are worse places to be homeless.

Sal's well aware of this, having tried it first-hand on those few occasions where she'd been between lodgings and found herself on friends' couches or in her tent behind some bushes or even, for a particularly memorable week, living in a little-used disabled toilet at a suburban cricket ground.

By comparison, her spot on powder-soft white sand beneath waving palm trees is quite acceptable. It comes with access to outdoor beach showers, spectacular ocean views and fairly regular access to free beer whenever backpackers set up nearby in conveniently accessible party-crashing proximity.

It is a particularly nice spot to return to this evening after an unpleasantly sticky day of wandering the city on foot in search of tourists she might scam into paying for walking tours. They've been a little thin on the ground, but she's ended the day with twelve American dollars, seven British pounds and fifty baht in her pocket, so she can't complain. Sal peels off her oversized hooded sweatshirt with pleasure, glorying in the sensation of cool sea breeze on her sweaty skin. Her increasingly bedraggled backpack is exactly where she left it, unconvincingly hidden beneath a small heap of palm fronds. Sal hauls it out and settles in to her usual sleeping spot, nestled against the trunk of a palm tree with the backpack providing a cushion against the rough wood. She briefly considers buying food, but quickly dismisses this idea in preference for just waiting for nearby backpackers to leave their food unattended. Free, she thinks, is always preferable.

The sun is just about to sink below the horizon when Grumpy English Bloke drops onto the ground beside her, sending a fine puff of sand right into her eye.

"Oh, fuck you," she says, blinking rapidly and picking bits from her eyelashes.

"Nice to see you too," he says.

"You got sand in my eye?" she says.

"What?" he says.

"You got sand in my... Oh fuck it, never mind," she says, wiping away sandy tears.

"You've been following me," he says without looking at her, apparently fixated on the skyline.

"Nope," she says. He looks at her now.

"Yes, you have," he insists.

"I have better things to do," she says with some disdain, "than follow your sad arse around town?"

Scepticism is clear on his face.

"Better things?" he says, "Better things like what?"

She ignores him, continuing to pluck tiny bits of sand from her eyelashes.

"Well, somebody's following me," he says, digging his fingertips into the sand and sending more flying.

"Would you stop fucking fidgeting?" she snaps. He looks

startled.

"Sorry," she says. "I don't deal well with small physical discomforts. It's a work-on?"

They sit in silence, watching colour spread across the horizon in the wake of the now-disappeared sun.

Remembering his bereavement, his suicidal confessions and his recent saving of her life, Sal starts to feel small twinges of sympathy.

"Sorry?" she says again. He shrugs.

In the dwindling light, the large silhouette of a shirtless backpacker weaves across the beach in front of them. Even in the gloom, his sunburn glows. Sam is quietly pleased to see that he made it out of the gutter.

The sunburned German carefully places a beer bottle on the ground, digging it into the sand and checking it's perfectly balanced before whipping out his penis and releasing an enormous quantity of urine onto the sand in the opposite direction. Even at a distance of several paces, Sam can smell alcohol on the German's piss.

"Jesus Christ," Sal sighs. "Fucking tourists?"

There is a clear expression of disdain on her face, but this doesn't stop her from snatching up the forgotten beer bottle as the German totters off back towards the water. She downs most of the bottle before passing the dregs to Sam, who's more than happy to finish it off. There is a significant amount of sand in the beer and likely a similar amount of spittle, but Sam is not about to look a gift horse in the mouth.

"So," he says, tucking the empty bottle out of sight under a nearby bush, "You definitely weren't following me?"

She shakes her head.

"Even after all that bollocks about redemption and connections and you have a duty to save me from myself?" He tries to make eye contact but she's evasive, seemingly fascinated by the sand between her toes.

"The person following me everywhere I went today; that wasn't you trying to save me?"

"Well," she says, "I may have been a wee bit drunk?"

"You followed me because you..."

"No, dickhead,"she interrupts. "I might have been a wee bit drunk when I said the things about nature and messages and karma and so on?"

"So you don't need to save me after all?"

"Well, it still seems like a good idea," she says. "You know, quid pro quo?"

He nods slowly.

"But you can't really be bothered now that you're sober?"

"Well, not exactly *sober*," she corrects him. "But quite a lot less drunk..."

It's hard to make out in the dark, but there's a shape down near the water that looks an awful lot like a small figure with a large hood. Sam squints and leans forward in an attempt to see better.

"You see that?" he hisses under his breath. There's no answer.

He glances over to see that Mad Australian Woman has passed out against the tree and is snoring softly, mouth hanging wide open.

There's a stranger following him. He's stuck in a foreign country where he doesn't speak the language with no money and three days before he can catch his flight back home. He has nobody and nothing and the only person who's professed any desire to help is a clearly insane Australian woman, homeless and sleeping on a Thai beach. It's all going horribly wrong, but for some reason Sam can't seem to make himself feel any sense of real concern.

Instead, he lies back in the sand and sleeps for ten glorious, dreamless hours.

When he wakes, the hooded figure is nowhere to be seen and somebody has stolen his wallet. Again.

Chapter Thirty-Four

Sal is firmly of the opinion that fried chicken tastes better cold. This particular plate had sat, untouched and cooling, in front of a pair of sunburned backpackers for a good twenty minutes while they argued and uploaded posts to Instagram. Now that they've spotted something share-worthy and disappeared off down the street, Sal makes short work of their abandoned chicken. An older couple at a nearby table seem to have noticed the sudden change in patrons and stare at her in horror. Nobody else seems particularly bothered.

Sal sits back, licking grease from her fingers, and takes a moment to savour the sensations of a belly full of chicken and the heat of the sun on her skin. There is also a distinct waft of unwashed body that Sal suspects is coming from herself, but she blocks this out and focuses on all she has to be thankful for. As soon as she gets back to her spot on the beach, she thinks, she will salute the sun in the correct practically-qualified-yoga-teacher manner in which it deserves to be saluted. She wonders whether an impromptu yoga lesson might also lead to a gathering of tourists keen to absorb her teachings in exchange for cash tips. Or beer. Or chicken; she'd happily accept more fried chicken.

An abandoned bottle of Coke shines in the sunlight, tiny beads of moisture dotting the cold glass. Setting aside her dislike of carbonated beverages and her general scruples against the Coca-Cola company, Sal downs the bottle in one and follows with a resonant belch.

She is gnawing the last flecks of chicken from the bones when there's a startled squeal from the street as the backpackers return to their table at pace. Sal makes herself scarce.

A few blocks away, Sal slows to a casual jog and starts to look around for the next possible source of abandoned food. She has found that the backpackers of the area - loaded up with valuable foreign currency, gullible, and often high - are a ready source of food, drink and money. Now that the days of homelessness are ticking over into weeks though, she has started to think that she might need to consider next steps. Her chemical-free, dairy-free, gluten-free vegan diet has certainly taken a turn for the worse since she left the yoga school and a small part of her is wondering how long she can sustain this before terminal cancer sets in. She has a distinct memory of telling a New Mums Yoga class back in Melbourne that one Big Mac had the same carcinogenic profile as an entire pack of cigarettes. Even at the time she was fairly sure this was wrong, but the idea of food as poison is sufficiently drummed into her that she can't help feeling a little queasy even as she eyes up the melted chocolate bar smeared across the pavement in front of her.

Eventually, she finds a half-eaten takeaway container of pad thai dropped in a gutter. Thoughtfully, the litterer has even left a plastic fork wedged into the noodles. She sits on a bench outside the bus station and eats cold pad thai as she watches pale backpackers arrive on buses and sunburned ones leave. A few days ago, she would've been looking out for potential targets for her local colour tours, but today she finds that she just can't be arsed with any of it. Even the idea of beachfront yoga has lost its appeal and she doesn't feel quite herself.

A pasty middle-aged man with a small paunch boards a bus nearby, on the way to the airport. She's pretty sure it's Grumpy English Bloke. There is a faint twinge of guilt somewhere inside Sal as she remembers her previously heartfelt intention to educate Grumpy English Bloke on the beautiful mysteries of life and the importance of following one's journey to personal enlightenment even in challenging times. It is only right, she thinks, that he should be saved from his own suicidal intentions by the same woman whose life he saved on a beach in Thailand. Really, she should fling aside the cold pad thai and chase after him right now. But she's still hungry and she can't be bothered and she's overwhelmed with a sense of general hopelessness so instead she just watches his bus leave.

It's probably the MSG.

Chapter Thirty-Five

By the time his in-flight meal arrives on the tray table in front of him, Sam hasn't eaten in more than forty-eight hours. He flings the little foil covers aside with such gleeful abandon that they end up in the row behind him, to the vocal disapproval of the passengers in those seats.

There's overcooked, grey chicken on a bed of gritty mashed potatoes. There are tiny, puckered peas in some kind of bland gelatinous sauce. There is custard in a shade of yellow so intense it appears radioactive.

Sam has never enjoyed a meal so much in his life.

Finished in less than five minutes, he washes it down with a warm beer before turning to the elderly woman beside him in search of seconds. She obliges, handing over the mushed-together remains of her own meal, clearly mystified by his absence of taste buds.

When he finishes that one too and requests a third meal, the flight attendant is so pleased with the unexpectedly positive feedback that she deposits two more in front of him. The beef, as it turns out, is so flavourless and overcooked it resembles chewing gum in his mouth. He groans with happiness in a manner so unintentionally sexual that the woman in front of him turns to glare daggers. He has a vague desire to explain but his mouth is so full of saliva and half-chewed beef that it's impossible.

By the time the flight attendant returns to retrieve the trays stacked high on Sam's tray table, he is snoring emphatically, head leaning heavily on the shoulder of the elderly woman in the next seat.

* * *

It's not until Sam is back at home - tucked into bed between the same gritty, sweaty sheets he hasn't washed in months - that the sickness sets in.

At first it's just a minor discomfort and he squirms around a bit in an effort to dislodge what feels like an awkward gas bubble. The bubble does not budge. Sam heaves over onto his front with an audible groan and quite unexpectedly, follows through with a startling quantity of vomit.

Still half-asleep, he opens one eye to see the bedside table liberally splattered in the remnants of three airline dinners, two beers and the four glasses of water he'd downed before bed in an effort to settle a slightly dodgy stomach.

There is vomit on the wall. There are pools of vomit on the carpet. There is a substantial amount of vomit strewn across the pillow, his face resting stickily in the middle of it. It seems very clear that he should get out of bed immediately to shower and clean up the mess.

Instead, Sam closes his eyes and goes back to sleep.

Three hours later, he wakes on the carpet in a new pool of vomit. He is covered from head to toe in a cold sweat. His legs are shaking uncontrollably. His hair is plastered to his face with sweat and vomit. He does not feel well.

Sam tries to crawl to the shower but can't seem to maintain balance or any control of his limbs. Instead, he twitches and seizes his way across the bedroom carpet, trailing a mess of bodily fluids behind himself. At some point, he passes out again.

Sam wakes to find himself curled in a foetal position on the bathroom lino beside a mysterious green streak and a dusty pile of pubes. This floor has not seen a mop in some time.

He slides across the dusty floor and into the shower, where he flings one arm at the controls until a torrent of freezing water blasts down on him. Sam crawls his way back into the foetal position, his back braced against the shower door. Shivering and sweating, he lies in the shower, moaning quietly and leaking bodily fluids onto the shower floor, until morning.

At some point, Sam must have passed out because he's woken by a twisting sensation in his gut so agonising he can't seem to breathe. His mouth gapes open and a strange little sigh emerges, quickly followed by a stringy mess of spittle and stomach acid. This seems to Sam an encouraging sign; surely if there's nothing left in his stomach there is nothing to make him feel sick any longer and the vomiting will stop.

This proves to be incorrect.

Seconds later, the twisting pain returns but this time it's accompanied by a tearing sensation and a stabbing heat in his lower back. More bodily fluids spurt their way across the floor of the shower. Sam passes out.

It's unclear to Sam exactly what happens over the next twenty-four hours, the time passing in a disorienting fever dream of stomach cramps and violent bodily expulsions. Sometime the next day, Sam finds himself standing upright under a cold shower. The cubicle around him shows graphic evidence of his sickness but his body - goosebumped and shivering - is mercifully clean.

He gulps back mouthfuls of tinny-tasting shower water until this triggers another bout of vomiting. Not a quick learner, but an effective one, Sam uses the next mouthful of shower water to rinse and spit instead.

Eventually he emerges on shaky legs and returns tentatively to his bed where he curls up amongst vomit-streaked sheets and sleeps for twelve hours. He dreams that Claudia is alive again, but he has died. He smiles beatifically in his sleep.

Chapter Thirty-Six

Four days after his return from Thailand, Sam finally manages to leave his bedroom.

It's not that he's recovered exactly, but more that the raging hunger has started to outweigh the nauseated need to remain completely still at all times. He crawls on all fours down the hallway, swaying heavily from side to side. At the top of the stairs, he repositions himself and gingerly places both hands on the top step before slowly shifting his weight onto the left hand and moving the right down onto the next step.

He moves at a glacial speed, ever-so-slowly working his way down the staircase while his gut churns in painful circles. About halfway down, Sam's elbows buckle and he slides face-first to the bottom of the staircase with a worrying series of cracking and snapping noises.

Convinced he's broken several bones, Sam lies motionless on the floor and waits for the agonising pain to set in. Beyond a vague bruised ache in one elbow, nothing happens. He waits a little longer. And he starts to smell something objectionable.

After four days in his sickbed, surrounded by a constant

stench of vomit, sweat and diarrhoea, Sam is in no position to criticise other aromas. There is, however, something distinctly garbagey- smelling about the downstairs floor of his home. Slowly, he raises his head from the floor and sniffs.

It's an eye-watering blend of earthy, composty, damp *decay*. It's like the smell of the mouse that died under the dishwasher last year and rotted for a month before Claudia found its mummified little corpse. It's a bit like the smell of the chicken Sam had tried to cook four days past expiry - a sulphurous stench so strong it invoked immediate gagging. There are elements too of the smell of a cabbage in a plastic bag, discarded at the bottom of the pantry for so long it had half-melted into a reddish-brown ooze and caused a near heart-attack when Sam mistook it for a decapitated head.

It's like all of these things and yet somehow it's worse than anything Sam has ever smelled in his life. This is the smell of the gates of Hell in all its horrifying, maggot-ridden rotting-flesh glory.

Ever so slowly, Sam inches his way across the carpet towards the kitchen in search of food. He has a distinct picture in mind of the chicken noodle soup frozen in a Tupperware container at the bottom of the freezer. Of indeterminate age, the chicken noodle soup waits for him in all its bland, watery glory. He is sure that this will be the answer to all his problems: the one thing that will sit happily in his stomach without invoking violent revolt. He will take it from the freezer and put it in the microwave and then...

But then he reaches the kitchen and realises that there is nothing edible here.

The lino is a pool of black swamp water, frothy with grey lumps of something ungodly. The swamp appears to have leaked out of the fridge, which is growing some kind of fluffy green mould across its base and in wide streaks up its sides. There's an odd pressure building in Sam's sinuses and an aching feeling behind his eyes – it seems that the loss of his chicken noodle soup has brought him close to tears.

As he stands in his stinking kitchen in stained underwear, surrounded by a rotting mess of old food, Sam has something of a lightbulb moment. The ice-cold showers. The bedside lamp that won't turn on. The eerie silence throughout the house. The stinking mess of defrosted fridge contents on his kitchen floor.

Following several months of non-payment, it would appear that the power has been cut off.

Chapter Thirty-Seven

Once upon a time, one wintry night in January, they'd slept the night out here. It must've been four or five years ago - back in the days of kids' bedtime routines. Bath-and-teeth-and-story-and-bed. Night after night. Rinse and repeat.

He'd come down from story time to find Claudia sat on the outdoor sofa, pink-nosed in the cold while it began to snow. Snowflakes swirled around on gentle breezes, gusting around to dust Claudia's hair and shoulders despite the small porch roof above.

Even back then - when they'd still been a little team united against the onslaught of their two small children - even then, it had been a rare treat to see her smiling. He'd pulled a fluffy blanket from the armchair indoors and gone out to sit with her.

He remembered so distinctly the feeling of sitting with her in the snow. He remembered the warmth of her under his arm and the achingly cold breeze against his face. He remembered the feeling of utter exhaustion - they were always exhausted back then - and the sensation of drifting off to sleep in glorious snow-muffled silence as the back garden turned white around them.

They'd woken at dawn to the sound of Avril screaming the house down, having tried to crawl into their cold, empty bed upstairs. The snow had melted. The dog was squatting on the sodden lawn at Sam's feet, defecating copiously. Claudia awoke with a jolt, slamming her forehead into Sam's chin.

And so, life had returned to normal.

Today it is not snowing.

It is unseasonably cold, grey and misty. There's a strong chance of icy rain in the forecast, but it's definitely not snowing.

Today, Sam sits on the same old outdoor couch in his underwear, grease running down his arms as he shovels down slice after slice of pepperoni pizza. To the pizza delivery man's credit, nothing was said about Sam's clothing choices or about the ungodly stench within the house. Sam had rewarded this remarkable show of discretion with a tip in the form of a handful of sticky change scooped from the coffee table in the lounge room. Pizza delivery man had barely flinched.

Following a fairly desperate online transaction with his only remaining card, via his 2%-battery-remaining cellphone, power and internet services have been restored. While Sam has no current intention to do anything about the rotting pool of filth in the kitchen, he harbours vague hopes that a re-chilling of the fridge contents might stop things from getting too much worse.

Halfway through the first pizza, Sam is seized by uncontrollable cramps and rushes back to the bathroom where he somehow shits half a pizza back in the toilet. It is quite remarkable, Sam considers, that half a pizza can pass through his complete digestive system in less than ten minutes, emerging in almost exactly the same condition it entered. It really does look like someone chewed up some pizza and spat it into the toilet bowl.

Sam's stomach cramps again, this time with unbearable hunger pangs and he weeps on the floor of the bathroom for a while before returning to his now-cold pizza and consuming another half.

Later, back on the toilet with his laptop perched upon his knees (complete with insistently flashing battery warning), he becomes aware within a few seconds of scrolling that something big is in the works. The storm of the year, absolutely, but maybe even the storm of the decade.

Keyboard warriors from across America and around the world are frantically booking themselves plane tickets or fuelling RVs or finding any way they possibly can of getting to a sparsely inhabited corner of Kansas. Despite very practical stay-at-home warnings from the Weatherman (who is already nearby in his mobile weather station, broadcasting live), storm enthusiasts are flocking.

It would appear that some shit is about to go down.

Sam just needs to figure out a way to stop shitting himself for long enough to fly back across the Atlantic and throw himself into the path of this storm.

* * *

Sprawled across a very expensive leather sofa in a borrowed silk bathrobe, Sal eats cold pizza and drinks beer in front of a ridiculously large television that she can't figure out how to change from the Weather Channel. Panoramic views of the coastline surround her through giant floor-to-ceiling windows and banana palms wave gently in the breeze outside.

It's not exactly what she had intended for her trip to Thailand but on reflection, she decides that there are many different ways of taking one's soul on a journey of self-enlightenment. Hers just happens to involve an older rich man and a mansion on the beach.

The Very Wealthy Man snores resonantly from his spot on the sofa beside her, impressive gut poking through the gap in his silk dressing gown.

While it's true that this man is twenty years older and fifty kilograms heavier than her usual type, Sal would argue that he is in possession of a number of unique charms. He speaks four languages fluently. He demonstrates excellent taste in decorating and furnishing his home - or at least, he hires people with excellent taste to do this for him. He knows all the best food and drink places in town and is able to magically summon decadent feasts to the door within minutes. The cold pizza is symptomatic more of Sal's hesitance to wake the sleeping giant than it is to any lack of better options.

The glorious mansion on the beachfront and the obvious excess of material wealth are, of course, completely irrelevant to Sal's interest in Walter. Or Gunther. Or maybe it was Gunnar?

Names are also irrelevant, naturally.

Wedged beneath the sizeable thigh of the sleeping man, Sal's right foot has fallen asleep. Wincing at the electric-shock fizz of pins-and-needles, she focuses on pulling the foot very slowly out with minimal disturbance. Eventually, her foot pulls free and she starts massaging numb toes between greasy fingers.

The TV has been babbling away at her for hours and she's managed to tune it out completely but all of a sudden, the meaning of all that babble becomes clear.

There is a storm coming to Kansas. It is a very, very large storm. There are big red warnings running along the bottom of the screen advising residents to flee the area. There are traffic jams on the way out of every major city in the storm's projected path. Crazy stormchasing weirdos are flocking from all parts of the globe to experience the absolute clusterfuck of weather expected to make landfall in around 48 hours' time. A grizzled old man in a large cowboy hat is being interviewed: "The Weatherman: Local Storm Expert" reads the caption. In an unexpectedly soft-spoken, polite manner, he exhorts all weather enthusiasts to stay away unless experienced and properly equipped.

Sal can think of one person in particular who is neither experienced nor properly equipped but she would bet her last five dollars that he's on his way to Kansas at this very moment.

With the pained sigh of someone tormented by conscience, Sal peels herself away from her comfortable spot on the comfortable couch beside the very wealthy man and goes back to the bedroom to dress and pack her bag. She stops for a moment to book herself a Business Class flight (no need for the excesses of First Class) on the Very Wealthy Man's credit card and to leave him a note in lipstick on the bathroom mirror. She's always wanted to do this, but finds herself unexpectedly lost for words. Pausing, lipstick in hand she considers the situation at length before writing *Gone out for a bit. Karma calling. Thanks for everything.* This seems suitably vague.

* * *

The Weatherman is in front of a moron with a television camera for what feels like the thousandth time today. Having been introduced to the moron and told she was a "Meteorologist for Channel Seven News", The Weatherman had expected some basic understanding of Meteorology and has been sorely disappointed.

"So what should our viewers expect when the typhoon hits the area?" she asks, eyes bright.

"Not a typhoon," The Weatherman says. "Like I already said, they're called hurricanes in this part of the world."

"Oh I know," she whispers, leaning in close. "But the producers don't like that we keep using the same word. They want us to switch it up a bit."

She winks and gives a grin so full of large white teeth, The Weatherman flinches.

She repeats the question about typhoons.

The answer is the same.

The Weatherman begins a long and detailed explanation as to the differences between a tornado, a tropical storm, a typhoon and a hurricane. It is a very clear and concise lesson in meteorology for beginners. There is no room for confusion. It is a triumph of science and reason over journalistic mediocrity.

"So, if this hurricane does make landfall when we suspect it might, then I'd say we should expect quite a show." The Weatherman concludes with a charming and self-deprecating smile.

A few hours later, the footage appears on the channel's website having been edited to remove the entire explanation.

"So what should our viewers expect when the typhoon hits the area?" the moron's voice asks.

"I'd say we should expect quite a show," The Weatherman smiles from the screen.

The banner reads "The Weatherman - Metoerolgst".

Perched on a stool at a local bar, nursing a double whiskey, The Weatherman pauses for a quick banging of forehead on the bar. It is not a clean bar. There is some sticking of skin to old stale beer spill.

The barman takes the hint and places another whiskey on the sticky spot.

The Weatherman throws back the whiskey and imagines the offices of Channel Seven News being obliterated by a tornado. It's hard to tell under the battered brim of the cowboy hat, but The Weatherman seems to be smiling at the thought.

Chapter Thirty-Eight

Due to his current need to remain near a toilet at all times, Sam has found plenty of time to make phone calls and sort some overdue life admin.

The insurance company, as it turns out, are perfectly reasonable once he bothers to call them back. Aside from a brief enquiry into his health, they don't seem bothered by the ongoing noises of diarrhoea and his accompanying groans. There are some questions about his mailing address and housing situation, something about his previous experience in caring for the disabled, something else about his outlook for future employment. It seems they mostly just wanted to check that he was still alive, having failed to make contact with him in several months.

The man on the phone ("Call me Colin!") seems a little confused when Sam asks whether the insurance company has had him followed in Thailand. It would seem that the company's jurisdiction does not include south-east Asia and their traditional methods of contact run more along the lines of phone and email than to physically following customers around the world.

Colin enquires as to whether Sam should perhaps be speaking to the police about this matter, but Sam has largely lost interest at this point.

While far less pleasant than Helpful Insurance Man Colin, the lady from the bank reluctantly agrees to reactivate his accounts and issue new cards. He is almost disappointed to hear that nobody has bothered to fraudulently use his stolen credit cards, although Grumpy Bank Lady points out that they were almost maxed out already so probably not a lot of use to anyone.

The bank also seems somewhat reassured by the evidence of Sam still being alive and also profess no knowledge whatsoever of anyone following him through the streets of Thailand. Grumpy Bank Lady shows far less interest in this than Helpful Colin, with no such concern for Sam's welfare.

By ten in the morning, Sam has sorted his finances, confirmed the insurance company's continued payment of all Avril's medical bills, transferred a large chunk of life insurance money into one of the few bank accounts he can easily access and paid an eye-watering sum for a last-minute series of flights to Kansas, departing in a few hours' time.

What Sam has come to realise over the past few days is that he has approximately three minutes from the time he eats or drinks anything until he will need to violently expel said food or drink into the toilet. As such, he is perfectly capable of trans-Atlantic travel. Just as long as he does not eat or drink for at least the next fifteen hours.

Waiting for an Uber to the airport (because he's loaded again, so why the fuck not?), Sam consumes an entire family-size bag of Doritos - Claudia's favourite Cool Original flavour, found stashed at the back of the pantry. Two minutes and fifty-three seconds later, he's expelling said bag of corn chips again.

He weeps quietly on the bathroom floor for a while. This has become quite standard behaviour: eat, shit, cry due to extreme hunger, eat again.

Then his phone dings to tell him his ride is here, so he wipes his eyes, flushes away the Doritos and heads off to face oblivion in Kansas.

Chapter Thirty-Nine

Sal emerges from the glory of Business Class travel feeling more refreshed and in tune with the universe than after any yoga class she's ever experienced. Standing in line at immigration, she considers that maybe she's been on the wrong path all this time.

Perhaps, she considers, the path to enlightenment is found not through sacrifice and self-reflection and healthy living and meditation, but rather through the possession of shitloads of money.

After twenty-one hours of top-class service, gourmet meals and as much free champagne as she could drink, Sal is now feeling significantly reduced in circumstances as she stands amongst a crowd of sweaty, exhausted economy-class passengers. This whole process of getting into America is remarkably democratic and egalitarian. Sal does not like it.

"You think Lady Gaga has to stand in this line?" she asks the small Thai woman in front of her in the line.

There is no response.

Sal repeats herself.

The woman looks up in clear exasperation.

"Lady Gaga is American," she says very slowly, as if explaining to a child. "Americans go in a different line."

Sal snorts.

"Racism," she says.

It is not a fast process to clear customs and immigration and by the time Sal is cleared to enter the United States, her Business-Class glow has largely worn off and it feels as if she might as well have flown cattle class after all. There had been no Business Class option for her connecting flight to Kansas, so by the time she arrives in Wichita, all traces of the pleasant champagne buzz have long worn off. She stands in the arrivals hall with aching feet, smelling distinctly of stale sweat and spilled alcohol. It's a little after 2am and it's pitch black outside the terminal.

She eyes the drivers holding signs with some envy. None of the signs show her name. Sal had harboured the tiniest hope that Very Wealthy Man might've funded some transport and accommodation, but the rather blunt text message she received after disembarking made it quite clear that his credit card was no longer accessible for her use.

With a sigh and a grimace, Sal hoists her backpack and makes her way out into the dark, heading for the bus stop.

* * *

Skye always knows when things are getting serious.

Perched on the passenger seat with both paws on the door-frame, she presses her muzzle against the small gap at the top of the window and whines quietly at whatever it is she can smell. Her stubby tail thrashes back and forward, catching The Weatherman in the arm with enough force to leave tiny bruises.

"Storm coming, girl?"

Skye turns away from the window for a fleeting moment to give a big doggy grin, then goes right back to it.

Outside, there's a thin drizzle falling from cloudy skies in the dim light of early daybreak. There's nothing to indicate any kind of impending disaster, but Skye knows better.

Fleetwood Mac comes on the radio and The Weatherman cranks up the volume, fingers tapping in time against the steering wheel. The GMRS radio unit continues to crackle with the exclamations of storm chasers shit-talking across the county, but The Weatherman turns up the music again to drown them out.

Skye turns away from the window again for a moment to grin her approval, large ears standing to attention and pink tongue lolling. She's always been a sucker for classic rock.

The Weatherman is not one for company, instead cultivating a solo lifestyle where Skye provides more than enough social contact. There are the podcasts of course, the online videos and the discussion boards but it's much less painful dealing with people from the safety of a computer screen. After today, there will be no more television interviews and no more talking to morons.

So it is a strange aberration from normal behaviour when The Weatherman pulls over to pick up a scruffy forty-something female hitchhiker a few hours outside of Wichita.

* * *

After four hours of attempted hitch-hiking, Sal is seriously pissed off with this ridiculous country. A veteran of more than twenty years thumbing rides around the world, Sal is well accustomed to waiting. She is very familiar with the apologetic sorry-I'm-in-a-hurry wave (often accompanied by pointing to a watch). She's also received many of the vague-gesture-to-the-left-or-right, clearly meaning that the driver is about to change direction and will be of little use in conveying the hitch-hiker to their intended destination. There's also the gesture towards to back seat (sorry, we're all full up already!) or the side-eye towards the passenger seat (wife/husband doesn't like hitch-hikers) and the always-mysterious thumbs-up gesture, which could mean almost anything at all.

What Sal hadn't experienced until today is the quite unexpected disdain, anger and vitriol directed at her for even attempting to hitch a ride. Roughly every third vehicle has pulled the finger at her. Six separate vehicles have swerved close enough that she's had to leap aside to avoid serious injury. One driver threw a half-full cup of flat cola out of the window at her. Four people have leaned out passenger windows to shout things at her; while some of these were a little garbled and not clearly intelligible, Sal is fairly sure that none of these things were compliments.

Americans seem offended by the idea of hitch-hiking. She's never seen anything like it.

As a large vehicle slows to pass her, Sal readies her middle finger to return the anticipated gesture but it doesn't come. Instead, the truck stops just ahead of her. The passenger window slides open and the grizzled salt-and-pepper face of a grinning dog emerges, large ears flapping slightly in the breeze. It looks distinctly like a dingo, but Sal suspects she might be hallucinating.

The passenger door swings open and a gruff American voice calls out.

"Want a ride or not? We're on kind of a deadline here." The engine revs slightly to emphasise the point.

Sal hobbles over, legs aching after hours of standing on the roadside. It's only once she's standing right beside it that she realises quite how large this vehicle is.

Seizing a handy grab-bar, she swings herself up into the passenger seat, the dog shuffling over quite agreeably to make space.

"Bloody big ute you've got here, mate," she says.

"Can't understand a word you're saying,"the driver mutters, pulling back into traffic.

Looking around, Sal lets out a low whistle. There are monitors and screens and flashing lights everywhere. It's like being in the cockpit of some kind of high-tech spaceship. But also a bit like driving a tank. The dog settles itself onto Sal's lap and shoves its nose out of the window. The dog smells like wet mushrooms and is balanced on hard little claws that dig into Sal's thighs with every movement of the vehicle.

"Why do you have a dingo?" Sal asks.

"You Australian?" the driver asks, eyes still focused on the road ahead.

"Sure am," Sal smiles.

"Then you should know an Australian Kelpie when you see

one," the driver mutters.

The dog does not seem offended by this oversight. Sal pats hesitantly at its head and receives an enthusiastic lick on the face. The dog's breath smells like a compost bin.

"Not really a dog kind of person," Sal says, although she's secretly pleased to have come across a fellow countryman. She gives it another little pat, only slightly disgusted by the sticky, gritty fur.

"I'm trying to get to the place with the storm," Sal says.

The driver looks at her, eyebrows raised.

"You want to go to the storm?"

Sal nods.

"On foot?" the driver continues. "With no equipment and zero apparent knowledge of what this might entail?"

Sal nods again. "Sure," she says.

"You ever seen a hurricane before, lady?"

"Funny you should ask," she says. "Because a couple of weeks ago I was in Thailand, right? And..."

The driver turns up the volume on the stereo, apparently uninterested in Sal's story.

"I love Fleetwood Mac!" Sal shouts. Neither driver nor dog seem to care.

They drive towards a dark shadow in the distance as it begins to rain. Sal looks around the vehicle and tries to deduce what any of these gadgets might do. Beyond the obvious conclusion that this equipment is worth a huge amount of money and the certainty that it has something to do with weather, Sal is clueless.

Eventually, the song ends and the driver turns the volume back down. In the quiet, the voices bursting from the other radio become much more insistent. As the storm approaches, they are reaching fever-pitch levels of enthusiasm.

"So that's a ham radio?" Sal asks. "Like truck drivers use?"

"No," the driver grunts.

Sal doesn't much care either way but decides it may be time to stop attempting to make conversation. She gives it one last go.

"I'm Sal," she says. "From Melbourne. And you are..?"

"They call me the Weatherman," the driver still doesn't look at her.

"The Weatherman?" Sal repeats blankly. "But doesn't that kind of imply..."

The driver glances at her with one eyebrow raised as Sal trails off into silence.

"Never mind," she says and settles in for a silent trip to the tornado zone.

Chapter Forty

The flight goes surprisingly smoothly. Having plumped for First Class (because again, why the fuck not?), Sam has slept like a baby and feels quite pleasantly refreshed upon arrival early morning in Kansas, where a man in the arrivals hall is holding a board with Sam's name on it. The man with the board has brought Sam one of those magical iced coffee concoctions with sprinkles and whipped cream. Sam throws it back with gleeful abandon and glories in the eye-popping sugar rush for all of thirty seconds before remembering that he is currently unable to eat or drink without severe and immediate consequences.

There is an ominous rumbling noise from Sam's bowels. The very soul of discretion, sign-holding man seems suddenly very interested in his shoelaces.

He makes it to a toilet with seconds to spare, then marvels at the ability of rainbow sprinkles to have travelled through his digestive system and emerge largely unaffected. Although the colours have run a little, he notes.

A brief sobbing fit follows as Sam is filled again with the conviction that he will spend the rest of his life in a state of permanent hunger, but he is cheered up shortly thereafter by the idea of his impending death in a hurricane. After all, he won't be hungry once he's dead.

* * *

Sign-Holding Man turns out to be a remarkably proficient driver in possession of a very large and very shiny vehicle. Sam sits up front so that he can get the best possible view of the irresistible in the distance as they get closer and closer. There is a small fridge between the front seats, packed full of soda cans and chocolate bars. Sam is halfway through his third chocolate bar when some aggressive noises from his digestive system remind him that he can't actually eat things any more.

The driver is most accommodating about finding a rest stop at seconds' notice.

Violently expelling chocolate in the truck stop bathroom, Sam reflects again that he is not a fast learner.

Back on the road, Sam feels the need to explain his current digestive situation to Sign-Holding Man, who nods sagely, eyes fixed on the road and says "Sounds like typhoid to me, my friend."

It had not previously occurred to Sam that he might actually be seriously ill, but upon reflection it does seem out of the ordinary for food poisoning to have lasted more than a week.

"Want me to stop by a medical centre?" Sign-Holding Man enquires politely.

Sam considers this for a moment before deciding that it's largely irrelevant whether he dies with or without diarrhoea in his pants.

"No thanks," he says. "Let's go see that storm first."

Sign-Holding Man shrugs and nods.

It's an hour of pleasant silence, coasting along the road under a dark purple sky. After he's dropped off on the outskirts of a tiny town, Sam feels a tiny pang of distress at the departure of Sign-Holding Man but it's soon drowned out by the electric tingles of anticipation fizzing through his body at the sights and sounds of impending storm all around him.

Chapter Forty-One

He wants to be in the centre of everything. He wants to be out in the open with nothing but himself and the storm.

He clambers onto a large farm gate, then wobbles precariously at the top as he realises the gate is not actually closed and is now swaying under his weight. With a strangled yelp, Sam leaps from the top of the gate to fall in an undignified tangle of limbs onto very hard ground. Adding insult to injury, the gate sags after him, the solid metal frame smacking him on the back.

Sam tentatively gets to his feet, relieved first to find that he has sustained no severe injuries and second to find that he has managed not to soil himself in the fall. Upon further reflection, he has decided it would be preferable to die *without* shit in his pants, if possible.

He dusts himself off and walks further into the field, limping over cracks and craters in the sun-baked earth. It's so dry that little bursts of dust puff up from the brown patches of dead grass as he kicks through them. Eventually he reaches a higher point in what feels like the middle of the field and he stops walking. Slowly, he turns a full 360 degrees. He breathes deeply, inhaling the heady combination of drought-affected pasture and cow shit and the heavy ozone smell of impending rain. All around him, the world seems thick with anticipation and Sam feels like finally, he is exactly where he's meant to be.

He doesn't hear the noise of the approaching engine. He's so focused on the glorious satisfaction of having found his place in the world – grinning like a madman with his eyes squeezed tight shut – that he doesn't see it coming.

It's only as it knocks through the sagging gate, sending it spinning off across the field, that Sam notices the large truck speeding across the field towards him. He blinks slowly. He smiles stupidly.

It's a surprise and yet at the same time, it feels like this is how it always had to go. The truck he's seen a thousand times in online video clips, the setup he's read so much about on the message boards. He knows that deep gash in the passenger-side door is from a chase in 2012 in Alabama. He could draw from memory the huge sticker plastered across the back window; Dorothy's house spinning in a cartoon tornado. The tall wires extending high into the air above the roof in a tangle of aerials and antennas – he knows what these are for. So when the driver's door opens and a pair of heavy work boots emerge, he knows that the Weatherman has come for him.

It's almost too much for Sam to take in. His mind feels like one of those plasma balls the kids always liked – electricity shooting all over in random bursts of colour. It's the Weatherman. Here. Now. If the Weatherman is here, then everything will be OK.

The driver swings the car door shut and approaches Sam at a cool saunter. He wears dirty old jeans and a flannel shirt. There's a battered old cowboy hat tipped forward over his face because of course there is. This is the Weatherman. He's the Clint Eastwood of storm chasing.

The Weatherman lifts the hat in one hand, a heavy braid flopping out across one shoulder. So cool, Sam thinks. Siouxstyle.

The Weatherman extends the other hand and says "Sam Frost?" in an unexpectedly soft voice.

Sam is shaking hands enthusiastically before he realises.

The Weatherman smiles at him, showing a perfect row of small white teeth in a dirty face framed by soft grey ringlets. Dark eyes sparkle at him from nests of fine lines in dark weathered skin.

"They call me The Weatherman," she says.

"They sure do,"Sam says, for a lack of anything better to say.

"Sam!" calls another voice from the truck. There's a series of rustles and bangs as a second person extricates themselves and bounces over to the clear spot where Sam and the Weatherman stand.

"Oh Jesus Fuck," Sam moans despite himself. The Weatherman laughs.

"I told you,"he says. "I don't like Australians in general and I really dislike you in particular."

She seems to interpret this as some kind of compliment and wraps him in an uncomfortably gropey bear hug.

"Sammy!"she says, as if to a long-lost family member.

"Mad fucking woman," he mutters.

The Weatherman drops her head, politely hiding an involuntary smirk beneath her hat. Clearly she has spent enough time with Mad Australian Woman to understand where he's coming from.

A dog with ridiculous ears jumps down from the truck and squats beside Sam, peeing into the dry dirt with sufficient force that some blows back onto his shoes. Normally, Sam is quite fond of dogs but in this case he is unconvinced.

"Right then," he says with some finality. "Nice to see you and all, but you can bugger off again now."

The Weatherman frowns and sucks her teeth.

"I'm not so sure that's a good idea," she says.

"No, no," he smiles in what he hopes is a reassuring manner. "It's a great idea. This is perfect."

"It's just that..." she says, then frowns in obvious irritation when he interrupts.

"This is where I need to be," he says, feeling very Zen.

She sighs and bends down on one knee to pat the dog, who seems to have finally finished peeing. Clearly she is not accustomed to being interrupted.

"This is not where you need to be," she says.

She raises one arm and points dramatically at the horizon, "In fact, you need to be around fifty miles that-a way".

Sam looks in the direction she's pointing and sees a rapidly darkening smudge spreading across the horizon. In the opposite direction, he sees blue sky and sunshine.

She's right. The storm is running away from him.

He looks back at the Weatherman, to see that she's already

half-way back into her vehicle.

"You coming?" she shouts back at him.

She doesn't have to ask twice.

Chapter Forty-Two

The Weatherman has a friend named Joe, who is of indeterminate age, ethnicity and gender. Joe is a person of few words, which Sam finds most refreshing after ten minutes spent in the same car as Mad Australian Woman.

Joe sits opposite Sam at a scarred Formica table in a diner so ridiculously American that it feels to Sam more like a movie set than an actual restaurant. Pausing ten minutes into their journey to stop for breakfast is not a decision that Sam agrees with in any way, but his protests have been overruled due to a lack of action on the storm front coupled with the need to meet up with Joe to attain the use of Joe's vehicle, in addition to the Weatherman's stated requirement for "a whole shit-tonne of caffeine" before spending more time in a vehicle with Sal. This is something that Sam can appreciate.

He gazes in wonder as Joe works their way through a comically large stack of pancakes, pausing only to gulp steaming hot black coffee from a chipped mug that passing waitresses top up every few minutes. The result of this is that the level of liquid in Joe's cup never visibly drops below full, despite consumption that Sam estimates at around three litres of coffee so far.

Joe wears a baseball cap emblazoned with the logo of a stormchasing company, pulled down low over sunken eyes dark with lack of sleep. There appears to be a large bruise covering the lower half of Joe's face but it's equally likely that this could be dirt or possibly just stubble. Joe is something of an enigma.

"Good pancakes?" Sam asks.

Joe doesn't bother looking up and continues shovelling, syrup dripping from fork onto table. There's a subtle movement of the shoulders that could possibly be interpreted as a shrug but might also have been a figment of Sam's imagination.

Joe takes another large slug of coffee. A waitress appears out of nowhere and tops the mug back up to brim-full. Sam watches in wonder as Joe eats.

There is a distinctly audible growl as Sam's stomach spasms painfully. Saliva collects in Sam's mouth. He watches Joe eat and imagines the same piled-high forkfuls of pancake and syrup churning around in his own mouth. He looks away and blinks, trying to focus on anything other than Joe's food.

At the next table, Mad Australian Woman is attacking a plate of bacon and eggs with a fervour not often seen in those professing to long-term vegetarianism while the Weatherman picks at a steaming dish of huevos rancheros. He can smell the eggs. He can smell the bacon. He can smell the pancake syrup. He can smell the coffee. Sam has not digested food in close to two weeks.

It doesn't feel like a particularly sensible decision, but he seems to have lost all conscious control of himself and instead observes himself with some concern as he places an order for orange juice, hash browns, bacon, sausages, biscuits and gravy. And a bottomless coffee.

Never in his life has Sam eaten so much food in such a short period of time. He cannot remember ever having eaten anything that tastes as good as this glorious extravaganza of fatty, salty, meaty delight. He can feel spittle dribbling down his chin as he eats but it all tastes so incredible that he cannot possibly pause to wipe his face. The coffee is so hot that it burns all the way down but he keeps drinking it anyway and the waitresses keep topping it up and he drinks more. It is like a fever dream of Americana and cholesterol and caffeine. There is a mixture of gravy and syrup and grease dripping from his chin and elbows as he shovels in more and more food.

And then, after a good ten minutes of uncontrolled eating frenzy, something very strange happens.

Sam starts to feel full.

For weeks now, Sam has been hungry. For every minute of every day, he has been hungry.

The hollow feeling in his stomach has suddenly disappeared and it is wildly disorienting for him.

There is a very familiar gurgling sensation from the depths of Sam's digestive system.

Slowly, he puts down his fork and wipes the gooey, fatty mess from his chin. There is an awful lot of bacon fat smeared through his stubble.

He sits and waits patiently for the spasms to begin.

Nothing happens.

He takes another sip of burning hot coffee.

Nothing happens.

Tentatively, he picks up the fork and spears half a sausage.

He chews and swallows.

Still, nothing happens.

Sam begins to feel euphoric. It seems that this particular combination of grease, meat and carbohydrate has formed some kind of brick in his gut that refuses to be shifted. He is wedged full of American breakfast. Uncomfortably full, in fact.

It is at precisely this moment that something changes and everyone else in the diner slams their laptops closed and leaves, abandoning half-eaten plates of food and - in Joe's case - a full-to-the-brim mug of steaming black coffee. Sam struggles to get up, incapacitated by an uncomfortably bloated stomach and hip joints that seem to have seized up completely after his ungainly fall from the gate earlier that morning.

Just as he reaches the door, Sam is seized by a familiar cramping sensation and diverts course to the bathroom where he loses half of his breakfast to yet another bout of diarrhoea. He still feels uncomfortably full afterwards and takes this as an emphatic win.

When he gets to the car park, Joe is almost tearful with frustration at having waited for Sam while every other vehicle has gone. Sal, the dog and the Weatherman have apparently long fled and Joe is making small, indignant squeaking noises as Sam nears the truck.

Joe sits, fidgeting and squeaking on the right-hand side of the truck, so Sam swings himself up on the other side, flopping into the seat in a bloated and ungainly manner. Unexpectedly, there is a steering wheel in front of him. Even more unexpectedly, the steering wheel is encased in some kind of fluffy, leopard print fabric in a startling shade of magenta.

"I'm driving?" he asks. Joe looks across with the strained patience of a saint.

"My gout," Joe says, in a tone of voice that implies this has been explained at length already.

Sam has some concerns about driving a large vehicle on the wrong side of the road, seated on the wrong side of said vehicle while the dashboard blinks in an array of unfamiliar lights and switches. The somewhat inclement weather seems unlikely to help.

"Excellent!" he says, thrusting the transmission into Drive with a loud grinding sound. Joe does not seem pleased by this sound.

Sam drops his foot to the floor and the truck leaves the car park in a flurry of sprayed-up gravel, narrowly avoiding collision with a large trash-can on the way out.

Chapter Forty-Three

The drive through the narrow streets of small-town Kansas is a disorienting and frustrating experience for Sam, with Joe's regular squeaks of disapproval a less-than-helpful cue to approaching hazards. There is a close call at a four-way stop crossroads before Joe explains the frankly ridiculous concept of first-in-goes-first. While Sam suspects this is some kind of ridiculous prank, there does seem to be a lot less honking of horns once he embraces the idea.

Before too long, with zero actual damage to Joe's truck (despite several instances of slammed brakes), they're outside the town limits and barrelling down red dirt roads across miles of empty farmland. There is a heavy layer of cloud extending as far as the eye can see, the sky below the cloud turning a dark muddy purple-grey. Joe has transitioned now to a different type of squeak - this one expressing barely contained excitement as they tear down narrow back roads towards the strange little shapes emerging from the wall of cloud in the distance.

There's a large camera on the dashboard in front of Joe and they alternate between peering through the camera and muttering something indecipherable into the large headset connected to said camera. Sam is still unclear as to whether Joe is narrating the footage or whether there's someone else speaking back through the headset but all in all, it doesn't seem particularly important either way.

The truck engine roars with such a deep, throaty resonance that Sam feels a very unfamiliar stirring in his very soul – he's never really been one for cars, but speeding down this narrow, furrowed path at ridiculous speed behind the wheel of several hundred horsepower is making him feel decidedly *male.*

The weather has turned as they near the cloud wall, the warm, still air of the town cooling and rain spattering the truck's dirty windscreen with steadily increasing ferocity. The steady motion of windscreen wipers has cleared a window for Sam to peer through, but it's ringed in dark red mud and the truck's other windows are opaque with a mix of dirt and rain.

Joe's squeaking has risen to a fever pitch and they're gesturing towards the cloud wall with kid–at–Christmas levels of excitement. Sam sees it. There, at the base of that giant wall of cloud are two distinct pyramid shapes, the cloud pointing down at the ground.

"Tornadoes?" Sam breathes in awe.

Joe nods, waving one hand dismissively in Sam's direction and continuing to chatter into the headset.

On the console beside Sam, his cellphone vibrates and he glances down momentarily to see it lit up with "Fuckhead calling". Of course Claudia's father would call right now. Of course he would ruin the one beautiful, fleeting moment when Sam had actually almost forgotten why he was here. He mashes at the phone with one hand in an attempt to reject the call and is horrified to realise that he has in fact answered and

Claudia's father's voice is now resonating from the truck's sound system.

"Sam?" blares the ridiculously upper-class voice. "Sam? Is that you?"

"Hello?" Sam replies, somewhat distracted by driving around potholes in a dirt road at 80 miles an hour.

"What?" the disembodied voice bellows.

"Sorry, I'm driving," Sam shouts back. "Also, it's a bit rainy."

"What?" Claudia's father thunders. "Just pull over and pay attention for five minutes!"

Joe is seriously displeased with this turn of events and is glaring at Sam while making a throat-cutting gesture. For a startled moment, Sam interprets this as some kind of death threat, before realising it's more of a pointed suggestion to end the call.

"Well, I can't really talk right now," Sam says, swerving to avoid an unidentifiable rodent flattened on the road.

"I know what you're doing," Claudia's father says in something of a Bond Supervillain tone, "I know where you are."

Somewhat surprised by this turn of events, Sam makes a startled gurgling noise in response.

"Look," Claudia's father continues to shout, "Just get yourself back from whatever nasty little corner of Southeast Asia you're hiding away in. We need to talk."

Sam blinks and looks again at his surroundings. It certainly doesn't *look* like Southeast Asia, what with the endless fields, the dirt road and the distant tornado funnels. He makes a noise of protest.

"I know you've got no money," Claudia's father sneers. "We'll pay for the ticket."

Sam presses the End Call button and there is a return to glorious silence, broken only by the sound of rain on the truck's roof and windows. Joe nods and flashes a brief thumbs-up in Sam's direction.

"I think my father-in-law stole my wallet," Sam says slowly. Joe looks somewhat concerned.

"I mean, I think my father-in-law paid a small ninja to steal my wallet. In Thailand." Joe nods decisively as if this has cleared things up and returns to peering at the dashboard camera, muttering quietly into the headset.

As the truck barrels towards an intersection, Joe points to the left. Sam slams on the brakes and throws the steering wheel hard. There's a very satisfying squeal of tyres and a big red cloud of mud thrown up in the air as they clear the turn with millimetres to spare.

Suddenly it seems that the cloud wall has moved much closer. The two triangle shapes protruding from the bottom have become more defined. At the sight of those distinctive tornado funnels, Sam's heart races, his blood feeling electrified as it races through his body. They're so close.

The funnel to their left is visibly moving right, closer and closer to the road they're currently speeding down. The funnel to their right is somehow moving the opposite direction, the two tornadoes approaching each other and the road between them at high speed.

Joe is bouncing and twitching in obvious excitement, chattering now into the headset at a rate of knots and interspersing the chatter with bursts of hysterical giggles.

A distinctive shape emerges out of the dust in the distance;

the Weatherman's truck is speeding along the same road a few miles ahead of Sam and Joe. Spotting the vehicle, Joe makes a particularly excited squeak and babbles into the headset. It occurs to Sam only now that Joe may be talking to the Weatherman over said headset.

Lightning flashes in the cloud wall ahead of them, bright shapes branching across the dark grey for milliseconds before disappearing. The rain is heavy now, bucketing down and streaming across the windscreen so thick and fast that the wipers can't possibly keep up. Their truck bounces, the suspension presumably taking something of a pounding from all the cracks, ruts and potholes on the road beneath them. Sam can see the truck ahead of them rocking alarmingly in a similar manner, occasionally leaving the ground completely. He presses the accelerator pedal further to the floor and the juddering of the truck worsens as they close the gap to the vehicle ahead.

They're just a couple of hundred metres away when it happens. As Sam looks on, the right wheel of the truck ahead dips dramatically into a large pothole and the left side lifts dramatically into the air. He slams on the brakes with both feet as the leading truck begins to skid across the road, the left side still up in the air. There's an audible intake of breath from Joe as the Weatherman's truck tips further and further, spinning out of control. Sam's truck comes to a grinding halt, mud spraying up in all directions and he can feel himself holding his breath as they watch the other truck teetering on the brink of tipping.

And then it topples, landing hard on the passenger-side door and continuing to slide fast through thick red mud. It tears through the post-and-wire fence on the side of the road and ploughs through more mud and dry grass before smashing into a large tree.

Chapter Forty-Four

Sal has absolutely no idea what's going on.

The fates have brought her to this place, obviously, to provide wise counsel to Sammy and prevent him from committing a great injustice to himself and his family by suiciding into a tornado. Being picked up by a woman closely associated with Sam and then finding him all alone in the middle of that field – well, it had seemed like things were going pretty well to plan. But now, somehow, Sal is in one truck while Sam is in a different one and some idiot has decided to put him in the driver's seat.

Sal is in the passenger seat of a truck equipped with so many beeping displays and flashing lights that it's basically more computer than vehicle at this point and there's a dog sitting in her lap with very sharp claws. The grey-haired woman in the driver's seat is an absolute *maniac* as far as Sal's concerned and every time she throws the truck into another skidding, high-speed turn, the dog's claws dig into the tops of Sal's thighs. She is clinging to the handle above the door for dear life, but it's not doing much to prevent her from being thrown bodily from side to side with every corner. There's also a creeping sensation beginning in her gut that feels like it might just turn into full-blown car sickness at any moment, but she's doing her best to ignore that.

"So," Sal says, keeping her tone as casual as possible, "You do this for fun?"

The Weatherman turns to her – *dear god keep your eyes on the road* Sal thinks – and flashes a huge grin, teeth bright white in that deeply tanned face.

"Sure do," she says. "To be fair, there is some pretty good money in it too."

This had not occurred to Sal for a second but now she looks around and considers that none of this equipment looks like it comes cheap.

"You get paid for driving around in storms?"

The Weatherman shrugs. "Basically, yeah."

She turns back just in time to avoid a large boulder right in the middle of the road. Sal's head bounces off the window with a jarring thump.

There are a number of cameras positioned around the cab so Sal takes a wild guess.

"For the videos? People watch that on the internet?"

The Weatherman nods.

"And TV channels will pay to use the footage. Plus some-times I'll have someone like you tag along; they pay pretty well for the privilege." This seems a bit pointed.

"Well thank you for the free ride then," Sal says, slightly distracted by the vomit rising in the back of her throat.

The truck bumps up and down as they tear down a narrow dirt road at what seems to Sal a wildly unsafe speed. Rain pelts against the windscreen and pieces of debris whip across the road ahead of them. In the distance, Sal can see two shapes that look distinctly like tornadoes although she's very aware that the closest she's come to a tornado before this is seeing the hand-drawn version on Saturday morning Roadrunner cartoons.

"Are those..?" she gestures ahead towards the shapes in the distance. The Weatherman grins again and nods enthusiastically.

In the rear-vision mirror, Sal sees the shape of Joe's truck emerge out of the clouds of dust behind them. It must be roaring up the road at an ever faster pace than the Weatherman's, because it's gaining on them quickly.

She feels an immediate and overwhelming sense of utter despondency. Sam saved her life. It's her duty to look after him and yet she's done nothing to prevent this from happening. She watches as Joe's truck gets closer and closer in the mirror.

Then the dog farts.

It's an ungodly stench, like old socks mixed with compost and it brings tears to Sal's eyes.

"Jesus Christ, dog," the Weatherman says, winding down the windows a crack and waving a hand ineffectually in the direction of the dog.

Sal giggles, but then she feels the vomit rising again and she doesn't think there's anything she can do to stop it.

"I think I might need..." she manages to say before it's too late. It's like every vomit scene you ever saw in a movie. It's Mr Creosote from Monty Python in vivid technicolour. There are torrents of puke so thick and continuous it's hard to believe it could all come from the same person.

Vomit pours from Sal uninvited, splattering the dog and the dashboard. Vomit coats the inside of the windscreen and drips from the mirrors. Vomit is beginning to pool on the floor at Sal's feet.

Unable to see properly, the Weatherman loses control of the truck when they hit the next dip in the road. The truck leans to one side, vomit sloshing while the Weatherman fights the wheel to try and regain control. Then it tips and Sal finds herself looking up at the Weatherman while the truck slides across the road, rocks scratching the glass of the passenger window and red mud coming in through the gap at the top. They bump across the road and then out across a field, still moving at what feels like breakneck speed until there's an earth-shattering thump as the truck hits something solid and comes to a sudden, whiplash-inducing stop.

Sal looks up at the raised side of the vehicle, where the Weatherman sags heavily against her seatbelt, one arm thrust across the steering wheel and the other hanging down towards Sal. The dog, apparently unharmed, whimpers in Sal's lap. The horn blares out into the storm.

Chapter Forty-Five

Sam looks at Joe, open-mouthed. For once, Joe is still. Completely mute, ashen-faced Joe slowly removes the headset and stares out at the crippled truck, face a picture of complete devastation.

Just ahead of the truck, so close that Sam feels like he could almost reach out and touch it, the left-hand tornado approaches the road. It's a mile away, or maybe two. If he starts right now and just drives straight ahead, he's pretty sure he'll hit it straight on. His foot drifts back to the gas pedal but his gaze is fixed on the crippled truck partly bent around the tree, steam rising from the staved-in hood.

Joe seems to snap out of their trance and scrambles for the door handle, throwing open the door and stumbling out into the rain. They slip in the mud, then make their way across to the side of the road, rain-soaked and splashed in red mud.

Now is his moment. Sam puts the pedal to the floor and the truck jumps forward, tyres sliding a little in the mud. There's the sound of a horn blaring from the Weatherman's damaged truck and he slams the brakes on again.

He looks ahead to see the tornado in spitting distance from the road, so close he can see objects spinning inside the funnel.

He looks back to see Joe reach the crashed truck, scrambling up to reach the driver's side door and yank at the handle. He looks ahead again to see the post-and-wire fence torn from the ground, a mass of wood and wire whipping around in the sky. He looks back again to see Joe wrestling with the door handle while the downed truck's hazard lights flash. His impending doom beckons to him just a few minutes down the road in a churning mass of wind and spinning debris but with one last, longing glance, he stamps on the foot brake and jumps out of the truck into the storm.

Just like Joe, his feet slide from under him and Sam slams down arse-first into a sloppy mixture of mud and gravel. It's a jarring collision, the impact felt all over his already stiff and aching body and he struggles to get to his feet, even with the truck right there to use as a crutch. Rain has stuck his hair to his face in thick wet sheets and the wind whips up everything around him so that he can only open his eyes in a strained squint. Holding onto the side of the truck with one hand, he slowly makes his way over to the break in the fence where the Weatherman's truck ploughed its way through.

Joe raises a hand and makes a gesture that might be welcoming or might equally be another version of the middle finger, but Sam waves back and continues across the field towards the damaged truck. He pauses for a moment, one hand raised over his eyes so that he can open them a little more against the pelting rain and screaming wind. He looks back over to the spot just up the road where the tornado is crossing, whipping up mud and stones. He gazes in wonder.

Joe makes the loudest squeak Sam has heard from them yet and it's only as he is struck by lightning that Sam realises it was a squeak of warning. Everything goes bright, hot white for a fleeting second and then everything is gone.

* * *

Sam wakes up in the muddy grass, with the worst headache of his life and his heart pounding uncomfortably fast in his chest. The Weatherman, squatting next to him, hands him a water bottle and he takes a few desperate gulps, then leans back hard on the tree that someone seems to have propped him against.

"Sammy!" Mad Australian Woman booms from a few feet away, where she is inspecting the exposed underbelly of the Weatherman's truck. "Back in the world of the living I see?"

The Weatherman smiles and passes him the water bottle again.

"Not... Dead..?" Sam groans through parched lips. The Weatherman shakes her head with a wry smile. Mad Australian Woman taps a fist against the thick rubber soles of the boots he'd borrowed from Joe earlier in the day.

"Insulation?" she says.

The Weatherman is shaking her head.

"Rubber boots won't make much difference," she says. "Some people just get lucky."

"Fuck's sake,"he mutters.

"90% survival rate," Joe adds. "Not usually fatal."

Sam tries to get up but nothing happens.

"I can't feel my feet," he says slowly, looking down at them in fascination.

"Keraunoparalysis," Joe says. "It'll go away."

Joe seems to have become quite the chatterbox following Sam's near-death experience.

"Burns?" Joe asks.

Stopping to consider this for a moment, Sam realises that his skin feels oddly tight, as if he has been sunburned all over his body. He raises his hands in front of him and sees that the skin has turned an alarming shade of pink.

"Yes," he says.

Something strange is happening to his hearing, everything echoing as if he's hearing it from underwater. Sam closes his eyes and tips his head back against the rough bark of the tree. Opening his eyes again he gazes up through the branches of the tree to see clear blue skies with thin wisps of white cloud high above. There are birds in the tree above him, singing while a gentle breeze rustles through the leaves. Looking around, Sam sees no sign whatsoever of any storm. The skies are clear. The sun is shining.

It almost feels as if the whole thing was a figment of Sam's imagination, except for the evidence dotting the landscape around him - trees snapped like twigs; random assortments of timber and iron and fenceposts piled in the middle of fields; the Weatherman's truck tipped over and clearly worse for wear. On a distant hill, a wind farm has been mostly toppled. Snapped beams and blades litter the hillside like discarded Meccano pieces. One turbine stands undamaged amongst the mess, blades turning lazily as if nothing has happened.

It is suggested by more than one person that Sam should probably stop by a hospital, but nobody is concerned enough to push the issue in the face of Sam's blanket refusal so instead, once the lower-body paralysis wears off, they go for a beer.

The Weatherman's truck is left in the muddy field from where, apparently, it will be retrieved by the insurance company and panel-beaten back into some semblance of its former glory. The lack of distress shown by everyone involved leads Sam to believe that this is not the first time the truck has ended a chase in a less than dignified position.

After three pints of ice-cold, flavourless American beer and half a bowl of chilli fries, Sam can no longer feel the tight tingling burn across his skin and his hearing seems to be returning to normal. At least, it feels more like there's a bit of pool water blocking his ear and less like he's submerged ten feet underwater and can't hear a fucking thing. It's perfect timing for an unwelcome phone call from his father-in-law.

"Yes?" Sam shouts into the phone, half-aware that he's talking too loud.

"Why are you shouting?" Claudia's father yells back.

"I got hit by lightning," Sam says. "Also, I'm in a pub and it's a bit noisy."

There is silence on the other end of the phone. The silence goes on for quite some time.

"Hello?" Sam says.

"Yes," Claudia's father says. "You got hit by lightning?"

"Sure did. But don't worry," Sam says, "I'm one of the 90 percent."

"Of course," Claudia's father says and Sam can hear the frown in his voice. "I've no doubt."

"How are you, though?" Sam asks around a mouthful of meaty, cheesy potato. "Keeping well?"

There is another stony silence.

Sam continues chewing. If he can survive being hit by lightning, he's sure he can survive his father-in-law's disapproval.

Eventually, Claudia's father clears his throat and speaks again.

"Avril's awake," he says. Then, always one for a dramatic exit, he hangs up.

There's a ringing in Sam's head and a plummeting feeling in his gut, as if he's just fallen down a very big hole. He takes another large gulp of too-cold beer and sits, staring blankly into space.

Eventually, he becomes aware that Mad Australian Woman's face is uncomfortably close to his own as she waves a hand back and forth in front of him and shouts.

"Sam? Sammy? Sam?" There are tiny flecks of spit flying from her far-too-close lips and her breath smells like onion rings.

"I think I have to go now," Sam says.

Mad Australian Woman sits back down, but looks no less mystified.

Sam drains the last of his beer and shovels down a final handful of chilli fries, then he leaves the bar and heads off across the car park in the direction of the highway.

Chapter Forty-Six

He's only just settled himself into a prime hitch-hiking spot, thumb out, when Joe's truck pulls in beside him. There's a sizeable spray of gravel that peppers Sam's lightning-burned skin in a way that is decidedly unpleasant.

The back door opens and Mad Australian Woman leans out with a drunken grin.

"You're riding with me, Sammy!" she leers.

He'd rather not, but beggars can't be choosers and he really does need to get to an airport. With a pained grimace, he climbs up into the back seat of Joe's truck and settles in for a couple more hours of unpleasant conversation.

The Weatherman is driving. Sam feels that this shows an impressive level of trust by Joe, considering her recent history of trashing vehicles. Joe is slouched in the passenger seat and appears to have nodded off already in the two-minute drive from the bar. The dog is balanced on Mad Australian Woman's lap, both front paws on the door and snout firmly stuck out of the small gap at the top of the window.

"So," the Weatherman calls back over her shoulder. "Where to?"

"Airport," Sam says.

She nods firmly and turns up the volume on the stereo. Led Zeppelin booms through the truck loud enough to shake the windows. Mad Australian Woman looks very much as if she'd like to say something but, thwarted by the volume of the music, she gives up and gazes out the window instead, absently scratching the dog behind its large floppy ears.

Why bother? Claudia's voice hisses inside his head and he's disappointed to find that loud music has no effect on the volume of the imaginary wife voice that only he can hear.

You never cared, Sam. You don't need to start pretending now.

He wants to protest, but doesn't know how.

You're such a fucking showman, Sam. So distraught. So overwhelmed with grief that you can't possibly live without us.

"It wasn't a show..." he mutters, hoping nobody in the truck will notice.

You didn't care when we were alive. You don't care that we're dead.

"I did! I just..."

This was only ever about you, Sam. Always playing the victim.

"I wasn't..."

You didn't even want your own daughter to recover. It was easier for you if we were all dead.

"That's NOT TRUE!" he roars and three startled heads turn to look at him.

The Weatherman turns down the volume.

They sit in silence for a few minutes, Sam's face growing more and more heated.

"So..." Mad Australian Woman begins, "What's not true, Sammy?"

He drops his head into his hands, shaking it slowly from side to side.

There is another awkward silence.

Five minutes down the road, there's a petrol station. The Weatherman pulls in, despite no apparent need for fuel and disappears into the building without a word. Sam silently endures the wide-eyed stares of both Joe and Mad Australian Woman, but is pleased to see the dog has no interest in him whatsoever.

After a lengthy absence, the Weatherman reappears with four enormous cups in a cardboard holder and a grease-spotted paper bag bulging with baked goods.

"Right," she says, "Everybody out."

It's a voice accustomed to being obeyed and it doesn't seem to occur to anyone to disagree. They pile out of the truck like a motley group of juvenile delinquents and follow the Weatherman to a roadside rest area where she has set the bag on a tabletop, torn open to display a whole lot of donuts in a frankly startling range of colours and toppings.

The Weatherman passes one of the cups to each of them and Sam is pleasantly surprised to find that he is holding an entire litre of coffee. Froth-topped, cinnamon-scented and peppered with tiny marshmallows, it is a perfect example of the ridiculous American petrol station coffee that Claudia used to love with a passion.

"French Vanilla creamer?" he hardly dares ask. The Weatherman digs into the pocket of her jacket and throws him two little plastic pottles. Sam pops them open and adds them to his coffee. Now, it is perfect.

The Weatherman takes a seat at the old concrete picnic table and gives them a look that makes it very clear they should also sit. They do. Even the dog sits obediently at the Weatherman's feet and is rewarded with a donut.

"It's a dog donut," the Weatherman sighs before Mad Australian Woman can say anything. "Liver sprinkles."

The concrete seat is cold through Sam's shorts. It is quite pleasant on the burned skin of his buttocks. They all sit in silence again and Sam wonders why the change of scene was necessary. They could all be sitting in awkward silence in the truck, on the way to the airport.

"Look," the Weatherman says and gestures towards the skyline where the sun is about to set. They watch as the sky lights up in brilliant shades of orange and yellow, small hills on the horizon forming dark silhouettes against the sunset. High above them, the sparse, fluffy clouds seem lit from within, a bright magenta against the orange-yellow of the sky. Sam sips at his enormous sugary coffee as he stares. The only sound is a dribbly snuffling from the dog as she demolishes her liver-sprinkled dog donut.

The Weatherman picks up a chocolate donut and starts to chew, washing it down with mouthfuls of coffee. Unable to move his gaze from the sunset, Sam flails vaguely in the direction of the donuts and grabs something sticky. He's already taken a large bite before it occurs to him that this might be another liver-sprinkled dog donut. There's a moment of panic before the flavours of custard and caramel flood his senses and he smiles with equal parts pleasure and relief.

They sit for some time at the rest stop, eating donuts and drinking coffee until the sunset fades to pastel shades and then to grey and finally to black. It's only as the first stars start to show in the sky that they begin to talk. There's something about sitting in the dark, Sam finds, when you can't really make out the faces of the people around you, that makes it feel like you could say anything at all.

"Why did you want to die, Sam?" Joe asks and Sam is surprised anew. Joe agreed to let a suicidal maniac drive their truck into a tornado? Joe may just be the most unusual person Sam has ever met.

"I just..." he takes another big bite of donut and pauses while he chews. "My family died. I mean, it's not just that they *died*, it's more that they got smashed into tiny little pieces. By a tornado."

Mad Australian Woman makes an *ahhhhhhh* noise of understanding, although Sam is fairly sure that he explained all of this to her already in the Thai hospital. To be fair, he supposes she had consumed a reasonable quantity of Thai moonshine at the time so probably cannot be blamed for gaps in her memory.

"So, you wanted to get back at tornadoes?" she says. "By dying?"

"Don't seem like the best way to make a point..." Joe says.

"No," Sam protests, but then has to sip more of his rapidly-cooling coffee while he seeks out the right words. "No, I just didn't want to be alive any more. Because they weren't."

"Seems easier to jump in front of a train," Mad Australian Woman observes. She's not wrong.

"Life insurance," Sam says. "My daughter needs the insurance money and they don't pay out if, you know..."

"But your family's dead," Mad Australian Woman says, and then adds "Sorry," when she hears herself.

Sam shakes his head.

"Not Avril," he says. "I mean, she was there and she got... well, she was there."

CHAPTER FORTY-SIX

Another mouthful of coffee. Will this cup never end?

"She was in a coma and they said... Well, I thought... They said her brain was gone, basically."

"Oh Sammy," Mad Australian Woman says. "That's awful."

He shakes his head and raises a hand in protest.

"No," he says. "No more of this *poor me* bullshit."

You don't deserve to be alive. Claudia's voice whispers inside his head. It's almost right but it's not quite right.

"I don't deserve," he starts. "No, I didn't deserve..."

Another gulp of coffee. The too-sweet milkiness of it sits uncomfortably on his tongue.

"It's just that I was shit." He smiles because it feels good to tell the truth. "I was a shit husband and an uninterested parent and generally just a pretty shitty human being and I really didn't care about anyone or anything and honestly what was even the *point* of me?"

There is another stunned silence. The Weatherman clears her throat and says, "So, you feel like you didn't deserve your family?"

Sam considers. This is almost right, but not quite.

We deserved better. Claudia whispers, and this is it exactly.

"They deserved better than me," Sam says. "They deserved to have someone who wanted to be there."

"Well, "Mad Australian Woman says, "I mean, nobody's perfect..."

"I didn't appreciate them," Sam says. "It didn't mean anything to me, having a family. They were just... A hassle. They seemed like something that made my life harder and I didn't care about them and I didn't really want them there and sometimes, maybe... Sometimes I think that maybe this is exactly what I wanted."

Exactly what you wanted Claudia's voice echoes inside his head.

"They deserved someone who wouldn't want to live without them."

"Nobody gets what they deserve," the Weatherman says, her voice so soft and quiet that Sam can only just hear her through his lightning-muffled ears. "Life doesn't work that way."

"Weatherman deserved a whole lot better than what she got," Joe adds. "Booted off the TV soon as she weren't young and pretty no more."

"You were on TV?" Mad Australian Woman pipes up. Sam is surprised anew at her obliviousness.

"Long time ago," the Weatherman says. "A lifetime ago."

"I'm a shitty person too," Mad Australian Woman says and Sam thinks it's the most honest thing he's ever heard her say.

"I go through life feeling like I'm owed something and thinking that I *deserve* all sorts of shit and I wait for great things to just land in my lap but I'm so fucking lazy and entitled that I never actually *do* anything."

"You were doing things in Thailand," Sam says. "Pilates or... whatever?"

"Yoga," she corrects. "Ashtanga yoga."

"Right," Sam says, as if he knows what these words mean.

"I prefer Vinyasa," Joe mumbles. "I like the flows."

And so the mystery of Joe deepens even further.

"But I was kind of just making it up," Mad Australian Woman says. "What do I know about yoga? I just printed off a fake certificate and started doing stretching exercises for posh women from Toorak."

"What's a toorak?" Sam asks, picturing some kind of terrifying flying marsupial. Nobody clarifies.

"And it didn't last long of course, because I can never stick to anything so then I leased this studio to get more customers but that didn't help because those Toorak women know a fraud when they see one…

And the studio lease was kind of pricey so I had to borrow from a dodgy ex to make the first payment and then I couldn't make the next payment but there was this teaching camp in Thailand so I thought, you know, two birds one stone…"

"Solid plan," Joe says.

"Sure," Mad Australian Woman continues, "Except that my credit card bounced so they kicked me out of the yoga camp and then this dickhead saved me from certain death but what was even the point of that because I only ended up homeless in Thailand until I found a rich fat guy who let me stay in his mansion but really the whole thing was kind of just a form of prostitution now that I think about it and honestly, I'm thirty-six years old and I still don't know what I'm doing with my life."

There is a muffled chuff of startled laughter.

"Thirty-six?" Joe asks.

"Fucking fine then," Mad Australian Woman says. "Forty-two. That's even worse."

"I was forty-two when they decided I was too old for TV," the Weatherman says. "Best thing that ever happened to me."

"So…" Mad Australian Woman seems confused. "You're saying that forty-two is alright?"

"I'm saying you better sort your shit out right now," the Weatherman says. "But if you do it now, you'll probably be

OK."

This feels like fairly solid advice to Sam.

"I'm forty-five," he says.

"Best get a move on then," the Weatherman says.

Chapter Forty-Seven

It feels like it's been a really, really long time since he last looked into those eyes. They're Claudia's eyes - intensely blue and framed by thick dark lashes - but somehow he'd forgotten that Avril had them too.

She's groggy and confused, struggling to stay awake for more than a few minutes at a time. Sam had been warned in advance that she might not recognise him. They'd told him to imagine a laptop being dropped down the stairs and then being restarted. Even if she were to eventually return to some semblance of normal, it seemed she'd always have what they euphemistically referred to as "challenges".

When he'd walked into the ward though, sweaty and red-faced after a ten-hour flight and a shockingly expensive taxi ride in early-morning rush hour traffic, she'd flashed a brief lop-sided smile and said "Dad" so casually it felt as if he'd only left the room for a few minutes. Then she'd gone back to sleep.

He'd sat in an orange plastic chair beside her bed, holding her hand while she slept and he'd cried again, but it felt different this time. Silent tears welled and slid down his cheeks but he was smiling because he'd forgotten *this*. He'd forgotten how it felt to just sit and watch someone sleep and feel completely at peace, even when the world's least comfortable chair was digging into the burned skin of your thighs. He'd forgotten how it felt to be called Dad.

She wakes again a little later and laughs at the white trails his tears have left on his filthy face. She asks for her Mum and he is stricken, horrified at the thought of having to tell her. But then she remembers and she cries for a while. They've told her about the accident, of course, many times.

"I'll remember now," she says sadly, but he knows she won't.

Claudia's parents arrive a few hours later, bearing armfuls of teddy bears and comic books and Get Well Soon cards. Avril blinks at them, then greets them politely but with zero recognition.

"We're your grandparents," Claudia's dad says. "Remember? We were here yesterday?"

"Of course," Avril says blankly. "I think I remember."

They stick around for an awkward half-hour of small talk, until Avril falls asleep again and they leave. Seconds later, she's awake again.

"I thought they'd never leave," she says, grinning wickedly.

"You don't remember them?" Sam asks.

"Of course I do," she says. "It's just funnier this way."

He has never been more proud.

He asks whether she remembers anything from her time in the coma. He asks whether she heard her grandparents reading to her, or visitors talking to her.

"They said you might be able to hear," he says.

She shrugs.

"I remember Disneyworld," she says. "And I remember being at a beach with Mum and Noah. And then nothing."

"It's just…" he clears his throat. "I wasn't really… well, I wasn't here much."

She smiles. "Yeah, Grandad said you've been off gallivanting."

"I'm sorry," he says and he really does mean it.

"I don't remember," she says. "So it doesn't really matter, does it?"

Later that afternoon, while she's sleeping again, he ventures out to the cafeteria in search of much-needed caffeine. Claudia's parents are there, reading newspapers and sharing a pot of Earl Grey tea. He sits with them and waits while the girl behind the counter struggles with the espresso machine.

He makes a half-hearted attempt at an apology, but finds that his father-in-law's condescending expression is just so incredibly frustrating that he can't quite finish. Claudia's mother pats the back of his hand and smiles, but her eyes are cold.

Claudia's father pulls an envelope from the briefcase that sits on the floor beside him. He passes the paperwork to Sam without comment and the same holier-than-thou expression on his face.

It's a custody agreement.

Sam laughs.

"We can give her a good home," Claudia's mother says. "She'll have everything she needs."

"All the best doctors and the best of care." Claudia's father adds.

"She needs stability," Claudia's mother says. "She needs responsible caregivers."

"What she doesn't need," Claudia's father says, "is a drunken, suicidal moron who couldn't care less."

With a smile, Sam picks up the document and, page by page, tears it into little pieces.

"That's not the only copy," Claudia's father points out.

"Don't really care," Sam says.

He drops the shredded pieces into a nearby bin and collects his takeaway coffee cup from the counter.

Sam stops at their table again on the way out.

"Thank you," he says. "For what you've done for Avril and for the memorials and for everything else."

Claudia's mother smiles that same cold-eyed smile and her father clears his throat as if he's about to say something.

"I really am grateful," he continues. "But she's my daughter. And you can fuck right off with this custody bullshit."

He does ask Avril later whether she'd rather live with her grandparents. The look of stunned horror on her face is enough to make him think he's making the right decision.

Sam spends three days straight by his daughter's bedside before she asks him to go home and shower. It seems that he is stinking out the ward and everyone else is too polite to mention it.

Chapter Forty-Eight

Returning home at sunset, Sam is surprised to find the house lit up and the smell of home cooking drifting from an open window. He's even more surprised to be greeted at the door by a bright-eyed Buddy pulling him into a bear hug so enthusiastic his rib cage creaks in protest.

"I heard about April!" Buddy enthuses. "It's a miracle!"

"Avril," Sam corrects.

Buddy hands him a cold beer, but Sam hands it back.

"Stopped drinking," he says. He hadn't actually considered this until right now, but it feels right.

Buddy gives him a formal salute. "Understood."

He pours the contents of the can down the sink, which seems unnecessarily wasteful but Sam appreciates the gesture nonetheless. It's only once he's standing in the kitchen, a chicken roasting in the oven and all surfaces shining, that he realises Buddy has cleaned up.

"The freezer!" he says, showing more excitement for a clean appliance than ever before in his life.

"Yeah, that wasn't pretty," Buddy chortles. "What the fuck happened there, mate?"

Sam is out of energy and words at this point, so he shrugs.

"Just life," he says, which strikes Buddy as uproariously funny for some mysterious reason.

They sit and watch football while the chicken cooks and Sam notices that the sitting room has been cleaned up too. Claudia's coat has been tidied away and the sofa seems to have been somehow washed to the point that it's returned to its original shade of beige, years of felt pen scribbles and general kid dirt having vanished.

Sam has absolutely no understanding of which teams are playing or who is winning. As far as he's concerned, the game is just bright colours moving around a screen. It's quite soothing to watch. A bit like a lava lamp.

"I haven't slept since Monday," Sam says at one point. "What day is it now?"

"Sunday, mate," Buddy says as if this should be obvious. "Sunday roast, innit."

As the football finishes, the door opens and Claudia's sister bowls into his house, pulling Sam's dog on a leash behind her. She's already halfway through a sentence.

"Oh my god, you'll never guess what happened," she says as she takes off her coat and hangs it beside the door in the manner of someone who's done this many times before.

"Dad tried to talk to Sam about the custody thing and he told them to get fucked! Can you imagine..."

It is very clear from the wide-eyed panic on her face and the sudden stop to the torrent of words that she did not expect Sam to be here.

"Bridget!" he says.

"Sam's home," Buddy adds, quite unnecessarily.

"I can see that, Mike," Bridget says through a strained smile.

There is something in the familiarity and frustration of her tone that makes it suddenly clear to Sam - Buddy and Bridget are *together*. And have apparently been living in his home for the past week, cleaning his sofas and cooking chickens in his oven and walking his dog. Despite everything, the thought makes him feel quite warm.

* * *

Sam and Claudia had never intended to have kids. When they were young and freshly married, they'd laughed at uni friends saddling themselves with eighteen-years-plus of responsibility. They'd shuddered at the thought of a house in suburbia, working dead-end jobs to pay a mortgage and getting up early on weekends to watch tiny morons chase a football around a frosty field. There had been nothing that appealed about the idea of parenthood. Absolutely nothing.

It had been a drunken weekend in Paris that messed it all up. Nightclubs and champagne and cocaine and bright lights and fancy restaurants and the poshest hotel either of them had ever seen in their lives. It had been everything they loved about their young, successful, child-free lives and all of the things their friends could no longer enjoy. They'd awoken on the Sunday afternoon, bleary-eyed in a trashed hotel room and then scrambled to leave in time for their flight. Neither had any memory of the previous forty-eight hours beyond a general sense of hedonism and wild dreams fulfilled.

The whole idea of children had been so incredibly unlikely, so opposite to everything they wanted in life that the possibility didn't really occur to either of them until much later than it really should've done. Twenty weeks after that fateful weekend in Paris, they were watching Iron Chef with a Thai takeaway and a bottle of New Zealand wine. It was midwinter and they were snuggled together on the couch under the ridiculous fluffy pink blanket that Claudia loved.

She'd wrestled around under the blanket and removed her bra, throwing it across the living room in a way that hadn't bothered him back then.

"God, my boobs hurt," she'd said. "Think I'm getting fat."

He'd grabbed at her almost unconsciously - any mention of boobs meant an instant desire to feel said boobs.

"I think they're bigger," Sam had said. "I like you fat."

"I'll get thin again for the summer," she'd said, shovelling down another forkful of green curry. She'd frowned. "Does this taste funny to you?"

She had been thin again by the summer, but she also had a newborn Avril screaming with colic at all hours of the day and night.

Sam lies in his bed now, exhausted but somehow unable to sleep. He stares at the ceiling, trying not to think about Buddy and Bridget fornicating in his sheets.

It wasn't all bad though, was it? Claudia's voice is back in his head.

"I was bad," he whispers into the dark. "I am bad. I'm sorry."

Sometimes it was bad. But sometimes it was good. Life's meant to be like that.

CHAPTER FORTY-EIGHT

It's true. Sometimes it had been good.

He remembers the sweaty, tired smile on her face when they'd lifted newborn Avril onto her chest and she'd been overcome by a completely unexpected wave of affection. He remembers something shifting in his chest too; not the overwhelming sense of paternal love he was supposed to have felt but something in that direction. A feeling that maybe the three of them might be OK.

He remembers a family holiday to the South of France a few years ago, when Noah was still in nappies and Avril toddling. They'd sat on the beach making sandcastles and watching the sun set over the Med, while Avril pointed at sunbathers and yelled "Boobies!". He remembers that feeling again, despite the young and childless holidaymakers frolicking about them; the feeling that maybe the four of them might have something good.

He remembers that morning on the beach in Florida, the sun beaming down on them while they basked in a renewed feeling of optimism. He's certain he could see it in Claudia's eyes too – the idea that maybe things could be better; the sense of good things on the horizon if they could just hold on to what they'd created together.

But then he remembers a night just after New Year, when he'd finished twelve beers in front of the TV while Claudia picked the kids up from school and fed them and showered them and put them to bed. She'd said something that morning, or done something, or looked at him a certain way perhaps. He didn't remember exactly but he'd been pissed off and decided to punish her with a cold shoulder and the kind of excessive drinking that she no longer had any tolerance for.

Inevitably, she was pissed off too.

She came down from putting the kids to bed and sat in the armchair opposite, stony-faced, feet tucked up on the seat and arms around her knees. She'd waited for him to say something, so he'd ignored her and continued drinking, staring blankly at the TV despite no interest whatsoever in the movie playing. After a while, he glanced over to see silent tears running down her face. This had only made him angrier.

"Well aren't you the fucking martyr?" he'd sneered.

She'd shaken her head and sighed.

"I'm so sick of feeling like a victim," she'd said. He'd turned up the TV volume to drown her out.

She'd walked over and unplugged the TV.

"I want a divorce," she'd said.

Then she'd plugged it back in and left the room.

"Oh fuck off," he yelled after her and thrown the remote. It bounced off the wall just above her head and when she flinched it hurt his heart to think that she was a little bit afraid that he might hurt her.

She hadn't mentioned it again, but it had hung over their marriage and he still wasn't sure - if they hadn't died, would they have left him anyway?

Just do the best you can her voice whispered inside his head. *That's all anyone can ask.*

"*OK,*" he whispers back.

He spends some time that night updating his will, giving legal custody of his house, his dog and his daughter to Buddy and Bridget in the event of his death. This does seem a lot of pressure to place on a fledgling relationship but he has a good feeling about them.

Then, finally, he falls asleep.

Chapter Forty-Nine

Sal has started over many times in her life. A new town, new relationship, new job – it's all become so routine for her that there's no longer much novelty in the idea of making a new start. This time though, it feels different.

She suspects that the Weatherman's advice to sort her shit out was probably meant more as a wake-up call to go back to Australia, pay off her debts, quit drinking and find a new career. Sal has gone instead for the approach of destroying her mobile, forgetting all previous acquaintances and setting off for a new life in a brand new country where nobody knows her. She had vaguely considered changing her name and acquiring a fake passport but this all seemed like a little too much work and she's fairly confident that neither the ex-boyfriend nor the Melbourne landlord to whom she owes money have the kind of international contacts required to track her down here.

As she waits in a line of tourists to board the ferry leaving Manila, she feels an overwhelming sense of being exactly where she's supposed to be. She's sticky and uncomfortable after twenty-three hours of flights and her over-stuffed backpack is heavy on her shoulders. There's a subtle pinching feeling in the side of her neck that she knows will develop into a full-blown problem in a few hours' time but she can't help smiling. The sun is warm on her face and she can hear tiny waves sloshing against the pier. There's not a cloud in the sky and the sea air is cool and fresh. It feels like heaven, but smells a bit more like fish.

Out of habit, she fishes in the back pocket of her jeans to check her phone but it's gone and instead of the usual panic at being disconnected from the world, she feels only a comforting sense of relief.

Something happens at the front of the line and people begin to move, jostling and stumbling a little in their hurry to board. Sal struggles to feel any sense of urgency but lets herself be moved along with the crowd.

On board, she finds a seat near the window and pulls out her embroidery work, settling in for a long trip. It's a new thing for Sal, embroidery – introduced by the mysterious Joe a few weeks back when Sal had admired the decorative pillows on Joe's couches.

She's currently working on a piece of cross-stitch that she plans to frame for the wall of her new home. Bordered with vines, leaves and tiny rosebuds and stitched in a calligraphic font made up of multiple tiny stitches, it will read "Cunt" once she's finished. She likes to think it'll be a nice reminder of her homeland, where the word peppers everyday sentences with a regularity unimagined in any other part of the world. The tiny bird-like Filipino nun who sits next to her on the ferry is apparently unfamiliar with this particular word, gesturing towards Sal's needlework with clear approval.

Sal is just adding the final touches to the "t" when the ferry docks and passengers start forming a queue to disembark. Sal can't quite figure out why everyone is in such a hurry but she goes with it and starts packing away her things. Tying off the last thread, she holds up the finished work to the nun, who gives an enthusiastic thumbs-up and a huge grin.

Slowly, stretching out her aching limbs, Sal makes her way across the cabin to join the end of the line, which moves remarkably quickly off the boat, down a ramp and onto a bus. Settled into the back seat, head against the window with the sun warming the side of her face, Sal nods off with a smile on her face.

Chapter Fifty

It's a little after nine in the morning and the sun is already high in the sky, hot enough to make tiny beads of sweat pop across Sam's forehead. It's a picture-perfect day. It is, in fact, the eighteenth picture-perfect day since he arrived in the Philippines eighteen days ago. All signs point to this being the best decision Sam has ever made.

From his position at their little construction site, he can see Sal further down the beach performing some kind of double-jointed, uncomfortable-looking contortions in the sun. A small group of tourists is gathered around her, making valiant attempts at the same poses. As always, a larger group of local children frolic in the waves behind Sal's students, mimicking their yoga poses and giggling.

Sam goes back to hammering nails. He's never been particularly good at woodwork and this hasn't changed despite a solid fortnight of hammering nails under the supervision of a very patient local man called Gabriel. This particular nail seems to have a mind of its own and is bending in a very strange direction despite Sam's best efforts to hammer it in straight. He gives it a last couple of whacks and moves on to the next nail, hoping that sheer numbers of nails will compensate for the crookedness of each and every one.

There are workers up on ladders doing something important with beams and studs, but it has been made very clear to Sam that he is not qualified to help with this task, so he sticks to hammering nails into pieces of wood around the sides of an entry ramp to what will one day be the front door.

"Sam?"

He puts down the cursed bloody hammer and turns to see Sandra, with a large mug of tea in hand.

"Not spiked this time, is it?" he asks. She smiles from beneath the hard hat that's jammed down over her silver curls.

"Yours isn't, love," she says and takes a healthy gulp from her own mug.

He's still not entirely sure how she found him, or whether it really was as coincidental as it seemed at face value – the happy widow making her way around the most remote corners of the world until her husband's life insurance money ran out right here on a beach in the Philippines. He doesn't much care, when it comes down to it. She's the best labourer anyone could ask for and her nails are never crooked, even after an entire potful of her "special" tea.

"Boss wanted me to check on the doorway width again," she says, wiping perspiration from her forehead.

"I told him," Sam says. "They have to be 900 wide, for the wheelchair."

"Yes," she says, downing the rest of her tea in one go, "But you've written down 762 for the kitchen door. And he does have teenagers of his own, you know, so he wondered whether maybe you wanted to keep her out of the food supplies?"

Sam grins.

"Nope, 900 for that one too please."

"You sure?" she asks. "Long way to the nearest supermarket…"

"I'm sure."

"Right then," she adjust her hard hat and turns to leave, then turns back.

"Almost forgot!" she says, pulling a handful of digestive biscuits from a pocket of her builder's apron. "Can't have tea without biscuits."

He sits on the sparse, dry grass for a while after she leaves, gazing down the beach to the lapping tide. Sal's class has officially finished but she's out in the water with a few student hangers-on, swimming laps to a battered orange buoy and back. The ocean's surface sparkles in the sunlight and the sky is huge and blue overhead, dotted with a few slowly circling gulls. Right now, there's nowhere in the world he'd rather be.

Finishing up the tea and biscuits, he returns the mug to the half-finished kitchen inside, where Gabriel is working on the 900-wide doorway and Sandra is screwing together cabinetry with pinpoint precision. Sam takes out his phone and video-calls Avril at the rehabilitation centre back in England. He takes her for her daily video tour of the house, pointing out the changes since yesterday and zooming in on the view from her bedroom window so that she can see Sal's yellow head bobbing in the sea. Gabriel mugs for the camera, but Sandra refuses to be distracted from her work with the cabinets with anything more than a cursory wave and a brief "Hello, love."

Avril shows him the wall planner beside her bed, a date eight weeks in the future emphatically circled in red felt pen, small stars drawn around the words "Move home". It will be quite the performance, returning to the UK to collect a disabled nine-year-old and transporting her, wheelchair and all, half-way across the world. But he can't wait.

* * *

Later that evening, after the builders have gone home, Sam and Sal sit in their usual spot on the sand just in front of the house. As usual, Sal's recliner faces out at the ocean view. Sam's is set at angle, pointing down the beach to face the sun.

"Typical fucking pom," Sal says, sipping home-made kombucha through a turtle-safe paper straw.

"You won't be saying that when I have a perfect tan and you have a stupid looking patch of sunburn on one arm," Sam says, struggling to sip his own drink through a soggy, rapidly collapsing straw.

"Pretty sure I'll still think you look ridiculous," she replies. "And those people up the beach think you're watching them."

At that moment, the family picnicking further up the beach gather up their supplies and disappear.

"You could say thank you for keeping the beach nice and deserted," Sam points out.

"Thank you, friendly neighbourhood pervert?" she cackles.

Sam spits the straw into the sand in frustration and gulps directly from the glass. This is a terrible mistake and he chokes on a mouthful of vinegary awfulness.

"What the fuck is kombucha anyway?" he says. "This can't

possibly be good for anyone."

"It's pina colada flavour," Sal says indignantly. "I added fresh pineapple juice and everything."

It does not taste anything like a pina colada.

She hands him a large bowl that appears to be full of crunchy green pieces of plastic film.

"Have some kale chips. Balances out the flavour."

He is sceptical but throws back a handful anyway. Suffice to say, it does not balance out the flavour.

In the distance, there's the faint sound of a siren.

"Stupid thing keeps malfunctioning," Sal says. "Every bloody day it goes off."

Sam lifts his sunglasses and looks out at the sea.

"No signs of impending tsunami, then?"

"I wouldn't sweat it," Sal says, crunching on a mouthful of kale.

Sam lies back on the recliner and closes his eyes, glorying in the feeling of warm sun on his face as a soft sea breeze ruffles his hair. After a while, he starts to snore.

Sal finishes her drink and then closes her eyes too. A late-afternoon nap has become a key part of their daily routine. In the distance, the siren continues to wail.

Neither of them notice when the tide goes out much, much faster than usual. It drains away so quickly that fish are left flapping on the sand, taken by surprise. There's a strange booming sound from out on the horizon and Sam stirs a little, but then goes back to sleep.

When it hits, it is ferocious. Moving at the speed of a freight train, a wall of water several metres high ploughs towards the shore. It smashes everything in its path, pushing driftwood and fishnets and pieces of ocean debris ahead of it. The wave hits the little island beach like something made of concrete and in seconds, everything is gone. Sam's house is shattered, blown apart like so many matchsticks and carried on floodwaters several kilometres inland. Sal's recliner is recovered a few days later from the topmost branches of a nearby tree. Sam's is found exactly where he left it, facing down the beach as if a pervert has just gotten up and walked away.

Sam himself is never found.

* * *

Enjoyed this book?

Sign up to Max Spanky's mailing list at maxspanky.word-press.com to become a VIP reader. VIPs will receive updates on new releases, special offers and other Max Spanky news, including sneak preview excerpts from upcoming novels.

If you enjoyed The Weatherman, please tell your friends! Even better, if you have a few minutes to spare, please leave an honest review on Goodreads, Amazon, or wherever you like to talk about books. I'm a struggling independent author without a marketing budget so your review can make the world of difference in helping other people find my books.

Thank you!

Max Spanky